MW01631490

Wolf Tales VIII

Also by Kate Douglas:

Wolf Tales

"Chanku Rising" in *Sexy Beast*

Wolf Tales II

"Camille's Dawn" in *Wild Nights*

Wolf Tales III

"Chanku Fallen" in *Sexy Beast II*

Wolf Tales IV

"Chanku Journey" in *Sexy Beast III*

Wolf Tales V

"Chanku Destiny" in *Sexy Beast IV*

Wolf Tales VI

"Chanku Wild" in *Sexy Beast V*

Wolf Tales VII

"Chanku Honor" in *Sexy Beast VI*

Wolf Tales VIII

KATE DOUGLAS

APHRODISIA
KENSINGTON PUBLISHING CORP.

APHRODISIA BOOKS are published by

Kensington Publishing Corp.
119 West 40th Street
New York, NY 10018

ISBN-13: 978-1-61523-192-8

Printed in the United States of America

Dedication

After I wrote "The End" on this book, I found myself sitting quietly in my office, thinking how quickly I'd come to the point where I was finishing up the fifteenth story (counting the novellas) in my series. It seems like only yesterday when my wonderful editor, Audrey LaFehr, said the series would be called Wolf Tales, with a Roman numeral to designate each book, and I made some stupid comment about having to learn my Roman numerals. I thought of that as I finished Wolf Tales VIII, and had to stop and look up the numeral for nine . . . it's IX, by the way! So here I am, getting ready to start the sixteenth title in the series, a novella I'm calling Chanku Challenge, and I still can't believe how much fun I'm having with my sexy Chanku. I owe so many people for this great opportunity and the amazing success of the series, from my terrific agent Jessica Faust of BookEnds LLC for seeing the possibilities, to my editor Audrey LaFehr for having the courage to run with it. Thanks too, to the Kensington art department for consistently giving me such gorgeous covers, and to Audrey's wonderful assistant, Amanda Rouse, who has managed to solve just about every problem I've tossed her way. Many thanks go to my longtime, keen-sighted beta readers—Ann Jacobs, Karen Woods and Sheri Fogarty—as well as my newest reader and MySpace buddy, Mospearet, aka Rose Toubbeh, for her eagle eye and wonderful sense of humor. I am forever indebted to my terrific readers who keep me coming up with new stories for characters who are fast becoming old friends. Most of all, my love and gratitude go to my husband, the man who has stuck by me all these years and is, in so many ways, the alpha male behind each and every one of my Chanku heroes.

Part I

Chapter 1

The narrow chin strap was uncomfortable, but it held her night vision spotting scope in place and made it easier to focus on the pair of wolves crossing the meadow behind the house. Even with the scope, it was difficult to keep them in sight for long. They moved like magic through the dark Montana night, and once they disappeared into the heavy overgrowth bordering the forest, she knew they'd be gone for hours.

Stillness descended as the last wolf slipped through the brush. Still, she watched, her vivid imagination taking her where eyes couldn't follow, taking her into a world of dreams, until exhaustion won out and the dark line of the forest lost its attraction.

Packing up her gear took only a few minutes. Climbing down the fragile rope ladder and raising it once again took a few more, but there would be other nights to watch. Other nights to contemplate the next steps . . . as many as were needed, now that their den was no longer a secret.

Father would be pleased to know she'd come this far. To know that her journey was almost over. She owed him this much, didn't she?

* * *

Head down, tail hanging, the dark wolf that was the wizard Anton Cheval trotted slowly through the towering trees with two things on his mind—the tantalizing scent of his mate and his own terrible failings. Keisha stayed just ahead, blatantly ignoring him. Without even trying, she still managed to entice him with her sleek wolven body and the musky perfume of her arousal. Her sensual appearance and seductive scent flaunted the invitation he'd felt in warm lips and soft breasts only moments before their shift.

He'd not embraced her then. He'd felt unworthy . . . almost unclean. Would he be able to here, in the depths of the forest? Here, where the feral side of his nature might finally overcome the issues confusing his woefully inadequate, deeply flawed human side?

For a man who'd taken great pride in his unflattering reputation as a presumptive, arrogant bastard, he'd certainly had the self-importance knocked out of him. Nearly dying could do that to a guy. Giving up and embracing death when those he loved still fought on, when even his infant daughter showed more backbone than he had . . . dear Goddess, that was even worse.

Would he ever find his way past the pain—the utter humiliation—of his own failings? He'd promised to keep his family and packmates safe, but he'd failed—intruders had breached the very walls of his home.

More than once.

There was no excuse for the fact that Keisha and her cousin Tia, pregnant with her first child, had been forced to defend not only their home and their own lives, but Anton's infant daughter.

They'd done an admirable job. A much better job than he or any of the other males had. As the so-called alpha of this pack of Chanku shapeshifters, he was a dismal failure.

Even now he felt that all was not well. Despite all their precautions, their nightly searches and increased surveillance, his senses jangled with the subtle awareness of some unseen danger hovering just out of sight.

Was it really a threat, or merely the fact that his personal world seemed to be spiraling out of control?

The first frost of autumn blanketed the ground and dried grasses crackled beneath their paws. Other than the sound of their passing, the night was silent . . . unless he considered the unwavering clamor of self-flagellation. Creatures stayed warm in their dens. The soft hoot of owls and whisperings of other denizens of the night remained curiously muted, as if the cold imprisoned their voices.

The chill wind didn't reach beneath his thick fur or cool the heat of his desire. No, he figured he'd manage to do that entirely on his own. Even Keisha's magic hadn't been enough to rouse him earlier. Now, her cool, amber-eyed gaze as she glanced over her shoulder drew him, even as his inner demons held him at bay. Still, he moved closer to her, drawn by love and respect more than sexual desire.

That alone reminded him all was not well. A creature normally ruled by his libido, Anton felt nothing. Nothing beyond a sense of terrible desperation.

Keisha slipped beneath a tangle of brambles and led him to a small glade protected from the chill night wind. There she waited, her feral pose as regal as a queen's, head held high, ears forward, feet planted firmly in the frosty grass. She was everything he desired in a mate. Everything he'd ever dreamed of, hoped for.

Everything he no longer deserved.

Anton trotted up to her. Ears lying back against his skull, he dipped his head and touched his nose to hers in an uncharacteristically submissive gesture. His long tongue wrapped around her muzzle. She tilted her head and acknowledged his touch, but her thoughts remained closed to him.

What more could he expect? He'd locked her out for days, an even more cowardly act than the one that had brought him to this point. He still wasn't certain if he was ready to open to the woman he loved. Not certain if he was brave enough to share the doubts and questions dominating his thoughts. For a man who embraced honor, integrity, and personal courage, the realization had come to him slowly—he was no longer worthy of her. No longer worthy of the esteem of his fellow Chanku.

Failure was a painful meal to swallow.

His packmates looked to him for guidance, for safety, for leadership. He'd failed them at every turn. Failed his pack, his lovers, his mate, and even his daughter. Failed to keep them safe, to protect them from those who would do them harm. In fact, he would have failed at life if not for the telepathic words of his child and the life-giving power of his packmates.

They'd shared their own life force to keep him from crossing through the veil when he'd hovered in that dark place between life and death. Seduced by the light and the peace it offered, he'd wanted so badly to follow. His people had given all they had to save his worthless soul when he'd been more than ready to leave this plane for the one that beckoned him.

It had taken the surprisingly powerful voice of baby Lily to force him to choose life with all its pain over the easy escape of death.

The truth unmanned him. The truth had nearly destroyed him. For all his abilities, all his empty words of wisdom and his arrogant orders to those who loved and respected him, Anton Cheval knew he had to face the truth.

He was a coward. Unworthy of the love and sacrifice of his fellow Chanku. Unworthy of their respect.

Unworthy of the woman who waited now, so patiently, for the physical love he couldn't bring himself to share.

Do you love me, Anton?

Keisha's question caught him by surprise. She doubted even that?

More than life. He met her forthright stare and once more felt unworthy.

Then love me. Here. Now. No barriers. No lies.

I've never lied to you. How could she even think that?

When you block me, when you refuse to open to me as my mate, you might as well be lying. Our bond is built on sharing, on complete and total honesty. You've been unforgivably selfish with your thoughts.

Her words were a coldly accurate assessment. They stung. Badly. Anton nodded in painful agreement. *Will you ever forgive me?*

Keisha's chest moved in and out with her slow, steady breathing. It terrified him, knowing she actually had to think about his request. Had he pushed her too far? Destroyed the finest thing that had ever happened to him? Without Keisha, there was nothing. Without her love, he would have been better to follow that seductive light through the veil.

Choosing death, not life . . . with all its pain.

Will you ever forgive yourself? There was no sympathy in Keisha's mental voice.

He hung his head.

Make love to me, Anton. Here. Now. Just the two of us, as open and free as we were when we first bonded. When you swore your undying love for me. When you pulled me out of my own hopeless pain. Do you remember how that was? Open your heart, your thoughts. Share what fears are holding you prisoner, the way you forced me to share mine. Prove to me that love is real, not just words without substance. Can you do that?

He trembled. Unbelievable! Anton Cheval, trembling before his mate, but he'd never been more frightened, not even when faced with his own mortality. To love Keisha here, now, with his barriers down and his thoughts open to her, was to show her the worthless creature she thought she loved.

She growled. *Give it up, Anton. You're wallowing in your perceived inadequacies. It's not all about you. What we have is bigger than you.* The sound rumbled up out of her chest and shocked him with the ferocity behind it. The anger. Her silent words stung.

The fur at her neck rose in an angry line along her spine and her lips peeled back to display sharp teeth. Anton's ears flattened against his skull. His hackles rose. Blood rushed in his veins. His lips curled back in a silent snarl.

She challenged him! Insulted him, belittled his fears. She stared him down with her legs stiff, her body posture aggressive and angry. He'd never seen her like this, not with her anger directed at him. How dare she challenge him!

Lust enveloped him. Fierce and ravenous, it rose in his veins, a feral hunger like nothing he'd felt in so very long.

Passion, anger, and arousal, all knotted together in a twisted tangle of want and need, of fear and confusion. He felt her questions battering at his mind, a demand that he grant her access to his deepest fears, his basest desires.

If he let her in, all was lost.

If he kept her out . . . all was lost.

His chest ached even as arousal blossomed, blinding him to everything but Keisha. His female, her body ripe with need, her scent a musky aphrodisiac enveloping his conscious mind, grabbing hold of his balls in a powerful, visceral grip.

He charged, snarling, teeth bared, saliva dripping from open jaws. Startled, she yipped and turned to run, but he was bigger, stronger. He caught the thick roll of skin at her neck between his teeth and clamped down. She twisted beneath him, and he searched for her thoughts.

Her mind was open, a blazing eruption of emotions, all the fears she'd hidden from him, the desperate needs he'd ignored for too long. His fault. All his fault!

Keisha tore free of his grasp and faced him, legs spread

wide for balance, head hanging low, breath charging in and out of her lungs. Her amber eyes nailed him and he felt her rage, the wolven equivalent of a powerful slap in the face.

No! The world does not revolve around you, Anton Cheval. The world is bigger than you. Our love is bigger than you! What is wrong with you? Where has the man I fell in love with gone?

Her angry words ripped a blindfold off his face and opened a window back into the world he'd fled. He saw himself through Keisha's eyes.

Saw himself through eyes of love.

Arousal surged. He reached for her. Gently, this time, his paw raked her back and she watched him warily. He mounted her as the blood rushed to his cock and when he slipped inside, it was with the amazing sense of truly coming home.

She was hot and slick, her passage ready for his entry. He felt her muscles clench as she braced herself to support his weight. His forelegs tightened around her shoulders and he filled her. His hips thrust hard and fast. The knot in his penis grew, sliding deep within her heat, swelling to fill her passage, binding the two of them together.

Arousal expanded, blinding him to anything and everything but the female he loved, the one who loved him. Power charged through his testicles, the sharp jolt of pleasure streaking from balls to cock as his orgasm swept over him, filled and overwhelmed him. Hot bursts of seed blasted into Keisha and she groaned, but he knew she hadn't found her own release.

Not yet.

Physically connected, his swollen cock locked tightly inside her passage, Anton searched her mind, opening his own thoughts to reach Keisha's. After so many weeks closed inside himself, he opened just enough to touch her spirit with his. He sensed it, then, her silent scream of pleasure, the climax she'd denied herself while she waited for this most intimate connection.

A connection even more powerful than two bodies locked together—the melding of two minds, the mating of reality and spirit.

Without warning, Anton tumbled gracelessly into her waiting consciousness. If he'd been human, he would have wept at the very moment the walls crumbled. The barriers he'd erected so many weeks ago dissolved and disappeared, leaving him naked and wanting.

No, my love. Never in my eyes. Never in the eyes of your pack.

He bowed his head until his muzzle rested against her shoulder. *They gave everything they had to save me when I'd already given up.*

If you'd truly given up, they wouldn't have been able to save you. Your life force, your *force, is stronger than that.*

I love you. You deserve better.

I love you, Anton Cheval. Now shut up and make love to me.

Did you just tell me to shut up? He bit back the unexpected laughter and they shifted as one.

The two of them lay together in the frosty grass with Keisha on her belly beneath him. His cock was still hard, planted deep inside her heat, but his mate pulled away from him and rolled to her back. "I want to see you when you make love with me. No more hiding."

Shamed once again, he hung his head as he knelt between her thighs. "I don't know what's happened to me. It's as if something is lost and I can't find it."

"It's your confidence." She reached for him. Her palm cupped the side of his face. He turned his head slightly and planted a kiss over her lifeline.

Keisha sighed. "You think too much, worry about too many things. It's all inside you, that innate ability of yours to trust in yourself. Make love to me now. We'll worry about it later."

He smiled. The first time he'd felt like smiling in ages. "Bossy, aren't we?"

She raised her eyebrows but didn't say another word.

He rolled his pelvis forward and the hard length of his cock slipped back inside, finding a familiar home between her damp folds. She raised her knees and tilted her hips, giving him perfect access to her slick passage. He clasped her hands up over her head and watched himself, watched his thick shaft slowly disappear deep inside, his skin so fair to her dark, dark chocolate.

Keisha's vaginal muscles rippled along his length, pulling him deeper, tightening around him until he'd buried himself completely inside her welcoming channel, until his flat belly rested against the soft swell of hers.

Already wet and slippery from their first climax, their bodies slid together in a saturated tangle of damp pubic hair and straining muscles. The ripe, intoxicating fragrance of sex and clean sweat filled his nostrils, the sound of their rapidly beating hearts, of breath rushing in and out of straining lungs rose to his ears.

If he thought about this, if he lost himself in the sensory beauty of the act of sex, he didn't need to think about everything that was wrong. If he thought about loving Keisha, his world was once again right.

Your world has always been right, you idiot.

Shocked, he blinked and stared at her. She stared back at him with a ferocious look in her eyes.

"Did you just call me an idiot?"

Keisha's full lips curled up in a smile. "Yes, I did. Want to make something of it?" She tightened her vaginal muscles as if to emphasize her dare.

He groaned and slowly shook his head. "I have been an idiot, haven't I? I'm not really certain what went wrong."

She pulled one hand free of his grasp, reached up and

stroked his cheek with her fingertips. "I'm not either, but almost dying can have a powerful impact on a person. I've been there, remember? I know what it's like. Then to absorb so much from so many people who love you, their fear for your safety, their determination to make you live . . . All of that lives inside of you now. I imagine it's a horrible responsibility, living your life for so many other people. Why don't you try, for a while, anyway, to live for Anton Cheval?"

He thrust forward, filling her completely. Slowly he withdrew. "And who is this guy? This Anton Cheval?"

Keisha's smile grew wider. "Why, he's the man I love. The father of the world's most beautiful little girl. He's the one who's taking me real close to a fantastic orgasm right at this very moment."

"He is, eh?" Anton drove forward, tilting his hips just enough to slide his cock directly over her clit. He felt her shiver and knew it had nothing to do with the icy ground.

"Oh, Goddess. Yes. He is!"

Again he filled her, and yet again. Keisha's back arched and her eyes closed. He slipped quietly into her thoughts and found nothing but love. No sense of condemnation, no anger at his foolish, self-centered behavior. She loved him, warts and all. He had no choice. None whatsoever.

No matter what, he would be worthy of the woman who called him mate.

This time, when they reached their peak, they found it together. With a fearsome cry, he arched his back and drove deep inside. Her body tightened and held him. Her nails dug into his shoulders, her ankles locked behind his thighs and she milked him with her warm sex, squeezed him tighter with each contraction of her climax, each beat of her heart.

For the first time since the night he'd almost died, Anton Cheval was finally fully, gloriously alive.

Chapter 2

"Yeah, we're all worried about him." Holding the phone to his ear, Stefan Aragat leaned back in the deck chair and rested his heels on the railing. The forest loomed dark and inviting, but little Alex was being a pill and Xandi had her hands full with the baby.

There'd be no running through the woods tonight, damn it all. AJ Temple's voice was a welcome diversion to a man who would rather be deep in the forest making love to his woman. Of course, AJ in person wouldn't be a bad diversion himself.

"You want to send three of them up here? Why not all six?"

AJ's answer made perfect sense. There really wasn't a good place for six new Chanku shapeshifters to run in downtown San Francisco, especially since a recent attack in Golden Gate Park had everyone watching out for killer dogs. The last thing they needed was a wolf sighting. Millie and Ulrich had asked for two or three people to help with the wolf sanctuary in Colorado. Sending the other three to Montana should work out just fine, if the Montana pack was okay with it.

"I agree, AJ. Plus, I think it's what Anton needs. Three kids without a lick of sense to take his mind off whatever's bugging him." Stefan laughed. It hadn't been all that long ago he'd been just as stupid. He liked to think he'd smartened up in the past few years, but Anton might have another thought altogether.

"We'll see you guys at the end of the week. You say one of them is definitely a doctor? It'll be great to have a doctor around, even if it's just for a while. Maybe he can figure out why Alex is so colicky. Adam hasn't been able to help him much and Xandi and I are at our wits' end. I'll let Anton know we've got company coming. Give my love to Mik and Tala."

Stefan clicked off the phone and stared out into the forest. The attacks on the Chanku appeared to have ended, at least for now, though he'd not been able to get past a lingering sense of unease. Life should be settled and comfortable, but he missed his best friend and lover. Anton hadn't been the same since his near-death experience, but then neither had any of the others. They'd all come too close to their own mortality.

Stefan saw the fear in his mate's eyes and wondered if that same look was mirrored in his own. He wondered, too, if their concerns for their son's safety might be part of Alex's fussiness. Was the baby picking up their anxieties? It was still hard to relax, knowing there were nuts out there just waiting to capture a real shapeshifter. The constant worry was making all of them a little crazy.

He'd never expected it to touch Anton. Anton Cheval was the one constant among them, the one who always seemed to have it together. But lately . . . Lately there'd been the sense that Anton was one step away from losing it entirely. Having three new kids here, young, brash Chanku without any of the baggage the rest of them carried from that harrowing period when they'd all been hunted . . . Stefan chuckled to himself. This could definitely be interesting.

Almost as interesting as the fact six new Chanku had

appeared at the same time, drawn together by their common heritage and the unusual varieties of grasses planted in a garden in Golden Gate Park. Grasses the Chanku needed to become shapeshifters. What were the odds of those six young people meeting up with Tala, AJ, and Mik, members of the San Francisco pack?

Pretty good, obviously, since one of them had shifted into wolf form and protected Tala from an assault—without knowing he even had the ability.

The more he thought about their visitors, the more Stefan liked the idea. That was, if Anton and Keisha didn't want to kill him for making the invitation.

He sensed Xandi's approach even before he heard her. "Is Alex asleep?"

Her warm hands slipped over his shoulders. "Yep. Thank goodness. Lily's out like a light, too. I swear that baby girl has a very old soul. I was so frustrated, I finally decided to try putting Alex down in the same crib with her, but he wouldn't stop crying. She woke up when Alex was fussing, reached out and touched him and he immediately settled down and went to sleep."

Stefan covered her hand in his. "Let's hope that works when they're teenagers and learn to shift." He tugged on her fingers.

Xandi slipped around the side of the chair and plopped herself down in his lap. "We're going to need to figure that one out—I'm not so sure I'll ever be ready for sexually active teenagers."

Stefan laughed. "I know. Anton and I were talking about sending them off to separate boarding schools until they're at least twenty-five."

Xandi jerked around and glared at him. "You wouldn't dare!"

"Kidding! We were just kidding." He cupped the back of her head and pulled her close. "I love you." His fingers tangled in her shiny, russet hair and he traced her lips with the tip of his tongue. She tasted sweet. There was no other way to describe his woman's flavor. He sipped at her mouth, ran his tongue along the seam between her soft lips and slowly gained entry.

She turned in his lap and draped both arms over his shoulders, kissing him with slow, steady sweeps of her mouth. The side of her breast pressed against his chest and he was sorry for the thick sweatshirt he wore against the evening chill.

He'd much rather be naked with his woman right now. Naked and buried deep inside her welcoming heat. Naked and pressed tightly against all her warm, feminine curves, naked and . . .

"So, this is how he babysits when we're away."

Stefan and Xandi jerked apart.

Anton stood beside them, bare-ass naked and laughing, with Keisha right behind him. *Laughing*. Anton was laughing. *Praise the Goddess* . . .

"I finally got both little beasts to sleep. Don't you dare wake them up." Xandi leaned away from Stefan and kissed Anton soundly on the mouth.

"Looks like you guys had a good time." Stefan glanced at Keisha and raised one eyebrow. She grinned back at him.

"I slapped him around a little, got him off his high horse," she said, jabbing an elbow into Anton's ribs.

Anton slipped his arm around Keisha's waist. "Actually, she reminded me what a horse's ass I've been. I'm sorry if I worried you guys. I'm still not sure what . . ."

Stefan grabbed Anton's hand. "You went through a hell of a lot. No need to apologize. Of course, I may owe you one."

"What for?"

"For telling AJ we'd take three of the new pups they've got. Remember the six homeless kids they found in Golden Gate Park? They need a place to run, to learn the ropes, and the park's not safe. Ulrich and Millie are taking the other three. At least we get the doctor, but we also get one with his leg in a cast. Broke it."

"They're coming here? When?"

"This week. And they're all yours."

Anton leaned over and grabbed Stefan's face in both hands. He planted a big, sloppy kiss on his mouth. "Thank you. Perfect. That's absolutely perfect." He turned to Keisha. "Don't you think so? It'll be fascinating to teach them what they're capable of, to show them . . . Keisha? Don't you agree?"

She held her hand over her mouth in a futile attempt to quell the giggles. "Perfect," she said, and then she lost it.

Anton stared at her as if she'd lost her mind as well. Even Xandi's body had started to quiver as she fought her own laughter. Finally, Keisha managed to pull herself together. "Yes, Anton," she said, sounding absolutely prim. "It will truly be fascinating." Then she looked at Xandi and both of them started giggling all over again.

Anton frowned. He glanced from Keisha to Xandi and back at Keisha. Then he looked at Stefan and shrugged. "I don't get it."

Stefan shook his head. "Me neither," he said.

But he did get it. After more than a month watching their mentor fade into a shadow of his usual dynamic self, Keisha's giggles were an obvious sign of her relief. Anton was back.

Their lover, their teacher, their leader, the one they counted on to find the answers to all their questions, had finally returned.

She jerked awake when the sound of a strange vehicle coming up the drive sent the images scrambling. A quick glance toward the big house told her there was an unusual amount of activity on the front porch. It was enough to snuff out the last wisps of yet another of those strange dreams that were more like hallucinations, so filled were they with vivid night sounds, the scents of the forest, and the sensation of thick grass bending beneath broad paws.

If only the disturbance had snuffed out the tingling remnants of sensual longing, the unusual arousal that always accompanied the dreams. Stretching carefully relieved some of the tension from her long hours in the confines of the hunting blind perched high up in the tall spruce, but it didn't help the throbbing sense of unfulfilled desire.

At least a hand was good for that. A hand with nimble fingers accompanied by a vivid imagination. Later. For now, a twist of the lens focused the spotting scope on the big house. As always, watching them helped to take her mind off the inevitable sexual frustration.

The sun was still up and the day comfortably warm. A bunch of people milled about on the broad front porch. Generally they stayed on the back deck during the daylight hours, or inside, most likely sleeping. They were so active at night.

They, or the wolves. Even with the scope, there'd been no proof yet they could actually shift. Was her information wrong?

No. Father had been a man of facts. A brave man. A powerful man, brought down by one of them.

Proof would come, eventually. It would happen, and one of them would forget the risk. They'd forget long enough to shift within full view.

Father had always cautioned patience. She would prove she could be as patient as he. Given time, she would prove her worth.

Adam Wolf stepped out on the front porch when the dusty SUV rolled into the yard. He called out to anyone within hearing distance, "They're here." Then he waved and headed down the steps. Eve, his mate, followed closely behind, along with Keisha and Xandi.

Adam couldn't help being curious about the three young Chanku, part of a group of homeless youth who'd banded together near the memorial garden Keisha had designed in Golden Gate Park. They must have been drawn by a subconscious need for the nutrients in the Tibetan grasses Keisha had used in her design, nutrients their bodies craved long before they knew anything at all about their amazing birthright.

Of course, they'd learned the hard way, when one of them had attacked a guy who assaulted Tala Quinn.

Attacked and killed—as a wolf.

He'd shifted without knowing he even had the ability.

Bet that shocked the hell out of his buddies. Not to mention the thug who'd attacked Tala.

He hadn't been so lucky, but his death had been blamed on gangs with dangerous dogs. No one suspected a shapeshifting wolf.

Thank goodness Mik, AJ, and Tala had gotten the kids away from the mangled body and far from the park, long before the police arrived.

Now three of them were in Colorado with Ulrich and Millie, and the other three were here in Montana. All of them capable of shifting, but without any knowledge of their heritage or the responsibilities that went with their amazing birthright.

No wonder Anton was excited about the challenge.

Adam spotted Oliver and Mei. Hand in hand, they crossed the driveway from their little cottage. Oliver waved to someone behind the big house. Adam turned and spotted two large wolves he recognized as Anton and Stefan, trotting across the meadow. He wondered if they'd found anything suspicious on their run. All of them had sensed something out of sync the past few nights. A sense of something not quite right. After the attacks right here on the property barely a month ago, everyone was still on edge. It didn't hurt to be careful.

Anton was proof you couldn't spend your life living in fear. You had to live it as best you could, or it would destroy the better part of you.

Anton had come so close to letting fear overtake him, but somehow Keisha had hauled him back from the edge. The love of a mate was a powerful thing. Adam squeezed Eve's hand and grinned at Oliver. "Nothing like hitting the newbies with the whole crew, eh Ollie?"

Oliver clipped Adam's shoulder in a light punch. "It's Oliver," he said, laughing. "Let me maintain at least a little dignity."

Mei leaned over and kissed him. "Too late, sweetie. I know what you've been doing for the past two hours."

Adam raised his eyebrows. Oliver turned brick red.

"Wow, Ollie . . . I didn't know you could blush like that." He lowered his voice and turned to Mei. "Details?"

The doors on the SUV were opening. "Later. I will say that the time frame in question included handcuffs and a treasure trove of battery operated implements."

"Enough, Mei." Oliver flashed her a stern look, and she broke into giggles.

Grinning broadly at the two of them, Adam tugged on Eve's hand and continued across the driveway to the visitors' car. Mik and AJ climbed out of the vehicle and stretched. Both men turned to give Adam and his mate a hug. A lanky young man with shaggy, dark brown hair and a plaster cast on his right leg that stretched from midthigh to ankle climbed awkwardly out of the middle seat. He reached in to give Tala a hand. Another dark-haired man came next. He was tall, though a few inches shorter than the first one, and he looked a bit older with his hair cut military short. Adam figured he must be the doctor. He was followed by a striking young woman of mixed heritage. She straightened up and stretched her arms over her head, emphasizing her height. Adam figured she had to be at least six feet tall, and her lean, athletic build added to a totally impressive package. Her hair was long and glossy black like Mei's, but her skin was almost as dark as Oliver's.

AJ had told him she'd been a victim of the sex trade, brought to the country illegally as a small child. Lucien Stone, head of Pack Dynamics, the Chanku-run investigative and search and rescue agency in San Francisco, was still working on getting identification for her.

The newcomers milled about, stretching after the long drive and collecting their few pieces of baggage. Adam stepped back when Anton and Stefan came down the steps wearing nothing more than loose sweatpants, all they'd grabbed after their run.

Anton greeted Tala with a hug and a kiss. "You're early. We didn't expect you until later tonight."

She laughed and kissed him back. "Over twenty hours, straight through. AJ actually let Mik drive for a while. I'm still in shock."

"So am I, but I think it's because of Mik's driving." AJ gave Anton a quick hug and then stepped closer to Adam with a pensive smile on his face. "I've missed you," he said, and there was a world of meaning in his words.

Adam flashed back to a morning not so long ago when they'd not only had spectacular sex, they'd shared an amazing out-of-body experience that continued to haunt him. He wondered if AJ still dreamed of that mysterious morning encounter.

I do. It never leaves me. Nor does the second event, when we shared it with the others. I'll never be the same.

Adam stared into AJ's dark amber eyes and his body hardened, immediately aroused. He smiled, leaned close and kissed AJ's lips. "Later," he said, but when he turned away, AJ's mental touch was like a stroke along his very erect cock.

Adam bit back a grin, actually thankful for the tight fit of jeans that helped control and disguise his aroused state.

"Adam, I want you to meet Christopher March, otherwise known as Deacon." Tala tugged on the tall kid's hand and dragged him forward. Long and lanky, he nodded his head, obviously embarrassed to have been singled out. "Deacon hasn't shifted yet. Little problem with a compound fracture, but we know he's ready. We're hoping you can work your mojo on him and help him along."

She smiled and reached for the young woman. "This is Jazzy Blue, and no, I have not gotten shorter. She's just real tall." Tala grinned up at her.

Jazzy laughed and patted the top of Tala's head. "I think you're shrinking, Little Bit."

Stefan laughed. "You let her get away with that, Tala?"

Tala winked. "You'd be surprised what I let this girl get away with. Believe me, I am really sorry she's not coming home with us." Her smile left little doubt in Adam's mind where Jazzy's talents lay.

Tala reached for the dark-haired man standing quietly behind Jazzy. "This is Logan Pierce. I'm sure he'll tell you more about himself later, but Logan's a doctor. A general practitioner from Los Angeles."

Logan nodded. "It's nice to meet all of you." Instead of shaking hands with any of the Montana pack, he reached for Jazzy's hand and held on to her. His dark eyes shifted over each of the men, obviously staking his claim.

"Are you bonded?"

Adam grinned. It would be Stefan who'd ask.

"We are. Jazzy is my mate."

Stefan nodded. "Congratulations to both of you. Happened fast, didn't it?"

Logan merely shrugged. "So did finding out I was a wolf . . . and a doctor."

"You didn't know you were a doctor?" Oliver held out his hand. "I'm Oliver, Logan. This is my mate, Mei. That's

Adam's mate, Eve Reynolds. Stefan Aragat and Xandi, and these two are Anton Cheval and Keisha." He took a breath after the introductions. "How could you not know you were a doctor?"

Logan's smile was brief and reserved. "Amnesia. I was mugged almost a year ago and didn't find out what I'd been before the attack until Jazzy and I bonded."

Tala snorted. "Yeah, he gets his memory back and finds out he's a doctor. How come when mine came back, all I remembered was being a whore?"

Mik slung his arm around her shoulders and kissed the top of her head. "Because you were a whore, sweetie. A damned good one."

AJ looked up from his conversation with Anton. "Well of course she was a good one. What do you expect?" He laughed and shook his head when Tala stuck her tongue out at him.

Laughing and talking, everyone headed up the steps to the main house. Adam fell into step beside Deacon. "You're handling the crutches really well," he said. "How long has it been since you broke it?"

"About three weeks, now. Ever since the others started shifting. It's healing, but not fast enough. They don't want me to try shifting because the cast won't make it through, and the bone's too badly damaged to go without the cast." Deacon's frustration was obvious in his long, drawn-out sigh.

Adam nodded. "If you'll give me some time later this afternoon, we might be able to speed things up."

Logan stepped behind him midway up the long staircase. "Mik and AJ mentioned that. You're saying you can make a bone knit faster? How?"

"Yep. I use a link, but with the body, not the mind. I actually go inside, to the source of the injury and repair it on site. It's sort of telekinesis and mindtalking at the same time. I'm not really sure how I do it, but it seems to work.

You're welcome to piggyback and go with me." He shrugged. "Maybe you can help me figure out just what the hell I'm doing."

Logan stopped in his tracks and stared quizzically at Adam. "You'd do that? Show me how?"

"Of course I would. Hell, you're a doctor . . . a healer, right? I'm a fuckin' mechanic! You have no idea how much I've wished for more medical knowledge when I'm trying to put someone back together. It's a lot more complicated than a valve job."

Deacon broke in. "Do I have anything to say about this? It's my leg . . ."

"No."

Adam shot a quick look at Logan—they'd both answered Deacon at the same time. When Logan finally stopped laughing he slapped Adam on the back. Adam felt as if he'd passed some sort of test. "And you're laughing why?" he asked, fighting back his own laughter.

"It finally makes sense, the way Tala says the Chanku healer 'fixes things'."

Pretending to grumble, Adam continued on up the stairs. "Well, that's what I do. I fix things. Just ask Oliver."

He left that line hanging and wondered if Logan would ask. He didn't know of a single doctor who'd ever successfully replaced a missing pair of testicles on any man.

And he *would* put Deacon's leg back together.

As he reached for the front door, a shiver raced along Adam's spine, powerful enough to stop him in his tracks. He turned with his hand on the doorknob and glanced down the long driveway, toward the forest. The voices around him faded away as he studied the dark trees and listened to the uninterrupted chatter of birds. Nothing. Nothing at all out of the ordinary. He took a deep breath and shrugged off the uneasy feeling.

Then he opened the door and went inside the house.

Chapter 3

She jerked back from the eyepiece on the spotting scope. That was too damned close! Those brilliant amber eyes had gazed straight at the camouflaged blind for much too long a time for it to have been an accident. They'd appeared so close, magnified as they were through the lens, even though the man was over a quarter mile away.

Discovery meant almost certain death. Her father was proof of that. He'd learned their secrets and he'd died. They showed no mercy, but they were animals. All of them, predators.

Of course, what they couldn't find, they couldn't kill. She gazed at the forest around her, at the thick branches of the big blue spruce concealing her perch. Then she gave the scope a subtle twist of the lens and focused once more on the house.

"I'm going to help Oliver and Keisha get dinner on." Eve leaned over the edge of the bed and gave Adam a kiss. Before he could respond, she pulled away. "Later," she said, in her soft, southern drawl. "You distract me too easily."

"I try." He watched her go, and then crawled out of bed. By unspoken agreement, they'd all taken naps once their guests were settled. Of course, napping with Eve had nothing to do with sleep.

The past couple of hours had been absolutely magnificent. Feeling unusually mellow, Adam showered and threw on a pair of warm sweats. Temperatures had dropped the past few days. Fall was definitely in the air, but Anton intended to run tonight, which meant Adam needed to find Logan and Deacon.

They were both out on the back deck having a cold beer. Adam plopped down in one of the chairs next to Deacon. "Got a few minutes? I thought I'd take a look at your leg before the rest of them come wandering out here."

Deacon nodded. "Logan talked to Oliver."

"Ah. Good. What did he say?"

Logan shook his head. "What he said was fucking impossible. That you gave him a set of balls he'd never had. How?"

Adam shrugged. "That's the problem. I really don't know. I'm assuming he told you he'd been castrated when he was a child. I wanted him to be complete—a whole, intact man. Not for the sex, so much, but so he could shift. Once we linked I was able to help him become a wolf, and the wolf had balls. Luckily, they stayed when he shifted back."

"Damned lucky. In fact it's almost scary." Deacon stared at his beer for a few moments. "I'd like for you to try and fix it, Adam. It kills me to watch everyone shift at night. They go off and leave me at the house and I feel like they've ripped something out of me."

Logan frowned. "God, Deac . . . I'm sorry. You never said . . ."

Deacon shook his head. "Not your fault. There wasn't anything anyone could do about it, but if Adam can help me heal faster . . ." He sighed. "It's a compound fracture—I could be in this damned cast for four more weeks. I'm tired of waiting."

"How'd you break it?" Adam tried to see beneath the cast. He felt the injury, a raw, only partially healed wound.

"Walking down a trail in the redwoods, looking up at a bird." He glanced away and blushed. "I'm so tall . . . I've always been really clumsy. I fell into a ravine and caught my foot in some roots on the way down."

"Ouch." Adam shuddered. He'd picked up Deacon's memories clearly enough to make his own leg hurt. "Logan, put your hands on mine and link with me. Can you get into my head?" Adam pressed his hands against Deacon's cast, directly over the break.

"How'd you know exactly where it was broken?" Logan's eyes locked with his. His palms were warm and solid when he covered Adam's hands.

"I felt it." Adam shrugged. It was never easy to explain what he did. "It just feels wrong right here." He paused for a moment, searched for Logan, found him. "Okay . . . I've got you in my head." He glanced at Deacon. "Hold really still now, and open your thoughts. I want to make sure I'm not hurting you."

"Good idea," Deacon muttered, but his barriers were down and his mind wide open.

There was so much pain in this kid. So much loneliness. Adam slipped away from the more intimate, personal memories, closed his eyes and pictured the open wound on the leg beneath the cast—the flesh beneath the wound, the veins and arteries feeding blood to the bone, and the bone itself. There was some infection in the broken skin where the bone had torn through, and the break in the bone was long and jagged. It reminded him of the shattered bones in Anton's wolven body when he'd been shot by intruders last month.

Anton's fall from the cliff had caused more damage

than the bullet, and the repairs had taken everything Adam had. This was simple by comparison. He found the edges of bone and tied them tightly together, manipulating tissue, nerves, blood vessels, and bone on a cellular level until the separation between the two pieces was solid once again. In a way it reminded him of the jigsaw puzzles he'd loved as a kid, as piece after piece slipped into its proper spot. He removed all signs of infection where the bone had broken through the skin, and closed the wound with healthy tissues.

Logan remained a silent presence, hovering just on the fringes of Adam's consciousness. Deacon hadn't said a word. Adam wondered if the kid felt anything as the break in his leg healed. He stayed long enough to check the underlying bone, the one he thought was called a fibula. He wished he knew more about the human body—at least that bone looked and felt healthy.

Slowly backing his presence out of Deacon's leg, Adam checked blood vessels and muscles, passed through flesh and healthy skin and plaster cast. Back in his own reality, he felt Logan's consciousness slip away from his and blinked himself back to full awareness.

The first thing he saw was Logan. The shocked look on the man's face was priceless. "Amazing," he said. "Absolutely amazing."

"Not bad for your average auto mechanic, eh, Doc?" Adam laughed. "How do you feel, Deacon? Is the pain better?"

Deacon shook his head. "There's no pain at all. It felt warm when you were both spaced out, but the pain's completely gone."

"Spaced out? I guess that's a good way of putting it. Or spaced in. I think we can take the cast off. Shifting seems to promote healing, too, from what we've seen. There's going to be some swelling. I haven't figured out how to deal with that, but it's not going to interfere with the bone's healing. As long as you take it easy tonight, you should be able to run with everyone else."

Adam stood up to leave. Logan grabbed his arm. "I need to learn that. Can you teach me?"

"I can." Adam gazed steadily into Logan's eyes. Eyes exactly like his own. "I know you're new, that you've not been Chanku long enough to really understand that much about yourself, about all of us, but the easiest way for you to learn is to link at a deeper level."

"How?" Logan lurched to his feet, still holding tightly to Adam's arm. There was a desperate look in his eyes.

"A deep link during sex." Adam shrugged. "How else? Maybe tonight after we run?" He touched Deacon's shoulder. "I'd offer to saw the cast off, but it'll fall off when you shift. A lot easier on all of us, don't you think?"

Deacon blinked, his eyes going from Logan to Adam and back to his friend. "You mean it's not broken anymore? Just like that? I can try shifting tonight?"

Adam shrugged. "Just like that. And yeah, you should be fine shifting." He grinned at Logan. "What do you think, Doc? Can he shift?"

"I saw what you did, but I still don't believe it. Yeah, Deac. It looked totally fine." Logan stood up and grabbed Deacon's empty beer can. "I'm going to get us a refill. I don't know about you, but I could really use another beer. As far as your leg, I'll check it after you shift, but I think it's good to go."

They gathered in the great room after dinner. Logan glanced away from his conversation with Jazzy and Deacon as Anton stepped out of the kitchen. He had a stained, once-white dish towel wrapped around his waist and the front of his otherwise immaculate white shirt was spattered with water.

Logan snapped his attention back to his packmates. *He's doing dishes?*

Jazzy shrugged and Deacon just stared, but he'd been acting a little spaced out all afternoon, ever since Adam had repaired his broken leg and told him he'd be shifting tonight.

That had to have been a shock. Logan was still sorting through the unreal experience of actually taking a mental trip inside Deacon's leg.

"Anyone who plans to run tonight, be here in the great room in ten minutes." Anton tugged the towel off and dried his hands on it. "And yes, Logan. I've been doing dishes." He grinned. "Don't worry. It's a democracy. You'll get your turn."

He went back into the kitchen where Mei and Oliver were loading the dishwasher.

Logan watched until he disappeared through the doorway. "How'd he hear me? I wasn't broadcasting."

"He hears everything." Tala flopped down on the couch next to Logan and in a deep, mysterious voice, said, "Hears all, knows all, sees all . . ." Smiling, she added, "And he's one of the nicest men I've ever known. However, he used to scare the shit out of me."

Mik flopped his huge frame down beside Tala on the big leather couch and kissed her on the nose. "For what it's worth, he still scares the shit out of me. Deacon, you ready for tonight?"

Deacon shook his head. "I don't know. I've been waiting so long, been ready for so long. How come I'm such a nervous wreck?"

Jazzy leaned over the back of the couch and gave him a big kiss on the cheek. "Because you know we're all going to be watching you when you take your clothes off." She laughed and rubbed the top of his head like he was a little kid. "S'okay, though. You'll be great. And Deacon . . ." She leaned even closer and pressed her breasts against his shoulder. "After we run, I think Logan's going to spend a little quality time with Adam, so you're all mine."

"Oh, shit." Deacon looked at her wide-eyed. "Now I'll definitely screw up."

Quality time. Logan's stomach clenched into a tight knot. No way in hell would he admit it, but he was as nervous as Deacon. Not about shifting. Never about that—at least not anymore, but sex with Adam? He'd never done it with just a guy before. It was different when he and Jazzy brought another man into bed with them. She was the buffer, the one who made it all okay.

Would he ever get over his hang-ups? Hell, just thinking of that first time with Mik still made him hot, but he'd had Jazzy there too. Sort of as a "guy on guy" shock absorber. And since then, Deacon had joined them on a lot of nights and it was cool, but Deacon was a buddy and definitely not alpha.

Deacon and Matt were a lot alike in that respect. Both really great guys, but quiet and not at all aggressive. Logan wondered how Matt was doing with Nick and Beth. The three of them had flown back to Colorado to work on that wolf sanctuary with another group of Chanku. It couldn't be anything like it was here, not with all these different packmates, all of whom seemed to be pure alphas. It was amazing they got along so well.

Matt and Deacon were different. They accepted their Chanku birthright without any overt issues at all, but they hadn't even tried to get either of the women to pay attention to them. It was like the competition and aggression that most of the Chanku males accepted as their due didn't exist with the two of them.

But Adam? Adam was definitely alpha. Even Anton Cheval, the one everybody treated as the *uber-alpha* of the pack seemed to defer to Adam. It had to be the guy's amazing abilities.

Logan's stomach practically tied into knots just thinking about the fact Adam wanted to have sex with him tonight. Except it wasn't so much for the sex, it was to give Logan the knowledge he wanted. Knowledge he craved, information that would help him be a better doctor, better prepared to help his patients in a manner he had never dreamed existed.

So, if he wanted to think about it, it wasn't just sex for sex, it was sex for the sake of the link. For learning. Yeah, he could handle it easier so long as he thought about it as . . .

"You okay? You're a million miles away, and your barriers feel like a brick wall around your brain."

Jazzy's soft words in his ear dragged Logan out of his mired thoughts. "Yeah," he said. He turned his head just enough to plant a kiss on her full lips. Damn. He'd been so lucky to find her. So damned lucky. Everything about her seemed to fit him perfectly. "I'm just thinking about everything that's happened. Hoping it goes okay for Deacon tonight."

Jazzy slid over the edge of the couch, squeezed in between Logan and Tala and snuggled up close against him. "It will, now. That was so cool, how Adam fixed his leg." She ran a finger along his shoulder. Logan was convinced he felt the heat through his shirt. "I'll be thinking of you tonight. You and Adam. It makes me hot, imagining the two of you together."

Hearing Jazzy say the words sent a shaft of lightning from Logan's balls to his cock. He wasn't sure if it was her voice or the image of Adam and what they'd be doing in a very short time.

He'd never before been so anxious for a run to be over. Never been so apprehensive about his own sexual skills, his control . . . or lack of it. What if he . . . ?

"Everyone here?"

Anton's voice snapped him back to the present. Logan glanced around the room and realized it had filled up while he'd been indulging his libido with daydreams of Adam Wolf. Everyone seemed to be here except for Mei

Chen and Oliver, but they'd volunteered to stay and watch the babies for Keisha and Xandi.

Logan glanced over at Deacon and gave him a thumbs-up. He noticed Adam had moved closer to the young man, almost as if he were a doctor and Deacon his patient, which, in some ways, sort of explained their strange new relationship.

"We do the shift indoors, okay?" Anton was already working down the row of buttons on his shirt. "And stay alert. I've still got a strange feeling, as if all is not as it should be, but I can't put my finger on anything in particular. Keep an eye out for anything that feels the least bit sketchy. Have fun tonight, but don't forget to pay attention with all your Chanku senses. You smell anything, see anything, feel anything at all different, I want to know about it immediately."

He tugged his shirt off and started on his pants. Logan realized he was surrounded by people in various stages of undress, including his mate. Within moments, all of them were nude, and seconds later, everyone but Adam, Logan, and Deacon had shifted.

At well over six and a half feet tall, Deacon towered over both men in a room filled with wolves of all shades and sizes, all of them waiting to witness a new Chanku's first shift. "Are you ready, bro?" Logan stood to one side. Adam took the other.

"No pressure here, eh? Give him some space, guys." Adam touched Deacon's arm, steadying him once he dropped the crutches. The huge cast looked awkward and unwieldy. Deacon shifted his weight to regain his balance.

"Get inside my head," Adam said. "Watch what I do. Then do the same thing."

Deacon nodded. Adam shifted. Deacon took a deep breath and followed his lead. The plaster cast crumbled into dust. The large gray wolf sitting in the midst of the pile sneezed.

The sense of celebration and outright relief in the room was an almost palpable force.

Logan dropped to his knees and hugged Deacon's furry neck. "I knew you could do it. Is your leg okay? Any pain?"

The wolf shook his head. Lifted up his front paw and studied the long, black nails, the thick pads. *Shit. I didn't really think it would happen. My right rear leg doesn't hurt at all. That's the one I broke, right?*

"Yeah. That's the one you broke." Logan swallowed back a sudden thickening in his throat. He'd been part of this. He'd made love with this young man, had helped him when he'd been hurt. Had ached for him when they'd all shifted and Deacon remained behind.

He wouldn't stay behind tonight.

The other wolves milled about. Many of them approached Deacon, as if offering congratulations. It took Logan a minute to recognize individuals in the pack, but their personalities showed through even in wolf form.

You did it, kid! Stefan bumped shoulders with Deacon and moved aside when Tala, Mik, and AJ approached. They sniffed noses with the big gray wolf. The wolf that was Tala stayed a moment longer than the two guys. Logan wondered what she said to Deacon. It was obvious some private communication went on between the two of them. Finally she nuzzled Deacon's shoulder and turned away.

She paused a moment and looked up at Logan. *I told him we'll always have a bed for him in San Francisco. For you and Jazzy, too, and your three buddies in Colorado.* Before he could reply, she turned and trotted after Mik and AJ.

Finally, everyone's attention shifted away from the newest wolf. Regal even on four legs, Anton headed for the open back door, but it was his mate, Keisha, who led the pack out into the Montana night. Logan's head buzzed with all the mental conversations as each wolf followed their lead and slipped through the doorway.

Logan shifted and stood beside Adam, Deacon, and Jazzy. It happened so easily, the change from human to four-footed beast. So naturally.

It still embarrassed him, remembering how he'd practically called Tala, AJ, and Mik liars when they'd first tried to explain his Chanku birthright to him. He couldn't believe how stubbornly he'd resisted the truth, even though he'd already witnessed Nicky's change with his own eyes.

Well, no one ever accused him of not being a horse's ass . . . Logan glanced toward Adam and found the other wolf staring at him. A shiver raced along his spine. Damn. He usually wasn't this horny until after a run.

When they fell into line behind the others, Logan followed, but his mind wasn't on the frosty air or the sounds of wolves running on all sides. He wasn't mesmerized, as usual, by the pure joy of running on four legs with his beautiful mate at his side.

No. He was lost in Adam Wolf. Caught in the view of his lean, dark frame streaking through the forest. Trapped in his scent, which had suddenly become a seductive lure unlike anything Logan had ever known. Beguiled by the feral beauty, the mystery of their kind and the knowledge he and Adam would be together tonight, he followed the pack into the forest.

Damn. Dark shapes streaked through the artificially bright green meadow, clearly visible through the high-tech spotting scope. Even in the distorted light it was obvious the pack was huge, but at this distance a clear count was impossible. Were all of them running together? They wouldn't leave the babies unguarded, would they? Babies couldn't shift, at least not babies as young as theirs.

A light went on in the house. Then another at the opposite end. That meant more than one person inside. The rest of the pack would be gone for hours, but the house appeared well guarded. There'd be no chance of getting inside, at least not tonight. No matter. Wrapping up in a warm coat would have to do. Maybe the dreams would return, and with them the heat of sexual desire. Better than nothing . . .

Something was going on. She wished she knew, just as she wished she understood the strange dreams growing more vivid each night. At least once the wolves entered the forest, they'd be gone long enough to allow for a quick nap . . . a nap, and another round of dreams. Maybe the dreams held answers? If only Father were still alive. She'd never thought to ask him about the dreams.

Chapter 4

If wolves could laugh, Deacon knew he'd be howling with joy. It was unbelievable, a dream, a fantasy come true. All those nights when he'd awakened with the scent of the forest in his nostrils and vague memories of racing along dark trails with the sounds of critters scampering out of his way . . . all those memories were real! They were happening, here and now.

The cold wind chilled his nose but didn't touch his skin, protected as he was by his amazingly thick gray pelt. His feet . . . no, paws. Damn, he had huge paws, and they gripped the hard-packed ground while his powerful leg muscles propelled him forward.

The injured leg didn't ache at all. There was no sense of weakness, no pain, nothing to take away from the glory of this first run. He'd been so jealous when the others had gone out and left him home alone. He knew they'd felt guilty about it, even though his fall was no one's fault but his own.

Tonight made up for all those nights past. It made up for everything. For life on the streets from the time he was a young teen, to the uncounted times he'd sold his body in order to make enough money to eat, to the cold days wandering the streets and the colder nights huddled in a dark alley or run-down shelter, praying to survive until dawn.

This was beyond cool, running as part of such a powerful pack, as part of a family. At dinner tonight, Anton had welcomed them. He'd said they were all family. He'd looked right at Deacon when he'd said that, like he was personally assuring him he was included, too.

Damn, what a rush that had been. That feeling of family, especially with such amazing people. All of them smart and beautiful and loving. If he'd had the chance to choose a family, he couldn't have come up with anything better than Mik, AJ, and Tala, and the people he'd met today.

The trail was narrow here, and they ran in single file through groves of huge trees and thick stands of bushes. Such beautiful, strong bodies, and his was one of them. Deacon leapt over a huge fallen log and he must have cleared it by at least a foot! His front paws touched down lightly, his hind legs bunched under him and he practically flew through the forest. Usually he felt like such a shit, so tall and gangly without a lick of coordination. This body, though . . . This body could do almost anything.

Then it hit him like a punch to the gut. This body was going home to Jazzy Blue tonight. Jazzy and that long, lean, dark and gorgeous body of hers, all to himself. As much as he loved sex with Logan, he'd never once been alone with a woman like Jazzy. Never dreamed he'd have the chance.

Tonight. Tonight he had more than a chance. He already had Jazzy's promise. Jaws agape, ears forward, Deacon ran like he'd never run before.

They killed an elk, a huge beast they found in one of the upper meadows, but a dozen wolves made short work of the animal. Logan prowled on the fringes with the other males, snarling and growling while the females fed first.

Tiny little Tala had been the one to actually bring the

animal down. She'd circled around and surprised it, fearlessly charging in, avoiding the slashing hooves and locking her jaws around its throat. Keisha and Xandi went after hamstrings and Eve and Jazzy leapt on the animal's back, latching on to haunch and shoulder with their powerful jaws. The elk was already dying when it hit the ground.

A clean kill from what Logan could tell. It made his blood run hot. The females aggressively defended their meal while the males circled, snarling, occasionally snapping at one another.

Anton was the one who instructed them, who explained that theirs was a truly matriarchal society, that the females usually led in the hunt and the kill was theirs, to share as they saw fit. He held them back when Logan would have rushed in, anxious for his first taste of the freshly downed elk.

His human mind saw his behavior for what it was, a bloodlust brought on by the thrill of the hunt, the successful kill, the smell of warm blood. His animal side understood only that meat was hot and fresh, blood flowed and the scent of death meant a full belly.

Once the females let them feed.

Eventually all of them ate, leaving little more than scattered bones and strips of hide. They cleaned their muzzles, rubbing their faces in the dried grass and drinking from a nearby stream, rolled in the frosty grass and slowly broke away, each wolf to go off in his or her own direction.

Keisha, Xandi, and Eve, Adam's mate, headed back to the house together. Anton and Stefan chose to run farther into the woods, while Tala, Mik, and AJ headed in to get a good night's sleep. They were going back to San Francisco in the morning, without their three young Chanku.

Jazzy nuzzled behind Logan's ear and nipped the thick ruff of his neck. *Deacon and I are going back to the house. I love you.*

I love you, too. You looked magnificent, going after the

elk. He lowered his head and butted her chest. *I got hot, just watching you.*

Save it for Adam.

Her mental laughter filled his heart and soul, and then she was gone. Deacon trailed along behind her. He turned and glanced over his shoulder at Logan. Then he trotted into the brush right on Jazzy's heels.

Logan watched them leave with mixed feelings, expecting jealousy, finding none. He loved them both. He felt relief that Jazzy wouldn't be alone tonight, that she'd have someone with her who would protect her, watch over her . . . make love to her.

An owl hooted. He realized he stood alone in the meadow. Alone except for Adam.

Are you okay with Jazzy going home with him? Adam's muzzle rested on Logan's shoulder. *I hadn't thought about the fact you were newly mated.*

It's okay. I guess I'm surprised that I don't feel jealous. I love both of them. He shook his head in a very unwolf-like manner. *It's all new to me, my changing attitudes and feelings about sex. Having sex with a guy is new to me.*

A lot of us were bisexual before we became Chanku. It's that overwhelming sex drive we were all born with.

I wasn't. I mean, the drive was there, overwhelming at times, but I never even thought of sex with another man. There were always enough women. Logan turned and gazed into Adam's amber eyes. *Mik was my first experience with a guy. Then Deacon, but it's all still new. Scary, in a way. It's so intense, being with another man. Getting into his head. Tonight, with you . . . This is my first time alone with a man.*

Thank you for telling me. Quiet laughter flowed into Logan's mind. *I promise to be gentle. C'mon. Let's go back to Oliver and Mei's cottage. They're staying at the big house. Eve's staying with Keisha and Xandi tonight and we'll have the cottage to ourselves.* Adam turned away and trotted back along the trail they'd come in on.

Logan watched him for a moment, and then he followed. His body was already tight with arousal. It took everything he had to control the desire to stop Adam here, in the deep woods. Stop him and fuck him now, without the long run back to the cottage.

A question slithered into his mind—was this really about the knowledge Adam could give him?

Or was he lying to himself? Was it Adam Wolf he wanted? And was Adam's knowledge merely the excuse Logan needed?

Deacon couldn't think of anything at all to say, so he followed Jazzy in silence all the way back to the house. The night was cold and clear and the stars so bright they looked almost fake, hanging like silver ornaments in the midnight sky.

He hardly saw them. His entire focus was the she-wolf leading him through the forest. Her scent drew him onward, her lean body, the tilt of her ears, the way her tail moved with each step she took. He ignored the night sounds, the myriad scents, the life surrounding them in the deep woods.

There was only Jazzy. Only the wolf mattered.

They trotted out of the forest and crossed the meadow to the back deck. There were a few lights on in the house, but at first he sensed neither sound nor movement. He wondered if the others had gone to sleep.

Concentrating on Jazzy as she trotted up the stairs and headed toward the open back door, Deacon slowly picked out other sounds with senses much sharper than he'd had before. Women's laughter came from the end of the house where Anton and Stefan had their rooms and he recognized Mei, Keisha, Xandi, and Eve. A man's voice broke in . . . Oliver. Deacon would have laughed if he'd been human. So the guy with the new set of balls was in bed with four women? It seemed only fair.

Jazzy slipped through the door and shifted as soon as she was inside. Deacon followed her and suddenly he was a man again before he'd even thought to worry whether or not he could do it right.

Someone had cleaned up the remnants of his cast. It felt so good to walk without pain.

"C'mon. I need a shower." Jazzy grabbed his hand and tugged him down the hallway to their rooms. He started to head for his own room, but she pulled him into the one she shared with Logan.

"He won't be back for hours. Shower with me, okay? I know this is your first run, but aren't you hornier than you've ever been in your life? I can't believe how shifting makes me go so crazy."

She stood there, holding on to his hand and smiling at him, and he thought his heart would pound right out of his chest. Like an absolute dolt, he nodded in agreement and let her tug him toward the shower. He must look like a total idiot, but Jazzy had taken charge and Deacon wasn't about to say no to anything she suggested.

And she was right about being horny. Everything about him felt extra sensitive. Just walking turned him on, the way his cock bobbed against his belly with each step he took. The slight contact when his balls brushed against his thighs sent shivers along his spine.

Jazzy flipped on the water and he followed her into the shower. She was tall, but he still towered over her. He'd always felt so damned awkward with legs and arms too long, hands and feet too big and a cock so huge it scared most women.

Now the damned thing was even bigger than usual, swollen and hard, standing high and hot. His balls ached. If she so much as touched him, he'd lose it.

"Wow, Deac . . ." Jazzy brushed his dick with her fingertips. His whole body jerked. He moaned and flattened his hands against the shower walls.

"If you want me to last, Jazzy, you better not . . ."

She grinned up at him and rolled her thumb over the smooth surface of his glans. One finger slipped beneath the edge of foreskin caught just behind the head. He groaned and rolled his hips forward.

"Doesn't matter. If you come, you'll be hard again in less than a minute. I guarantee it. Just watch."

She slipped to her knees with the hot water beating down on them both and slipped his cock between her full lips. That hot, wet mouth, stroking tongue, and scrape of teeth hit him like a hammer to the crotch.

He cursed and grabbed at the slick tile walls for support. She sucked harder and her tongue snaked along the full length of his shaft. She cupped his sac in her palm and one long finger pressed against his asshole. Without any warning, his hips jerked, his balls tucked up tight between his legs and he blasted hot jizz down her throat.

Moaning, Deacon bent double, curling himself over Jazzy's kneeling body. She kept sucking and tonguing him and his cock kept shooting for the longest time. His legs felt like rubber and it was hard to catch his breath. Finally, she turned him loose and backed away, grinning. "See? Now watch what happens."

"Watch it? Shit, Jazzy. I can hardly stand up, much less see straight." But he glanced down anyway, too embarrassed to look her in the eye. He'd been dreaming about sex with Jazzy and now he'd already shot his load and . . .

"What'd I tell you?" Jazzy stood up, but she brushed her palm over his growing erection. "All ready to play again, and not nearly so impatient."

Impossible. Or not . . . The stinging spray calmed him down a bit, but he couldn't take his eyes off his suddenly rejuvenated cock. Finally he got it together enough that he rinsed his tangled hair and soaped his pits, but he kept glancing down to make sure the thing was still hard. Jazzy's hair was all white and frothy with shampoo. She smelled like vanilla and her dark body glistened. He wanted to touch her, but he didn't know if she'd let him or not.

So far, this was all Jazzy's show. He figured she'd been doing just fine. They got clean and rinsed beneath the spray without too much more body contact. Even though he'd already come once, washing his crotch was pretty dicey. He reached for a towel hung over the shower door, but Jazzy suddenly threw her arms around him. Her wet body slid against his and he hugged her tight to keep from falling, but it was like hugging a wet seal.

A very sexy wet seal with full breasts and a soft belly and lips to die for.

"Do you want me, Deac?" Jazzy's mouth was sucking on the soft skin between his neck and his shoulder, and she rolled her pelvis against him. The soft thatch of hair between her legs brushed over the underside of his cock.

"Oh, shit, Jazzy. Are you kidding?"

She laughed and her mouth and tongue slid wetly down his chest. She sucked on his left nipple and then bit down—not too hard but enough to make it sting. His cock twitched. He groaned and fought his body's reaction. The need was all-consuming, the powerful, gut-wrenching need to shove his cock inside her, to take her here in the shower, up against the wall and drive into her as hard as he could, as fast as he could. But she was Logan's mate and he didn't know the rules, so he fought it.

"Don't."

"Don't what, Jazzy? God, you're killin' me here." He arched his back and pressed his chest against her mouth, silently begging for her teeth, her hands, her lips.

"Don't fight it. Take me hard. Now. Right here in the shower with the water making us both all slick and slippery. Do it up against the wall. Just shove it in as deep and hard as you can. I want it now, Deacon. Want it like that."

"Shit. How'd you . . . ?"

"You're broadcasting, Deacon. I hear you . . . And I like what I hear. Can you do it? Is your leg strong enough to hold me?"

"Shit, yes." He groaned and kissed her, sucking her full lips between his, biting and feasting on her mouth. She twisted her hips and pressed her thighs against his. Her hand slipped between them and caressed his swollen cock, fingers encircled him and squeezed. Then she broke their kiss long enough to aim his hard cock between her legs, between the silky, swollen lips guarding her pussy.

A black haze filled his vision. Deacon felt the hot touch of her outer lips, the slick inner walls, and he thrust forward and up, so hard he lifted her feet off the tile.

Laughing, Jazzy wrapped her long legs around his hips and her arms went around his neck. Deacon braced her against the tile wall of the shower. The spray beat down on his back and buttocks and he plunged in and out like a wild man. He'd never have the balls to do this with Logan nearby, but now, just him and Jazzy . . . *Oh, shit, oh, shit, oh, shit* it was so damned good and she was already coming, already climaxing, her pussy rippling around his dick, pulling him in deeper, harder.

Her back arched and she pressed harder against him, her thighs squeezed the breath out of him. Her arms were like bands of steel, holding him close. She sucked him all the way inside, like his huge size didn't matter at all to her. He was in so deep she ground her pussy lips against his root and he felt the hard knot that had to be her womb pressed against his tip.

He'd never felt anything like this, never been completely buried in a woman, not like this. Tonight he was invincible, unstoppable.

Harder, faster, he pounded into her. The heat was boiling up from his balls, racing the length of his cock and Jazzy screamed! Damn, she screamed and bit his shoulder, latching on so hard he felt the skin break and he roared like some fucking wild beast. Roared and exploded, his cock blowing seed deep inside Jazzy, spurt after spurt while her muscles rippled and clenched, squeezing him so hard it hurt, squeezing every last drop and wringing him dry.

Her heels separated against his back and he felt them slowly slide down along his legs. It was all he could do to hold his own weight upright, much less Jazzy's. Somehow, though, he managed to keep from stumbling until she was standing in front of him, her arms still looped around his neck, her tongue caressing the place on his shoulder where she'd bitten through the skin.

"You're bleeding," she said, pressing her body close. "I'm really sorry."

"S'okay." He nuzzled her wet hair, reached behind her and turned off the water. "Damn. That was . . ."

"Amazing? Mind-boggling?" Jazzy laughed. "Shit, Deacon, where'd that come from? I didn't know you had it in you. You were like a wild man."

"Did I hurt you? Fuck, Jazzy, I'm really sor—"

She pressed her finger to his lips. "Are you kidding? I loved it. Logan would love it. Getting that cast off your leg really turned you loose!"

"You really didn't mind?" He grabbed a towel and rubbed her dark hair, then ran it along her body, between her legs.

"Absolutely not." She arched and groaned.

"Good." He stood up and ran the towel over himself, then he picked Jazzy up and threw her over his shoulder. "Because I want to do it again."

"Again?" She actually squeaked.

"Yep, Jazzy. Again. And maybe again after that." He carried her across the room and tossed her on the bed. His cock had already recovered, if it had even gone down. No matter. He'd never felt so powerful, so sure of himself.

The night was young and so was he.

And Jazzy was his—right now, for this moment in time. All his with Logan's full consent and permission. With any luck, Logan might show up before he was totally wiped out, and then he'd have both of them. Maybe he'd even call the shots this time. He looked down at Jazzy and grinned. Then he palmed his cock and stroked the full, fat length of it. It felt so damned good, he did it again, running his hand slowly up and down until it grew to fit his grasp, swelling hard and solid in his hand. Jazzy reached for him. Her eyes glowed with need. Need for him.

It just didn't get any better . . .

Chapter 5

The wolves had been returning all evening. One by one or in groups of two. Keeping count probably would have been a good idea. At this point, she really had no idea how many she'd seen.

Someone moved near the small cottage, the one across the driveway from the main house. Two wolves trotted across the drive and up the stairs to the front deck. They disappeared in the shadows. She tried to see where they'd gone, but the scope was slightly out of focus. She adjusted it quickly, but not fast enough. The view cleared just in time to see the door close behind the body of a tall, naked man with a wolf at his side.

Damn! Had that one shifted on the porch? Outside? Why not the other one? *Crap*. One more missed opportunity, all because the scope was out of focus! The first chance to actually witness a shift, missed. *Damn, damn, damn!*

Much too aware of Adam's nudity, Logan followed him through the door and shifted once he was inside. "I hope no one saw you."

Adam shrugged. "I know. I tried to be quick. I should have been more careful, but I forgot to leave the door ajar." He laughed and shrugged his shoulders. "I still haven't figured out how to open one with paws. You're right, though. We need to be careful. I can't get over the feeling someone is watching us. Guess I'm just being paranoid, but we didn't used to worry out here. We'd shift anywhere because we felt protected, as if we had all the privacy we needed. Not anymore."

Logan quietly closed the door. Talking about anything, even something this bad, was better than thinking about the fact they were both naked, both aroused . . . both well aware why they were here together.

And what they were going to be doing in a very few minutes.

"Mik told us about the attacks here last month, that they actually got inside the house."

Adam nodded. "They did." He led Logan down the hallway. The line of his back was long and smooth. A sheen of sweat between his shoulder blades and along his spine caught a reflection from the hall light . . . the same light that left deep shadows in the taut muscles of his buttocks as they rippled and bunched with every step.

Logan was mesmerized by the flow of light and shadow across Adam's ass, the muscles hollowed and dark as he moved ahead with such natural grace. His fingertips itched with the effort it took to keep his hands at his sides, so badly did he want to reach out and stroke Adam's sleek flanks.

"They could have stolen the babies," Adam said. His deep voice raised barely above a whisper. "As it is, they almost killed Anton."

"But you saved him, right?"

Adam paused with his hand on the doorknob to what was presumably a bedroom. He looked unbelievably handsome, every inch an alpha male, yet unaccountably conflicted. A chill passed over Logan. A line of heat surged through his groin and settled in his balls.

"Not really." Adam's soft reply caught him by surprise. "He was in bad shape when I got to him. I mended the broken bones and stopped the bleeding, but we would have lost him without the pack." Adam paused and closed his eyes a moment, as if the memories were physically painful for him. Then he turned his gaze on Logan. His amber eyes sparkled in the low light. Tears?

"I was exhausted . . . beyond exhausted, and I couldn't do anymore for him. Somehow Eve and my sister Manda figured out a way to channel their energy into me. So much of what we do is a learning process. There's so much we don't know, so much we might be capable of, if only we knew."

Adam shook his head, obviously frustrated by his lack of knowledge. "They did it so I could help Anton, but there wasn't much more I could do for him, not until everyone in the pack gave him as much of their life force as they could. That's what saved him. That and his daughter Lily."

"Lily? She's just a baby. And with so many injuries . . . how?" Channeling life force, healing broken bones from inside a body . . . It was all too much.

"Come with me and I'll show you." Adam held the door wide open.

"Said the spider to the fly." Grinning despite the butterflies in his belly, Logan stepped through the open door into the bedroom beyond. He fixated on the big, empty bed and his mind exploded with questions, but all he asked was, "Is this where you and Eve stay?"

"Sometimes." Adam ran his fingers along the bedpost. "A lot of nights we're in with Mei and Oliver, sometimes over at the big house. Some nights it's just the two of us, when we want to be alone. There's never any pressure for any of it . . . It's all up to the individual." He turned away from the bed and stroked Logan's shoulder.

Logan's body jerked.

"Relax. I won't bite."

"Damn. I was sort of hoping you might." His voice cracked and he felt like a damned fool. He looked back over his shoulder at Adam. Adam's eyes narrowed, studying him.

Logan took a moment to do the same, to inspect Adam's lean body, his fair skin darkened by exposure to sun and wind, his large hands covered in nicks and scars from working on things that were broken.

From fixing things.

And those things included people, with all their myriad injuries. Exactly what Logan wanted to understand.

Adam was heavily aroused, his cock standing dark and proud against his flat belly. The nest of hair at his groin was darker than the streaked blond hair that hung in tangles to his shoulders.

Logan was every bit as turned on, erect and swollen to the point of pain, but all he could do was stand there, trapped by Adam's gaze, caught by needs he didn't fully comprehend.

He bowed his head, a blatantly submissive gesture that somehow felt right. "I'm sorry, Adam. I don't know how to do this."

Adam grinned. "What? Fuck a guy or get into my head?"

Logan raised his eyes, smiled and shook his head. "Take the first step. Usually Jazzy leads the way."

This time Adam laughed out loud and Logan felt the tension begin to melt away. "Don't you love those alpha bitches?" Adam walked across the room and grabbed a bottle off a low shelf. "This might help," he said, pouring the golden liquid into a water glass and handing it to Logan. He poured another for himself. "They don't call it liquid courage for nothing. It's a trick I learned from Anton. A glass of good cognac releases a lot of inhibitions we still have from our human lives." He stretched out on the bed, grabbed a pillow and leaned against the headboard with his glass in his hand.

Logan sipped at the fiery liquid and felt the heat as it slipped down his throat. At Adam's unspoken invitation, he stacked a couple of pillows against the headboard and stretched out beside him.

"That's me," Logan said, staring into the golden liquid in his glass. "Full of inhibitions. The weird thing is, when I had amnesia, I got myself tattooed from one end to the other, pierced my nipples and my dick . . ." He glanced at Adam and sighed. "It's like I had this alternate personality that finally broke free."

"That was probably the Chanku part of you, tired of being roped in by conventions." Adam shrugged and set his glass aside. He'd almost emptied it. "After so many years of medical school, your internship, residency . . . I imagine that part of you was more than ready to break free."

"Could be." Laughing, he stared at his glass. "Then, the first time I shifted, all the tats just fell off, along with the piercings."

"Dust in the wind, right? Anything foreign to the body doesn't make the shift. Luckily none of us has had any fillings in our teeth." Adam rolled his head to the side and grinned. "Did Tala tell you what she lost?"

Logan nodded, laughing. "Her IUD. We've had fun teasing her, but she's a damned good sport." He took a big swallow of cognac. It burned going down and made his eyes water. His smile slipped as his mind shifted away from Tala, on to deeper things.

He took another swallow and turned his head. He wanted to see Adam's eyes when he spoke to him. He needed that connection, at least now, while he was sharing a part of himself he rarely gave up. "I remember back when I was a resident at Good Samaritan, a big hospital down in southern California, thinking about sex and being too damned tired to do anything about it. After I was injured—it happened during a business trip to San Francisco—I had no idea who or what I was. No identity, no money. Once I was healthy enough, they booted my ass out of the hospital and I ended up on the streets. I fell in with a group of homeless guys. Hell, they'd fuck anything that moved, but that didn't feel like me, either. Their lack of morality, of direction, bugged me. The ones I ended up with, Deacon, Jazzy, Nick, Matt, and Beth, were all smarter than the rest. More focused on survival, but surviving with a code of honor the others didn't have." He stared at his glass and took another sip.

Adam nodded. "There's an instinctive sense of integrity among Chanku. Ruthless, sometimes, but still honorable. An ability to kill without regret if the pack is threatened, to kill for food, but there's a powerful sense of family, too. It's something all of us seem to need. Probably what drew you to your friends in the beginning. A sense of something familiar, even though you didn't recognize it."

Logan nodded, mesmerized by the soft glow in Adam's eyes. He watched the steady tattoo of his pulse at the base of his throat and thought he actually heard the throbbing beat of Adam's heart, the rush of his blood through veins and arteries.

Without conscious thought, Logan reached for Adam, touched the pulse point in his neck, traced the broad stretch of his shoulder and ran his fingers down his arm. He felt Adam's thoughts in his head, his curiosity, his need to know more of what Logan had learned about medicine as much as his need to understand the kind of man Logan was now, after essentially living his life as two distinct personalities.

The dedicated doctor, the amnesiac slacker. Which one wanted to share his body with Adam Wolf? Logan set his empty glass down on the bedside table and reached for

Adam, vaguely aware he'd suddenly taken the more aggressive role.

Something about Adam drew him, whether it was the calm acceptance and understanding in his eyes, or the powerful sense of self that seemed so much a part of the man.

Adam knew who and what he was. Like Anton Cheval, he accepted his power and shared it without question, yet the need to learn more was a compelling force. The need to know more about others in order to understand himself.

Why Logan found that trait so seductive, he wasn't sure. Maybe it was the cognac. Maybe not. Without planning the move, he pulled Adam into his arms. Adam came willingly, all lean muscle and masculine angles and warm male flesh. Logan held him close, traced the seam of his lips with his tongue and explored the soft contours of his mouth.

Another man's mouth. He couldn't recall kissing Deacon. Maybe he had . . . or Mik, either. He had to taste Adam. Adam's lips were dry, a little chapped and weathered, just like the rest of him. Logan moistened them with his tongue, slipped between and touched teeth and tongue. Adam's big hand palmed the back of his head and held him close. His breath was hot, sweet, seductive.

Kissing wasn't really necessary, not for the physical coupling required to link, but Logan needed it, wanted the sense of connection that demanded a total union of taste and touch.

Adam threw one long leg over his thigh and pulled their midsections together. Hip to hip, cock to cock—when Adam's hot shaft slid across his, Logan gasped and thrust his hips forward.

They grappled, mouths fused, legs twisting and tangling in a sensual wrestling match for domination that brought their bodies closer. Logan's sense of power grew with each moment of contact, the innate feeling there was something about the two of them together that made each of them stronger.

Adam broke the kiss first, and power shifted. He slipped lower, biting at Logan's nipples, licking his belly and finally reaching his swollen cock. There was no subtlety, no finesse at all, just pure, male power when he wrapped his lips around Logan's cock and sucked him deep.

Logan arched his back. He cried out when Adam caught his balls in his hand and squeezed just to the point of pain, but it was pleasure that held him, desire that controlled him. Sucking harder, Adam's teeth scraped sensitive flesh, his tongue danced along the sleek length of Logan's shaft.

Adam took him quickly to the point of climax, but he pulled away before Logan lost control. He reared back on his knees, chest billowing in and out with each breath, his mouth and chin slick with his own saliva and Logan's precum. He wiped his face with the back of his hand and looked down at Logan where he lay, stretched out on the bedcovers.

"Whatever I want," he said. "Whatever I say. All right?"

Heart pounding, his cock wet and throbbing and his balls tight between his legs, Logan would have promised Adam the moon.

He nodded.

Adam reached into a drawer beside the bed and pulled out a wrapped condom and a tube of lubricant. He set the tube on Logan's belly as if he were nothing more than furniture and handed the condom to him. "Put this on me."

Adam leaned forward and planted his hands beside Logan's head. His cock bobbed obscenely between them. A white bubble of fluid dripped from the slit and landed on Logan's chest.

Logan shivered and bit back a groan. With teeth and shaking hands, he tore open the package and carefully wrapped his fingers around Adam's hot length.

Damn, the guy was huge. At least as large as Mik, if not bigger, and he was going to shove that monster up his ass. Logan's chest tightened, but it wasn't fear. Pure, unadulterated arousal, an almost manic desire for penetration surged through his body.

He raised his head and caught Adam watching him, watching Logan's face, not his hands. The two men stared at each other for a moment. Their thoughts were totally blocked, but if the longing written on Adam's face was as clear on his own, Logan knew there was no doubt of either man's intentions or desires.

Logan lowered his gaze first. He looked down at his hand, at the tight grasp of his fingers around Adam's thickly veined cock. The white bubble at the tip had become a steady stream, running down Adam's shaft, coating Logan's fingers. It would be so easy to jerk him off, to make Adam come before he had a chance to fuck his ass, but that wasn't why they were here.

He swallowed, took a deep breath, and placed the condom over Adam's broad glans, covering just the tip. The pure yet somehow forbidden intimacy of the act, of sheathing another man, made him even hotter. The muscles in his groin and between his legs rippled and clenched almost violently, but he managed to roll the condom down over Adam's length. He even remembered to leave enough at the tip so that it wouldn't tear when he ejaculated.

An image filled Logan's mind, a visual of streams of hot, creamy fluid shooting forcefully from Adam's cock, caught there within the latex tip of the condom. He imagined the taste . . . bitter, maybe, or even sweet, but he wouldn't know. Not this time. *As if we'll do this again.*

Logan swallowed convulsively as he smoothed the sheath over Adam's hard length. Knowing what was coming next, once the condom was in place, sent a stab of heat from the small of his back to his balls.

His buttocks tightened. He released Adam's sheathed cock and rested his hands beside him on the bed covers.

Adam sat back on his heels and grabbed the tube off Logan's belly. "Roll over."

There was no intonation at all in the clipped instructions. Logan had no idea what Adam was thinking, what he truly expected of him. Adam's mind was closed, the thoughts held back so that Logan acted in a complete void of knowledge.

Adam's easy domination made Logan's heart pound. His mouth went dry, his body tingled with expectation and excitement. He was such a control freak. Did Adam know that? Was that the reason he . . .

"You're broadcasting. Quit trying to analyze me or what the fuck we're going to do. Just roll over. I want your ass in the air, knees bent. Fold your arms and put your head down. Close your eyes. Don't talk and don't move."

Logan rolled. He took the position. Submissive, helpless. Cool air brushed his buttocks and for some reason he felt more naked, more exposed, than he'd ever been in his life. He was so hard, he hurt. His cock brushed his belly and the wet tip left a smear across his stomach. He wanted to grab it, to wrap his fingers around that swollen piece of meat and jerk off hard and fast before the pressure killed him, but he kept his arms folded and his forehead pressed against his wrists.

And he waited.

Vulnerable, more defenseless than he'd ever been with any other person. The ones who mugged him had knocked him out first. He'd never known what happened. Now he knew. Now he anticipated what was to come, the complete submission of self.

Submission to another man.

Adam knelt behind him. Logan sensed but couldn't read him. He felt the curve of Adam's calves brushing the sides of his legs, but nothing more. No mental contact, no other physical contact. He counted seconds that dragged on forever. Finally, after at least two full minutes, Adam roughly shoved Logan's legs farther apart. It threw him off balance and he knew his butt cheeks gaped wide. He felt horribly exposed. Unprotected. The taut muscle around his ass tightened, clenching and releasing in a rhythmic pattern that made his cock even harder.

Adam didn't move.

What the fuck was he doing? Just kneeling back there, staring at his ass?

Logan had never felt so defenseless. Not even when he was in the hospital, his head wrapped in bandages, no clue to his identity. This was worse, this sense of being totally under Adam's control. The sense of urgency, of knowing he was ready to do anything at all to please him, admitting to himself that it wasn't merely for the knowledge Adam had promised to share. No, he'd do it just to ease the ache, to satisfy the pure, carnal need for Adam Wolf.

Jazzy had tried to play the dominant partner, but they both knew Logan could overpower her anytime he wanted. Adam was physically stronger than Logan. Bigger. Kneeling here in the bedroom with the lights still on, his body entirely exposed, there was no denying the facts. He was entirely at Adam's mercy, his cock hard and dripping, his asshole winking an invitation.

He trembled, as much from fear as anticipation. His heart pounded, echoing in his ears. His senses, already Chanku sharp, seemed to sharpen even more.

When Adam ran his fingers down the sweaty crease of his ass, Logan jerked.

"Hold still."

He forced himself not to move. Not when Adam stroked him again, pausing at his hole, not when he forced a finger inside through painfully dry tissues.

Logan bit back a sigh when Adam added the slippery

lube to his fingers and pressed the broad tips against his tight sphincter muscle. Rubbing and pressing, he worked at the sensitive ring of flesh before pushing first one, then two fingers inside. In and out, slowly, methodically softening the taut muscle. Logan bit back a groan of pleasure.

Adam added a third finger, stretching, probing deep, forcing them all the way in. When he softly massaged Logan's perineum with his other hand, Logan wanted to cry out.

Pleasure? Pain? So closely aligned, one so much a part of the other he didn't know, but he bit his lips and breathed deeply, steadily through his nose.

Even that didn't work when Adam cupped Logan's balls in his hand and spread lube over the wrinkled sac and along his cock. Exquisite pleasure, unbelievable sensation enveloped him. A small whimper escaped in spite of all his attempts at silence.

At the first hint of sound, Adam's hands slipped away from his body. Logan shivered as all the parts of him covered with the slick lubricant reacted to whatever fragile air currents drifted through the room. They felt like cool fingers caressing his balls, slipping over his buttocks and down the sweaty crease, stroking his cock.

He heard Adam screwing the lid back on the tube. Cool air raised gooseflesh over his back and down his thighs. Still he waited, and the tension grew.

He sensed Adam's change of position behind him. The sense of waiting, of expectation grew, expanded, swelling until Logan felt as if he might explode with wanting. Then Adam was in his head, his thoughts crystal clear. Logan saw through Adam's eyes, felt with Adam's hands.

His body trembled and he gave up all sense of himself. Gave up the man who was Doctor Logan Pierce and became nothing more than a receptacle for Adam Wolf.

Chapter 6

Free now, open to whatever Adam asked of him, Logan tried to divide the sensations, the feelings that were Adam's, the need that was his own. His palm warmed to the length and heft of Adam's cock when he lifted the sheathed member in his hand, but it was Logan who trembled in expectation as Adam hovered a mere breath away.

When Adam finally pressed the broad glans of his cock against Logan's ass, the ease with which he entered was almost anticlimactic. Logan didn't even have time to tense, so intent was he on Adam's sensations, Adam's need to push just hard enough to enter, not enough to hurt.

His cock slipped through Logan's softened ring of muscle and pressed forward, deeper and deeper until his flat belly rested against Logan's buttocks, his cock so thoroughly embedded, their balls touched.

Logan sucked in a couple of deep breaths as Adam adjusted his angle of penetration and pressed even deeper. A low moan slipped from his throat when Adam reached under his belly and encircled his cock with strong, scarred fingers.

Then Adam began to thrust, slowly sliding his big cock in and out of Logan's ass. His fingers kept up the same rhythm, jerking Logan's lubed cock in time with each stroke.

Something in Logan's mind seemed to melt away. Was it his own ego? His inhibitions and fears, his need to control? He wasn't certain. He didn't care. His neural pathways were nothing more than a garden stroll for Adam . . . just as Adam's memories and knowledge opened wide for Logan.

The amazing eroticism of the sex act moved beyond pure sensation. It was a tool, a contrivance bringing them into complete synchronization, their bodies and minds so perfectly aligned, so perfectly aroused that the thoughts of one man were those of the other. One existence, one experience.

Logan saw with a most amazing clarity exactly how it was that Adam fixed things, from broken trucks to broken bodies, how he'd repaired his mate's terrible brain injury and Anton's badly damaged body. And during that learning, that gaining of knowledge, he knew Adam absorbed all Logan's years of study, all his training as a physician.

That and more. Adam's childhood, his discovery of his Chanku heritage, his love for his mate and the special bond he shared with his twin sister, Manda. The years he'd communicated mentally with the imprisoned young woman, unaware of their blood ties. All this and more became Logan's experience as Adam slowly, steadily, drove deep inside his body. The generosity of his mental link, the fact he held nothing back took Logan even higher into the pure beauty of this darkly sensual experience.

Pure, unadulterated trust, something shared so rarely between two powerful men. There was no longer a sense of domination over a lesser man. No need for Adam to exert his alpha status. Now, their minds linked in a bond almost as complete as that between mates. They were equals, no matter on what field they might chose to test themselves.

Logan suddenly understood the mechanics of replacing a bad carburetor in a truck as well as repairing broken bones and torn tissues, of manipulating damaged areas of the body so that they might heal and become whole. He absorbed Adam's knowledge of an unbelievable mental conversation Anton had shared with his infant daughter, a conversation that had convinced the dying wizard to choose life over death. He understood Adam's love for Eve, just as he gave up his true feelings for Jazzy, his own beloved mate.

All of this and more filled his mind, the knowledge to be sorted and fully comprehended later. He had no idea how much time had passed when he finally glanced back over his shoulder at the man driving in and out of his body. Adam nodded, and Logan knew they'd each assimilated and absorbed all the other had to share.

With that acknowledgment, Adam sped up his thrusts, slamming hard and fast against Logan's ass, his cock a thick battering ram staking its intimate claim. Adam had both hands on Logan, now. He squeezed his sac and his cock, pulling and sliding with the lube, building sensation into a blend of equal parts pleasure and pain.

Logan slipped once more into Adam's thoughts and discovered himself, his heat and his strong body, the way his cock felt, sleek flesh sliding across callused palm. He felt his own testicles, the solid orbs caught in Adam's fingers, and he knew the moment Adam's climax was upon him, the burning rush of semen from balls, through contorted tubes and vessels and down the length of his cock.

Shared sensation took Logan over the top. He arched his back and cried out as he pushed back against Adam, driving him deeper inside. His voice blended with Adam's, his orgasm blasted thick jets of seed between Adam's fingers and over his own belly and chest. It seemed to go on forever, the jerks and thrusts into his ass, the tightly clasped hand around his cock stroking slower now, rubbing semen along his shaft, over his belly, down to his balls.

They collapsed together and rolled to one side, chests heaving, mouths wide as they drew in great draughts of air.

"Shit, man." Adam's lips touched Logan's shoulder. His cock still pulsed deep inside Logan's body, yet as tightly connected as they were, the physical intimacy was nothing compared to the intimacy of the mental link they'd just shared.

"My feelings exactly." Logan pulled Adam's hands together over his belly and held them there. He didn't want to break either connection, not the mental link, not the physical.

Not yet.

Finally, long gasping moments later, Adam laughed. "You were a good student, weren't you? I can't believe everything you know. I was such a slacker in school."

Logan merely sighed. "I missed out on so much real life, though. I was doing it all on scholarship, so I had to get the good grades, be the perfect student, the best doctor. I didn't start living until I lost my memory." He laughed, but he knew there wasn't much humor in it. "I really came alive when I discovered I was Chanku. When I bonded with Jazzy. She's the better part of me."

"I know. I feel that way about Eve, and Oliver, too." Adam kissed his shoulder. "Do you see how I do it, now? How I fix things?" He slowly pulled himself free of Logan's body.

"I do. It's so simple, really." Logan rolled his legs around and sat up on the edge of the bed. His belly and chest were sticky with ejaculate and his ass hurt like hell. He still wasn't used to penetration, and Adam was big. He'd be sore in the morning, but the pain was worth it. His body still vibrated with the lingering effects of orgasm. "How about you?" He turned his head and gazed steadily at Adam. "Does the information you got from me make sense?"

"It does." Adam stood up and held out his hand. Logan took it and let Adam pull him to his feet. "And it will continue to make more sense as I incorporate it into my own thought processes. We all have different ways of using information, of finding conclusions. You'll do the same with what you've gotten from me." He glanced down at their clasped hands and slowly released his grasp. "We're going to do this again, you know. Maybe with the women, maybe not."

"Damn right." Logan raised his head and stared directly into Adam's eyes. The intensity in the other man's gaze took his breath and left him with a dark coil of need in his gut.

After a moment, Adam broke the visual connection. "I'll use the shower in Oliver and Mei's room. They won't be home tonight." He turned away, almost as if he regretted the small separation.

"Adam?" Logan pushed himself away from the bed and stood up. He wasn't certain what he wanted, what he was really asking when he said, "Don't leave."

Adam paused in midstep. He turned around. "Why?"

Logan shrugged. "I'm not really sure. I don't want to be alone right now. Will you shower with me?" He laughed, but the sound was strained, even to his own ears. "I'll scrub your back."

Adam grinned and shook his head. "Works for me. The one in Mei and Oliver's room is bigger. C'mon."

Feeling unaccountably shy, Logan followed Adam into the master bedroom. The bed in here was huge, even larger than the king they'd been using. Leather restraints were attached to the headboard and footboard, their padded cuffs open as if recently used. A variety of sex toys lay scattered about the bedside tables.

"So this is why Oliver's smiling all the time." He ran his fingers over a padded ankle cuff.

Adam slanted him a knowing glance. "Mei's into dominance, and Oliver's learned he thoroughly enjoys the submissive role. It's a match made in heaven."

Logan shook his head. "I've never tried any of that stuff."

"You might like it."

Adam flashed him a grin and headed into the bathroom. Logan followed, but his mind was on the big bed and the padded restraints . . . and images of Adam tied firmly in place.

The shower in this room was definitely larger, with plenty of room for both of them and spray nozzles at each end. Logan stepped into the billowing steam behind Adam as if they'd showered together for years.

Intimacy seemed to come more naturally once one man had been inside another's head . . . or maybe it was taking a cock up his ass. It didn't get much more intimate than that. Logan understood the man almost as well as he understood himself. He knew what he liked, what he needed.

What he wanted.

Once he'd washed himself, Logan grabbed a cloth and soaped it. Adam turned around and braced himself against the tile wall with his back to Logan. His shoulders were broad and tanned, the muscles strong and sleek under the stinging spray. Logan ran the washcloth over Adam's shoulders and slowly traced the bumps of vertebrae along his spine.

He hesitated at Adam's tailbone, then knelt down to wash first one long leg, and then the other. Adam spread his legs wider. Logan stood up and swirled the cloth around Adam's groin, carefully soaping his heavy sac. Hands covered in soap, he reached around Adam's waist and stroked his erect cock with his right hand while his left cradled his testicles, softly kneading the balls inside.

A low groan echoed against the tile walls. Logan searched for Adam's thoughts and found a slowly simmering kettle of desire, incoherent thoughts, and swirling images of lust and need. He concentrated on Adam's desires, pulling out individual images as they flitted across the man's conscious mind.

One in particular caught his attention. Logan grabbed the bar of soap and ran it across Adam's firm buttocks, over one tightly chiseled cheek and then the other. He slipped the bar along the dark crevice between, running it up and down the tight cleft until soapy bubbles trailed down Adam's inner thighs and his big body shuddered with each slick stroke.

Soaping his hands, Logan traced the warm valley with his fingertips, finding and pausing at the wrinkled edge of Adam's anal sphincter. He waited for Adam to say something, to tell him to stop, but the visuals expanded and the images came clear.

Adam wanted Logan, but he wanted it to be Logan's idea.

Logan swirled his fingertip around the taut muscle, pressing and retreating, softening the tight ring, pressing harder, easily slipping through into Adam's hot, wet passage.

He went deep with one finger, and then two, relaxing the tight muscles with each slow, easy thrust. Three fingers filled Adam, and he pushed back, forcing them deeper inside.

The shower pounded down on both of them, a seemingly inexhaustible supply of hot, steamy water. Logan slowly pulled his fingers free and replaced them with the broad head of his cock.

Adam shuddered with the first contact and his shoulders tensed. Logan wrapped his fingers back around the other man's cock, cradled his sac in his palm and pressed forward. He slipped easily through the softened ring of muscle, aware of the subtle ripple and flex of Adam's internal muscles clasping his cock, pulling him deeper inside.

Finally, long, slow moments later, Logan's dark tangle of pubic hair brushed against the smooth curve of Adam's ass. He withdrew and thrust forward once more, harder this time.

Deeper.

Adam grunted and pressed back against Logan. His

cock twitched in Logan's grasp. Logan felt Adam's sac pull up tighter between his legs.

He sensed Adam's need for more, for harder thrusts and he complied, pulling out almost to the very tip of his glans, then slamming back hard and deep, burying himself in hot, clenching muscle, his hands filled with hard cock and heavy balls.

He found a rhythm, a primitive dance with Adam swaying back each time Logan pressed forward. He felt as if he could go on forever, the two of them slamming together, pulling slowly apart, but tensions were rising, the sense of completion hovering just outside each driving penetration.

Water streamed over their bodies, the steam filled the bathroom and Adam's body visibly trembled. Still driving fast and hard against his lover, Logan opened his thoughts wide. He found only sensation—Adams's feelings, his needs, his unbelievable arousal as his body hovered on the knife's edge of orgasm.

Sharing his own rising passions, opening to the pure sensation of hard, masculine fucking, Logan felt his world expanding, felt himself changing, as if he was no longer a corporeal being, but merely a creature of sensation.

He blinked, and would have fallen if he'd been able, but somehow he'd become nothing more substantive than the steam rising from the shower, an entity of thought without form, hovering here against the ceiling, watching himself drive deep inside Adam's willing body.

What the fuck?

Relax and enjoy.

Adam's voice had the hint of laughter behind it. Logan sensed Adam's thoughts beside him, but he kept his gaze glued to the two men just beneath him. It was mesmerizing, watching himself, watching Adam and the steady thrust and retreat of two men caught in the age-old rhythm of sex.

What happened?

I have no idea, but it happens occasionally when the sex is really, really good. One of these days I'll figure it out.

Glad you think the sex is so good, but have you thought of maybe warning a guy? Logan felt himself begin to calm. Adam didn't seem to be the least bit concerned.

What? And have you run screaming out of the room? This time there was no imagining the laughter. *I think we're about ready to finish. Let's go back.*

Okay, but how?

Before he could finish the question, Logan was back in his own body. His muscles were screaming, his balls ached and he felt the familiar coil of heat running from the base of his spine to his sac.

He tightened his fingers around Adam's cock, squeezed his testicles just enough and thrust hard and deep as climax claimed him. His body jerked and froze in place while his cock pumped spurt after spurt deep inside Adam.

He'd taken him bare, without a condom, something Logan didn't think he'd ever done before. Thank goodness there was no risk of disease, but the sensation was exquisite, as much a mental rush as a physical one to experience that skin on skin feeling.

The sense of connection, a bond he'd not expected.

Adam's cock jerked between his fingers. A hot flow of ejaculate flowed over Logan's hand before it was washed away by the hot shower spray. Logan leaned forward and pressed his cheek against Adam's long back. His muscles quivered, his cock still twitched deep inside its dark passage, his heart thundered in his chest.

He felt cleansed, as if this experience with Adam had brought them full circle. He couldn't explain that weird out-of-body thing, but Adam hadn't seemed at all surprised, so Logan wasn't going to worry about it. Not now.

Now all he wanted was to dry himself off and go back to his room with Jazzy. Deacon was probably still with her, but that was good, too. He felt drained, his body replete, and if he didn't miss Jazzy so much, he'd crawl into bed here with Adam and sleep.

Logan pulled slowly, almost regretfully out of Adam. His cock was still partially tumescent, but his raging libido had stilled. He hated to give up the connection they'd shared, the amazing affinity, a bond both emotional and physical.

The water was finally beginning to cool, but he rinsed himself off and shut off the tap. Adam turned the one off on his end of the shower at the same time.

The silence that enveloped both of them felt like a benediction. The steady drip of water from one of the taps echoed in the stillness. Adam turned the handle a little tighter, and even that sound stopped.

Logan grabbed a towel off the rack just outside the shower door and handed it to Adam. He reached for a second one and dried himself. He wasn't sure what he expected after such an intense sexual experience, but it certainly wasn't this sense of ease, the feeling he was with an old friend, a man he could be himself with.

"You can, you know. Be yourself." Adam touched his shoulder and Logan turned around to face him. "We have no secrets between us after what we've done tonight. You've opened everything you are to me. I hope I've done the same for you."

Logan shook his head, bemused. "What happened? What was that, when we were both in the air, looking down at ourselves? Did it really happen?"

Adam nodded. "It did. It's happened before. I can't explain it. Don't know exactly how it works, but you never know when it might come in handy." He shook his head slowly. "We are a mysterious people, Logan. Even we don't know our own secrets. Not yet. We're trying to learn more about ourselves, but we just don't know what we're capable of. Personally, I think that if we believe something strongly enough, we can make it happen. The jury's still out on that. I don't really know."

He carefully hung the towel on the rack, leaned over and kissed Logan softly on the mouth. "Good night. I'm going to bed. If you want to stay here, you can sleep with me or take Mei and Oliver's room. They won't be back tonight." He cupped the side of Logan's face with his palm, smiled and winked. Then he turned away and walked out of the bathroom.

Logan watched Adam go with an odd sense of awareness. Since the link, he actually understood what made Adam Wolf the man he was. In fact, he knew Adam better than anyone else on the planet, besides Jazzy. The knowledge rattled him, yet left him feeling complete in some unexplainable way. He stared at the door Adam had gone through for a long, silent moment. Then he shook his head and laughed out loud.

Damn if his life hadn't taken some amazing turns.

Still feeling a little spacey, he headed down the hallway toward the front door. He knew what he needed, but he wouldn't find it here—a good night's sleep, back at the main house in that big bed with Jazzy. He wondered if Deacon was still there, if the two of them had gotten it on as hard as he and Adam had.

Or as often. Knowing Jazzy, he figured they might still be going at it. He had a lot to think about. A lot of fascinating knowledge he'd gleaned from Adam, even more he'd learned about himself. Amazing, he thought, how all your preconceptions can fly right out the window.

Adam was right. They would do this again. And again. Grinning, Logan opened the front door and stepped out into the quiet of the night.

Chapter 7

Startled awake, adrenalin surged and her muscles responded. There'd been some sort of disturbance, enough to override the dreams, but not enough to forget the reason for spending another miserable, chilly night in a hunting stand high up in the trees. It took only seconds to balance and focus the spotting scope, this time on the front door of the cottage just as it opened.

Earlier, a wolf and a man had gone inside. Now one man emerged. A different man than the one earlier, walking naked across the driveway toward the main house.

Didn't these people ever wear clothes? Of course, with a body that perfect, why cover it up? And how the hell was a person supposed to keep track of who belonged where? You needed a damned scorecard with all the players.

A shower and a good night's sleep in a warm bed sounded way too inviting. Impossible to get really comfortable in the small blind, but it was still the middle of the night and the wolves might be around. Just before dawn was a safer time to get out of here without detection. Then they'd most likely be sleeping. During the night you never knew who or what might be wandering about.

Naked. They were so often naked. But why? Not that she was complaining. No, not complaining one bit. That was one thing her father had never mentioned—how physically beautiful these people were. All of them perfect in every way. Except, of course, for the fact they were killers.

Gathering and packing the equipment only took her a few minutes. Now there was nothing to do but wait until all grew quiet once again. Wait, and hopefully, dream . . .

Stefan trailed behind Anton as they followed the property line from the western boundary to the main drive. Staying within the tree line, they slowly drew close to the house. They'd run farther than either of them intended tonight, but Stefan was well aware it had been a long time since Anton had felt like running at all.

Now he was filled with plans for their three young Chanku and his brilliant mind flipped from one idea to the next with almost ballistic speed. Stefan listened with only half his attention. When Anton got on a roll, there was no stopping him, not that anyone wanted to. The man was amazing.

Suddenly Anton spun around and planted all four feet. *You're not listening to a thing I've said, are you.*

Statement. Not a question. *Uh . . . some of it. Most of it.*

Anton shifted. He stood there in the darkness, tall and beautiful, laughing and shaking his head. "Ah, Stefan. I try so hard with you."

Stefan shifted as well. He sighed and tried his damnedest to bite back a grin. "I know. When will you realize I'm hopeless?"

"Never." Anton slapped his shoulder. "I promise never to give up on you."

"Okay. So what's so important that I should have been paying attention?"

"I was discussing our three young . . ." Anton's voice trailed off and he frowned.

"What?"

He put a finger to his lips. *Open your senses. Something's not right.*

Stefan immediately focused on the house just a quarter of a mile up the drive. *The babies? Xandi and Keisha?*

No. Close by. The thoughts of someone who doesn't belong. I sense . . .

Shit. Stefan raised his eyes, drawn to a towering spruce that grew beside the driveway. There, more than halfway up the tree, hidden in the branches . . . *a hunting blind?*

Anton nodded. *I see it. With someone inside. He might have heard us talking, but he hasn't spotted us yet. Link with me. We should be able to reach Igmutaka. I don't want to alarm the others.*

Igmutaka. That made sense. The Sioux spirit guide roamed freely now, his ancient intelligence in the body of a healthy young cougar. A very powerful cougar. Stefan took Anton's hand, marveling, as he always did, at the surge of power, the unmistakable strength of his friend. Their minds immediately linked. The call went out.

Igmutaka's response came moments later. He'd been trailing them through the woods most of the night.

Did you know that? Stefan shot a quick look at Anton.

Of course. And if you'd been paying attention, you would have, too.

Smug, Anton. You're sounding much too smug.

Anton merely raised one very dark eyebrow.

The big cat was suddenly there, not five feet away. Neither man had heard him arrive.

Damn, that's spooky.

Anton ignored him. He knelt in front of the cougar, his entire focus on the big cat. Communication with the spirit guide wasn't always a sure thing, but right now he seemed to understand Anton perfectly. Igmutaka raised his head and stared up into the spruce.

Then he walked to the base of the tree, sat beneath it

and screamed. His harsh cry raised the hairs along Stefan's spine.

A muffled curse came from the camouflaged hunting blind. Anton and Stefan melted back into the thick undergrowth. Both of them shifted. Anton nudged Stefan's shoulder. *I'm going to the house. I want to alert the others. I'll bring back Adam and the new kids. They need to know what threatens us.* He glanced upward once more, at the shadowed platform hidden in the branches. *Then we need to figure out how we're going to handle this latest mess.*

I'll make sure he stays put.

Don't take any chances.

Stefan stared over his shoulder at Anton. *You either, my friend. Now hurry.*

Growling and snarling, Stefan and Igmutaka prowled around the base of the tree. A good twenty minutes later, Anton trotted out of the woods and sat back on his haunches for a moment to watch. Dawn was breaking. The shadows of night faded quickly.

Igmutaka stretched his full length and raked the bark with razor sharp claws. Stefan growled. Fear radiated from the intruder trapped high over their heads. Anton trotted over and joined them. He howled and then circled the base of the big spruce with his fellow predators.

The sense of anxiety from whoever cowered in the hunting blind high above grew with each passing moment.

The sun was peaking over the mountains when Adam, Logan, Jazzy, and Deacon arrived in one of the SUVs. Disheveled, obviously just awakened, the three twenty-somethings glanced wide-eyed toward the wolves and wildcat.

"No," Adam said. "Look up."

"What the hell is that?" Jazzy shaded her eyes with her hand and squinted. "Is that some kind of tree house?"

"Well, in a way." Logan shook his head. "It's a hunting blind. A tree stand, actually. Sort of a temporary platform hunters use to hide from deer—or people they want to spy on." Logan walked around the base of the tree and then rejoined his companions. "This one is pretty sophisticated. He must have a ladder he can drop down."

Adam cupped his palms around his mouth and shouted. "You. In the tree. Come down now or I'm calling the sheriff."

"Not with those wolves down there." He didn't show himself. There was a noticeable tremor in his voice. "Or the cougar. You think I'm nuts?"

Adam glanced at Anton and raised an eyebrow in perfect imitation of Anton's typical response. "Well, yes, actually. I do. I'll call them off, but you get your ass down here now."

He sounds like a kid. Stefan trotted back, away from the tree, and sat beside Deacon. Now that his presence was no longer needed, Igmutaka slipped silently into the woods.

Anton stood next to him. *I wonder why he's watching us. At least it explains the sense of unease I've had all week.*

Stefan nodded, well aware it was a terribly unwolflike gesture. *The question now, is, what do we do with him?*

It all depends on what he's seen. Anton turned his head and stared directly into Stefan's eyes.

I won't kill a kid, Anton. There are limits.

I didn't ask you to. He turned his head away, but his thoughts were blocked.

Stefan stared up at the shelter overhead. They'd killed so many times over the past few years. There were bodies buried deep in the caves on Anton's property, more men Jake and Baylor, two of their packmates, had killed and hidden deep in the quarries near Jake's property in Maine. Then there was the reporter who'd been fixated on Keisha. He'd gone over the railing of the Golden Gate Bridge . . . with help.

At least they didn't have to hide his body. It had never

been recovered, but he and the others had died, just the same.

All to protect the identities and secrets—and lives—of the Chanku.

Stefan concentrated on the rope ladder emerging from the bottom of the shelter high above them. Watched as one large hiking boot followed by a skinny, jeans-clad leg slipped through the trap door at the bottom.

No matter what Anton decided, Stefan drew the line at kids.

Anton would have preferred to be in human form, but on the other hand, at least as a wolf he had sharp teeth and a short temper. Anger surged through him as he watched the intruder place one foot carefully on the first narrow step of the collapsible ladder, and then the other.

The balls of these people! Why in the hell wouldn't they leave his family alone? He thought of Keisha, sleeping soundly in their big bed with Lily beside her, so vulnerable and yet so ferociously protective now that she was a mother. His fear for her safety made his blood run cold.

If not for Stefan, he'd tear this interloper to shreds, and he'd do it without regret.

A sharp crack split the air. A curse. One of the steps had split down the middle, the guy's foot slipped. His hands scrabbled at the ropes, he hung for a moment before he lost his grip and fell.

Adam and Logan both rushed to catch the falling man, but his foot caught in the rope. Arms flailing, he seemed to hang motionless for a brief second out of time, eyes wide, mouth in a perfect "O" of surprise. Then time sped up, his body flipped and he slammed against the tree trunk upside down with one foot still tangled in the ladder. He went totally limp, his foot slipped free and he dropped head first at least forty feet to the ground.

Deacon actually got to him first, arms outstretched, but

the force of the intruder's fall knocked the kid to the ground. They lay there a moment in a crumpled heap of arms and legs before Deacon carefully extricated himself.

Logan knelt beside the unnaturally still and twisted figure.

Jazzy knelt beside Logan. "Is he dead?"

"No." Logan carefully removed the person's stocking cap. Long, dark brown hair tumbled free in a tangled mass of curls. "But *she's* badly hurt. Adam?" He glanced over his shoulder. "Can you diagnose? I don't want to go inside her in case I have to resuscitate. She's probably got a concussion from banging against the trunk." He raised his head and his dark eyes were shadowed. "I think her spine's injured."

Adam nodded and knelt on the girl's other side. He touched her shoulder and hip, and quietly slipped into a trance. Anton sat very still and watched. Who the hell was she and why was she spying on them? She looked young, probably close to Jazzy's age. Slightly built, her skin was a soft golden brown. He wanted to search her mind, but now was not the time.

She struggled to draw each breath, but her eyes didn't open. Adam stayed with her for a good five minutes while Logan continued to keep his fingers pressed to her carotid artery, checking her pulse. Anton wondered why no one had thought to call for an ambulance, but Logan and Adam acted as if they knew what they were doing.

Stefan nudged his shoulder. *I wonder what her story is?*

I have no idea. I don't want to interfere with their work, or I'd go in and find out.

Adam raised his head and sat back on his heels. "Her back's broken. Two of her vertebrae"—he glanced at Logan—"T4 and T5, I think, are out of position. They haven't severed her spinal cord, but they've compromised it."

Logan actually smiled at Adam, in spite of the dire situation. "That's what I was afraid of. You really did learn the medical stuff, didn't you? Good job. Now, can you fix her?"

Adam nodded. "I want to get her back to the house first, and I'll want you in there with me."

There was still no mention of calling for help. Anton sat back and observed while Deacon and Jazzy took the SUV and raced to the house. They returned in less than five minutes with a wooden door off one of the rooms. The young woman was carefully strapped to the hard surface and placed in the back of the SUV.

Anton trotted along beside Stefan when they were finally able to move her to the main house. Oliver was waiting, ready to help Deacon and the others carry their makeshift stretcher into one of the larger guest rooms.

Anton and Stefan shifted and grabbed sweatpants from a chair in the entry, but they both held back and stayed out of the way. This was not a time for interference, not when a young woman's life was at stake. When Logan suggested rearranging the furniture to make access easier, Anton helped Stefan move the bed into the middle of the room.

They decided to leave the young woman on the flat door to keep her back immobilized, so they carefully centered it on the bed. Adam immediately knelt beside her and placed his hands on her chest. Logan knelt on the bed on her other side, touched her shoulder and hip, and glanced up at Anton. "If you can get into her thoughts and keep her unconscious, or at least still, it'll make our work easier. We can't risk her moving while we attempt the repair."

Anton nodded. He pulled a desk chair to the head of the bed and sat down with his palms cupping the sides of her face. Her breathing was still labored, though not as bad as it had been when she first fell. Anton glanced at Logan and Adam. The men each nodded and turned their attention to their patient.

Anton slipped easily into her unconscious mind. He felt her fear, sensed her body's frustration at not being able to move and realized the extent of her injury . . . she was paralyzed from the middle of her chest down.

His eyes filled with tears. No matter that she was their enemy, spying on his family and his packmates, she was a beautiful young woman, her future totally in the hands of the two men who attempted to repair the terrible damage to her body.

Damage she'd brought on herself. But why? What possible reason could she have for watching them? Calming her fears with a soft, hypnotic suggestion, Anton waited until she slept before wandering through her memories. It was a simple process, after all. Unconscious, she was unable to block him, but the deeper he explored, the more his frustration and anger grew.

And the more powerful his hope that Adam and Logan would be able to make her whole once again, if only so she could answer his questions.

Anton wasn't sure when Eve entered the room. Adam's mate seemed to sense when he needed her and now, after two long hours spent working with Logan on their young victim, his need must be overwhelming. He looked practically gray with exhaustion, and Logan wasn't any better.

"Go now," Eve said, laying her hand on his shoulder. "Rest. You and Logan were up most of the night and you're exhausted. I'll stay with her." She glanced away from her mate and caught Anton's gaze. "You too, Anton. Go to Keisha. She's worried about you. About what's happened."

Anton nodded. He took one last look into the girl's thoughts, found her resting peacefully without fear, and slipped quietly out of her mind. She was tightly restrained, still on the wooden door to keep her healing back flat, and with her arms and legs held firmly with soft leather bands, she'd not be able to move.

Stefan and Oliver had gone some time ago, along with Deacon and Jazzy. After a final check to make sure none of the restraints were too tight, Anton, Adam, and Logan left together. The three of them walked down the long hallway, each man lost in his own thoughts.

There was no need to speak. They knew they'd done all they could. Now it was up to the girl.

Not just any girl . . . Daciana Lupei.

Anton knew she went by Daci, that she was all of twenty-five. That her mother had been a fascinating woman of Romanian descent, the mistress to a powerful man who'd kept her identity a secret from his wife. But Daci's mother had secrets of her own—secrets that somehow gave her power. Even so, she'd died much too young in a car accident.

Through her mother, Daci was half Romanian. Through her father, she carried a legacy of hatred. Anton wondered exactly how much of an influence the man still held over her.

Hopefully, she was more her mother's daughter than her father's, but that might be too much to ask. How the hell was he going to explain that she was the bastard daughter of one of their most hated enemies—the man who had ordered Ulrich Mason's kidnapping and who had kept Manda Smith imprisoned for twenty-five horrendous years? He couldn't believe that they'd just saved the life of the daughter of their enemy, the late Secretary of Homeland Security, Milton Bosworth.

The man was dead, but certainly not mourned.

At least, not by the Chanku.

Which begged the question: why was his daughter here?

Anton sensed his mate nearby. He raised his head and caught her worried glance just as Keisha met the three of them in the hallway. "I've got a fresh pot of coffee in the kitchen," she said. "Could any of you use a cup?"

Adam touched Anton's shoulder. "I know I could." He glanced at Logan. "Come with us, Anton. We need to talk."

Anton nodded. He kissed Keisha and took her hand, but his thoughts were far away.

Chapter 8

Sunlight streamed through the big windows where Stefan, Xandi, and Oliver waited in the kitchen. Xandi poured coffee as each of them took a seat.

"Where are the others?" Adam picked up his cup and sat at the counter where he could see everyone.

"Sleeping. Showering." Oliver shook his head. "Fucking. Whatever. Mik, Tala, and AJ left for California about an hour ago. They got called out on a job and had to bail even earlier than they planned." He sat at the table beside Anton. "We can fill them in later."

Adam nodded. He glanced at Logan, then sipped his coffee. "I think she'll walk again. Not right away. There's a lot of bruising, her spinal cord wasn't severed, but the pressure from the vertebrae we repaired will affect her until the swelling goes down."

"Any other injuries?" Anton's dark eyes flashed from Adam to Logan and back again. His fingers beat a nervous tattoo on the tabletop. "It looked like she hit her head pretty hard when her foot caught in the ropes."

Logan nodded. "While Adam was repairing her spinal damage, I checked her upper spine and head. No damage, but I did find something interesting." Once again he deferred to Adam. "You know more about this than I do."

"Logan was near her brain stem, looking for injuries," Adam said. "He happened to skirt the hypothalamus and discovered an anomaly."

Anton's eyes immediately shifted to Logan. "What kind of anomaly?"

"Something that didn't belong," he said. "At least not from what I learned in medical school. A small gland, undeveloped, but definitely not a tumor, not a growth of any kind."

"Do you think . . . ?" Anton's fingers stilled. He clasped his hands together so hard his knuckles turned white.

Adam and Logan both nodded. "I think she might be Chanku," Adam said. "When I was in Eve's head, when she had her brain injury, I remember seeing exactly what Logan described, only the gland was larger. However, she'd been getting the nutrients and had already made her first shift. I'm guessing that what Logan saw was the same gland, the one that governs our shapeshifting abilities, before it's been exposed to the nutrients that enable shifting."

"That would explain it." Anton steepled his long fingers beneath his chin. "The girl has many secrets, not the least of which have to do with her parentage." He glanced directly at Adam. "She's Milton Bosworth's illegitimate daughter. The man who held your sister prisoner for all those years had a daughter of his own, one his wife never knew about. Her name is Daciana Lupei, a name I find absolutely fascinating . . ."

There were soft gasps of surprise from Xandi and Keisha. Stefan's muffled "Oh, shit," was heard over Oliver's mumbled curse.

Pressure pulsed in Adam's skull, pounding faster and faster until he felt like he might explode into a million pieces. "I don't give a shit about her name." He stood up and stared toward the hallway leading to Daciana's room. "If I'd known that she was . . ."

"Bosworth's daughter?" Anton reached out and touched

Adam's arm. His fingers looked relaxed, but his grip was solid steel. "Would it have really made a difference, Adam? I think you would have fixed her injuries even if you'd known. The daughter is not culpable for her father's sins."

Adam's heart pounded. He listened for a moment to the rapid tattoo, each beat hammering out a memory of Manda's desperate life. "He tortured Manda. The things that bastard did to her . . ."

"Are no reflection on the girl. She was a child."

"She's old enough to stalk us, damn it all. We could kill her now, before she ever wakes." He glanced down at Anton's fingers, still wrapped around his forearm. "I could go back into her brain, make sure she never wakes up. It would be such a simple thing. A ruptured blood vessel and no autopsy in the world would . . ."

"No. Absolutely not. I have had no true sense of danger from her. None at all. No dreams, no warnings. Not as I have in the past when we were threatened. Merely a sense of unease that all of us have shared, the sense we were being watched, which is true. She has watched us, not harmed us in any way. For all we know, she's merely curious." Anton's fingers tightened once more around his forearm. Then he released Adam altogether and sat back down at the kitchen table. His eyes were dark pinpoints, gazing into Adam's soul.

"Let it go," he said. "I don't often invoke my status, but in this case . . ." Anton sighed and shook his head. "No. I won't go there. I will only ask you, as a friend and as a lover, to let it go."

Adam filled his lungs with a deep, calming breath. He felt his heart rate slow and reclaimed his seat at the counter once again. "Okay. I'll go along with what you want, for now. I don't like it, but I'll abide by your wishes."

Anton nodded. Adam turned away from him and glanced at Logan. "What do you suggest?"

"Eve's with her now. She should have someone with her at all times, at least until she regains consciousness." Logan's relief was obvious as he slipped directly into his medical professional persona, but he knew nothing about Bosworth's history with the pack. "We don't want her waking up and trying to walk, and we don't have any drugs to keep her sedated. She'll be out for a few more hours, I imagine, but she's still badly injured. I don't know enough about the process of repairing tissue and bones the way Adam does it, to know how strong repairs are in the beginning."

"I'll stay with her."

Adam swung around toward the sound of Deacon's voice. "Are you sure? Do you know what to say or do if she wakes up?"

Deacon shrugged his big shoulders. "Not really, but I can certainly keep a little thing like her in bed. Besides, I know what it's like to be recuperating from an injury when everyone around you is healthy as a horse, and it's not fun."

He grinned and glanced down at his leg. Adam just shook his head and looked away. He'd still rather the girl died, but this was one battle he wasn't going to win. That didn't mean he couldn't watch the woman closely. If she was anything like her father, he really didn't care what Anton wanted.

At least Deacon had a way about him, a calm and peaceful manner that could diffuse even the most intense situations. Adam met his steady gaze. "Okay. I give. What are we going to tell her, though? We still don't know why she's watching us."

"I'll try and find out while she sleeps." Anton drained the last of his coffee and set the cup on the table. "Deacon, do you want to come with me now? While she's resting might be the best time to get beyond her defenses." He paused a moment and looked at each of them, and his bearing was every bit that of a leader. The true alpha male of this pack.

"If I discover she is truly Chanku, I intend to add the nutrients to her food. I could never, under any circumstances, deny her the chance of knowing her true birthright."

Keisha rose to her feet and planted her hands on the table in front of him. "Not without telling her. You have to give her that choice."

"I agree, Anton. You know how we feel about sneaking the nutrients into someone's food. It's not right." Xandi stood beside Keisha.

Anton looked down at his folded hands for a moment, then directly into his mate's dark eyes. "We can't tell her anything until we know we can trust her. We can't begin to trust her until we know absolutely that she is one of us. We'll do this my way."

Keisha spun around and left the room. Xandi sighed and shook her head. "Oh, Anton. Why?"

When he didn't answer, she followed Keisha out the door.

The room was entirely silent when Anton and Deacon left. So quiet, Adam heard his own heart pounding in his chest.

Eve glanced up from the book she was reading when Anton and Deacon entered the room. "Shhh." She held her fingers to her lips and glanced toward the sleeping girl. She lay still and pale, tightly restrained on the wooden door in the middle of the bed. "She's quiet now, but she's been restless, almost like she's trying to awaken but can't."

Anton nodded and moved quickly to the head of the bed. He cupped his palms around the girl's face and closed his eyes. Everything else in the room faded away. He no longer worried about Keisha's anger, no longer sensed Eve or Deacon.

Only the girl. *Daciana.* The hypnotic suggestion he'd left her with should have kept her asleep for hours, but her mind was more powerful than he'd thought.

Thoughts swirled, images of wolves racing through the

night, of naked men slipping in and out of doors. He paused a moment and smiled. She'd certainly appreciated all the glimpses she'd caught of the various pack members without their clothing. It figured. She had a typically active Chanku libido, the kind that existed long before they'd had any of the nutrients that allowed them to shift. Still smiling to himself, Anton went deeper into her comatose mind. Confused at first as he assimilated her memories, he realized he was surrounded by the sterile glass and stainless steel of a small room that looked like a doctor's office.

No! It was a laboratory. That was all it could be, with its various machines and gauges and beakers lined along walls, with test tubes and examination equipment. And there . . . there in the corner . . . an examination table, similar to the one an obstetrician might use, only this one had powerful clamps and straps to hold the patient in place.

The girl remembered that table with horror. Not for herself, for someone else. Someone she'd seen strapped on, unable to move.

Restrained as she was now restrained.

She was remembering her father's lab! Almost afraid of what he might find, Anton leaned over and pressed his forehead to the girl's. Images, stark and painful in their clarity, leapt into his mind.

What he saw made his blood run cold. There, in a small cage in the corner of the lab, a creature cowered in fear. Only this was no ordinary animal. Horribly misshapen, with twisted arms and legs and a face that was a hideous parody of both human and wolf, it could only be Manda.

Frightened and lonely, caught in the middle of an incomplete shift from human to wolf, she'd been imprisoned and tortured for years. Anton knew this once-pathetic creature of Daciana's memory was now a lovely young woman, mate to Baylor Quinn . . . and Adam Wolf's twin sister.

Manda was one of them, now. Whole and happy in her

life as Chanku after a nightmarish childhood, after years of indescribable pain and horrible mistreatment.

Manda. Dear, sweet, loving Manda.

And this girl had known her. She'd been a child herself, obviously much younger than Manda, but she remembered the strange creature her father kept in a cage for so many years. Remembered her with sadness and a mind filled with questions.

Questions Anton hoped he might soon be able to answer.

He strengthened the mental suggestion to sleep and heal. Daciana relaxed into restful slumber. Slowly, thoughtfully, Anton pulled away from the girl and stretched. So, this was the purpose of her search, the reason she stalked the Chanku. A child's desire to prove her father wasn't the horrible man she feared, that he'd had a reason for keeping a strange young woman imprisoned for so many long years.

Too bad her father was everything she suspected, and worse. Anton motioned to Deacon. "Stay with her. She should remain asleep for at least a couple more hours, but call if you notice her becoming restless again. Do not, under any circumstances, tell her what we are or what she might be. She must not know. Not yet. I want to keep her just a bit off balance, for now."

Deacon nodded. He held up a book. "I've got plenty to keep me busy." He settled into the comfortable chair where Eve had kept watch.

Anton followed Eve down the hallway toward the kitchen, but he veered off and stepped into his office. There was an important call he needed to make. A call to the one person Daciana might actually believe, and possibly even relate to.

Sitting down at his desk, Anton quickly dialed Manda Smith's number. She and Baylor were in Maine, but it was only a few hours' flight from them, should she decide to come.

* * *

Daciana floated up and out of the most amazing dream. The wind was in her hair and the pungent scent of cedar and pine filled her nostrils. She frowned. There was something else. Something more powerful and terribly attractive.

An unfamiliar scent, yet her body responded immediately. Her breasts tingled and she felt her nipples rise to sharp peaks. She waited for the accompanying ache of desire between her legs, but there was nothing. Not even the slightest sensation from any part of the lower half of her body.

The dream exploded in a burst of reality when she tried to wriggle her toes. *Nothing.*

Her eyes flashed open. At once fully awake, adrenaline surged. She was strapped down, tied firmly to a flat, hard surface. Able to move little more than her head, she turned to her left and saw only a bare wall with a single window, shaded against the light.

To the right—so that was the source of the compelling scent—a man slept, his long, lean body sprawled in a large, overstuffed chair. A book lay open against his chest with the cover partially hidden beneath his hand. His lips were parted, his eyes closed, but even in sleep he had a look that reminded her of an old-time preacher—dark hair, fair skin, high cheekbones and a long, narrow face.

A strangely compelling face. She frowned. What was it about him that called to her? No matter. She would figure it out soon enough.

She tried to remember what had happened. How she had ended up here—wherever *here* was—a prisoner. Nothing. Her mind was a blank slate beyond the last few minutes in her hideout. A cougar and a wolf circling beneath her tree, the fear of discovery. Had someone shot her? She tried to move her legs, but there was no feeling at all from somewhere above her waist, all the way to her toes.

Had she broken her back? Her arms were strapped down, but she could wiggle her fingers. Their slight movement settled some of the agony in her mind, but not all. She lay quietly and stared at the ceiling while she slowly catalogued those parts she could feel. Her face. Shoulders and arms, her chest.

Those damned nipples that pressed against her shirt.

How in the hell could she be horny when she was absolutely terrified?

Or was she? There was something weird going on, as if her anxiety level was way down below where it should be. Had they drugged her? Maybe that was it. Maybe she'd been pumped full of drugs. She'd expect that sort of thing from people like these.

Her father said they had strange powers, that they could turn into wolves. They were killers, according to him.

They were the same people who had killed her father.

She'd watched them all this time, hoping to prove he was right, that he'd had a reason for the things he'd done, but she'd still not seen them shift. That didn't mean they couldn't.

Why hadn't they killed her?

She tried to pull her arms free, but the restraints were too tight. They were padded and didn't hurt, but they definitely held her in place.

She thought about screaming, or maybe just cursing at the guy who slept in the chair next to her. Rolling her head to one side, she looked directly into the most beautiful amber eyes she'd ever seen.

"Are you okay?"

He had a deep voice. Soft and soothing. Probably why they'd picked him to watch her. "Sure. Just dandy," she said. "I'm tied to a board and I can't move my legs."

"It's a door, actually, and it's for your safety. Because you injured your back, they wanted you on a hard, flat surface. Logan didn't want you to try to move before you were healed. I'll call him in and see if we can remove the restraints, now that you're awake."

"Fuck you." She turned her head away. Like untying her was going to make things better?

"No need to cuss at me. You might think of thanking me. I'm the one who caught you when you fell out of the tree."

Fell? She didn't remember falling. Reluctantly, she turned her head and stared at him. "What happened? I don't remember."

He shrugged his big shoulders and leaned forward in the chair. His amazing scent tickled her nostrils. She closed her eyes and inhaled before she realized what she was doing.

He's the enemy, you idiot. Her eyes snapped open. He could be one of them, a person who turned into an animal.

"We had your platform in the tree surrounded—you were, after all, spying on us on private property—and you were coming down. One of the wooden steps in your ladder broke. You lost your grip and fell forward, but your foot was caught. I think you smacked your head pretty hard before you came untangled from the rope. I tried to catch you, but all I managed to do was break your fall."

She thought about that for a minute. There was no memory of anything he told her, but she really had no reason to think he was lying. Not yet, anyway. "Am I in a hospital?"

He shook his head. "No. We have a doctor and a healer. They took care of you. Once the swelling goes down, you should be fine. You can't walk yet, but you will. Everything is still bruised. Your spinal cord was injured, but it'll get better. Adam and Logan can fix anything."

He said that with such an air of conviction she decided not to argue. "What are you going to do with me?" Damn. She hadn't meant to ask such a pathetic question. Sweat beaded her forehead. What if she didn't get better? What if she couldn't walk? What if . . . ?

"Ah, you're awake."

The man who entered her room was older, but so drop-dead gorgeous his age didn't matter. He seemed strangely familiar. She wasn't sure if she'd seen him before, but she still felt as if she knew him. As if he knew her.

"I'm Anton Cheval," he said, answering her unasked question. "I own the house you've been spying on."

He didn't sound angry, but . . .

"No. Right now I'm more curious than angry."

She blinked. Was he reading her mind? How . . . ?

"Yes, I am, Ms. Daciana Lupei. I knew your father."

"Did you kill him?" She clenched her fists and wished she had better control over her big mouth.

He shook his head. There was a patient, bemused expression on his face. "No. I believe the papers said he died of a stroke. I have no reason to discount their report, but I will be honest and tell you he was not mourned by any of us. Least of all by one of the men who saved your life, Adam Wolf, but that's a story for a later time."

She kept her mouth shut. Her mother had always told her she could learn more by listening than talking. Right now seemed like a good time to finally pay attention to Mom's words.

If only her mother were still here. She'd know exactly what to do. Her mother could do anything. Call the wind. Talk to the spirits, and other, secret things Daci wished she could remember. If only . . .

Cheval smiled and touched her forehead. His fingertips were cool and dry. Her skin tingled where he touched her. Weird. Definitely weird.

"I would like to have known your mother. She sounds like a fascinating woman."

"Quit doing that! Stay out of my head." Her mother could read her mind. Now this guy seemed to have the same ability. Daci gritted her teeth and tried to ignore the strange sensation where his fingers connected with her forehead.

This time he laughed. "I'm not in your head. You're broadcasting. Quite well, actually, for one who . . . well, we will leave that for a later time as well."

She blinked and focused on his face, on the brilliant amber eyes so much like the young man who'd been watching her.

So much like her own.

"What do you mean, broadcasting?"

"I hear your thoughts, much as if you were broadcasting them on a radio station only I am tuned to. I know you are confused, that you're frightened by your paralysis. Our healers assure me that you will walk again, probably within a few days. There was damage to your spinal column, but nothing that won't heal. Be patient and lie as still as you can for now."

"Why are you keeping me here? Shouldn't you have called 911?"

He shook his head. "Why were you spying on us? And traditional medicine isn't as good as the healers we have. Without them, you might be facing a lifetime of paralysis. As it is, you should be fine."

"My father studied people like you. He wanted to help you and you killed him." She felt a flush of heat across her chest and waited for him to hit her, to call her a liar, to deny her accusation.

He merely shook his head. "Your father was fascinated by things that were different, seemingly impossible. He imprisoned a young woman for more than half her life so that he could study her, much like a lab rat. Do you remember her? The creature he kept locked in a cage?"

She did remember, and the memories made her stomach hurt. "I remember," she said. "He wanted to help her."

"You know better than that, Daciana. Be honest. Your father did unspeakable things to her. His curiosity about her origins overwhelmed any hint of human compassion."

She blinked back sudden tears. "My mother protected her, when she could."

"I know. I wish I'd met her. You have amazing memories of her. She sounds wonderful." He sat down on the bed beside her and covered her hand with his. She was restrained or she would have pulled her fingers free. Still, she couldn't deny that the strength and warmth of his hand felt comforting . . . and he sounded sincere when he spoke kindly of her mother.

"She was. My mother was . . ." Her voice cracked and she closed her mouth.

Cheval nodded. "She died much too young. The creature, though. The one you saw? Her name is Manda, in case you've forgotten. I've called her and asked her to come see you. It may take her a couple of days to get here, but she promised to make the trip. She actually remembers you quite fondly, in spite of the horrible things your father did."

"After my mother died, one time when I was at the lab with the lady who raised me, I asked my father to turn her loose. He made me leave. I was never allowed back." She swallowed and wished her arms weren't tied down. Wished she could sit up and face this tall man who loomed over her. Who reminded her of things she'd rather forget.

He didn't speak, but he began working at the restraints holding her arms to the board. "Be still, and I'll release you. I don't want you to move. Our healers said you could injure yourself further if you put pressure on the section of your spine they've repaired, but I think you'll be much more comfortable if we can take off the restraints. Then I'll go and get Logan or Adam and we'll get you off of this door."

She nodded, almost afraid to say anything as he carefully released the padded restraints holding her arms. The tall young man was suddenly on her other side, undoing those straps as well. She held her breath. She didn't want to trust either one of them . . . she had, after all, been spying on them for the past couple weeks. Why were they being so nice to her?

Cheval's fingers stilled. Daci cringed. He'd heard her thoughts again.

There was no smile on his face now. "You should know," he said, "that we did think about killing you. Some of the others might still feel that way. I haven't asked. Personally, I decided against it once I realized who you are. Not because you are your father's daughter, but because you are your mother's. It is her legacy that lets you live. Keep in mind, though, that you are not yet accepted by us. Even I don't entirely trust you."

With that he went back to unfastening the clasp on her restraints.

Daci closed her eyes and wondered what in the hell he was talking about. Her mother had been amazing, but Daci was nothing at all like that fascinating woman. With that thought came the question—what in the hell was she going to do now?

Chapter 9

Manda Smith set the phone back in the cradle and raised her head. Baylor, her mate, watched her with his typically unnerving intensity. "It's okay," she said, before he could comment. "I want to go. I would like to see Daci again. It's been a long time. She was a sweet little thing. She wanted so much for her daddy to love her, but he was such a heartless bastard. I always felt sorry for her. It's hard to believe she's all grown up."

She glanced down at her long, slim legs, bare beneath her short skirt, and remembered the last time she'd seen the tiny, dark-haired girl. Then, her own legs had been twisted and ugly, covered in patches of dark fur. Her hands had been nothing more than misshapen claws, her face a horrifying mix of human and wolf.

Daci had been hanging around the lab since she was barely able to walk. Manda had known from the beginning that she was the daughter of one of the technicians, a lovely young Romanian woman with a calm and loving manner. She'd seemed to understand Manda's plight better than most and had done her best to protect her from some of the more profane experiments and tests the others had wanted to try.

So many horrible things. Memories flooded her mind,

and with them so much remembered pain. She sighed and brushed away a bit of nonexistent lint from her skirt. She wished she could brush away most of her childhood just as easily. Unfortunately, the nightmare that had been her life would never be fully consigned to the past. Not really.

"You're sure about this?"

Bay's soft question scattered her memories. Manda raised her head and smiled. "Yes. Daci was so sweet. Her mother was killed in a car accident when she was about seven. I only saw her once after that. She said something to her father that angered him, and he yelled at her. She was never at the lab again. I've always wondered what happened to her. She was so young, she didn't realize I was something scary. I was just the girl in the cage."

"Never again."

He touched her face with his callused fingertips and the look in his eyes made her stomach tumble. To think he'd actually looked at her this way when she'd still been ugly and deformed! Manda leaned close and kissed him. Baylor had fallen in love with her before she'd looked even remotely normal—he'd loved the real woman inside the twisted body.

Not many men would have been so generous with a woman who was nothing more than a freak. So patient he would put off his own pleasure until she was healed enough, strong enough, to share it with him.

Manda opened her mind to Baylor. Freed the memories she usually tried to block, even from the one who loved her most. Memories so painful she still shuddered when they swept over her conscious mind. Now, though, they were softened with the love her mate continually shared with her.

Love she felt day and night, no matter if they were together or apart. He reached out and touched her. His fingers stroked the line of her throat, the sharp edge of her collarbone, the soft rise of her breast.

Manda sighed. She felt the now familiar ache in her womb, the heat that flooded between her legs, the sharp tingle as her nipples peaked against her cotton shirt.

"I'll come with you." Bay punctuated each word with a small kiss along the line of her jaw.

Manda eased herself onto his lap and straddled his hips. Her skirt rode up above her thighs. Bay grinned when he realized she wasn't wearing panties.

"You planned this, didn't you?" He reached between them and stroked his finger between her swollen lips. Manda felt the shudder and clench of muscles reacting totally out of her control.

She tried to answer him. Wanted to say something silly that would make him laugh, but he'd found her clit and was rubbing slow, silky circles around the blasted thing, and she couldn't make a sound beyond the ragged whimpers that slipped from her throat.

She reached for his zipper, but Bay trapped her hands in one of his. "Not this time. I want to watch you." He settled into the chair and spread his legs just a bit. The change in his position forced her legs farther apart.

She hung there in his lap, skirt around her waist, legs spread wide over the tops of his jeans-clad thighs. He held her hands behind her back, tightly clasped in one, big fist. His right hand plundered her sensitive tissues. Three long fingers penetrated her now, and his thumb kept up the rhythmic assault on her clit. Manda gave herself up to sensation, to the gentle sweep of his thumb, the deep thrust of his fingers.

"Ah, I wondered what you two were up to!"

Manda jerked against Bay's fingers and swung her head around just in time to catch their packmate Jake Trent's cheeky grin.

"Can't you tell I'm busy?" Bay laughed, but he never broke his fingers' delicious rhythm.

"Shannon's still shopping. Mind if I help?"

"I don't think . . ."

Bay cut Manda off. "You're not supposed to think, remember? Sure, bud. Got any ideas?" His fingers continued their subtle strokes.

Manda arched against him. *So close!*

"Not yet, sweetheart." Bay slowed his strokes to a frustratingly light tickle. Manda whimpered.

Jake grabbed a kitchen chair and scooted it close behind Manda until her naked butt rested on the hard, wooden edge. Jake's muscular thighs encased her hips and spread wide, beyond Bay's.

His big hands fumbled with the buttons on her shirt. Cool air wafted across her suddenly naked chest and strong fingers plucked expertly at her nipples. "How's this?" Jake's whisper tickled her ear.

Manda moaned.

Surrounded now, encased in rough denim-clad thighs, her back pressed against Jake's hard chest, she swiftly evolved into a creature of pleasure, taking whatever her men were willing to give.

Bay's fingers stroked the inner walls of her vaginal passage, his thumb slipped over her wet and throbbing clit. Jake's palms cupped her full breasts and his fingers pinched her pebbled nipples into tight, responsive peaks. Bay's hand still clasped her wrists, sandwiched now between her back and Jake's chest and she was caught there, a prisoner of sensation and desire, her body arcing into a taut bow of pleasure.

She sensed the moment they decided to take her over the top, the silent agreement of two men entirely familiar with her body's responses. Bay's fingers sunk deeper inside, Jake's pinched harder.

The sharp bite of pain forced a gasp of surprise to her lips and she jerked back against Jake's solid chest. He twisted her nipples, sending jolts of sensation straight to her clit. Bay's fingers worked their magic, dragging her higher, pitching her into a mindless frenzy. Writhing between the two men, she whimpered and pleaded as Bay slipped his fingers free of her pussy and released his grasp on her wrists.

Jake pulled her completely into his lap and stretched her legs wide on top of his thighs. He held her in place, helpless, panting, crazed by their touch. A sheen of sweat stuck her unbuttoned shirt between her back and Jake's broad chest. He held her firmly with her breasts cupped in his palms, her nipples pinched painfully between strong fingers.

Her clit throbbed in the cool wash of air. Jake spread her thighs farther apart with his own legs, and tugged at her nipples. Manda felt like a string stretched to the breaking point, as if her body might shatter and scatter in all directions, trembling as she was on frustration's raw edge.

She rolled her head back on her shoulders and whimpered. Jake's soft chuckle warned her, just as Bay's hot mouth covered her sex and a cold, wet nose bumped her clit. Shrieking with laughter, Manda tried to close her thighs as his tongue swept deep inside her channel, deeper than was humanly possible, but Jake held her legs spread wide.

Laughing, bucking against the overwhelming levels of sensation, Manda glanced down at the black wolven head between her shaking thighs and gave in. She loved him so, no matter what form he took.

But, she loved him most like this, with his pointed ears pressed back against his fine skull while his long, wolven tongue swirled around her clit before plunging back inside her sex. This was the better side of the perfect man who had saved her. The side that linked them in a love more enduring than time, more powerful than life.

His tongue laved her swollen labia and circled the taut nub of her clitoris. Jake's fingers rolled the turgid peaks of her nipples and Manda gave in to sensation, gave up what little control she'd convinced herself she still retained.

With a harsh, almost guttural cry of completion, she hurled herself into yet another amazing climax, surrounded by the two men she loved the most.

Panting, gasping, almost numb with completion, it took her a few minutes before she struggled to open her eyes. Baylor was back in his chair, naked now, but human. His cock stood proudly against his flat belly, and he was grinning, looking toward the front door. Immediately Manda knew someone else had entered the room.

Shannon? Blinking, Manda glanced over her shoulder as their packmate walked in with her arms laden with grocery bags.

"Yep. It's me . . . and it looks like you've been busy." She leaned over and kissed Baylor lightly on the cheek, then planted a long, wet kiss on Jake. When she pulled back, there was a twinkle in her dark green eyes. "Manda, I made the long, lonely trip to town and shopped while you were here being entertained. Just look at the mess you've left! Do you mind putting the groceries away while I take care of the guys' little problems?"

She held out her hand. Manda grabbed it, giggling. "Works for me." She glanced down at Baylor's huge cock and the visible bulge behind Jake's zipper. "Though I don't think either problem is all that small . . ." She ran her fingers over the swollen front of Jake's jeans, then leaned over and kissed the tip of Baylor's erection. "We're taking a trip in a couple days, to Montana. Bay will tell you all about it."

"Montana? Life's never dull when we go visit Anton." Shannon sighed and handed the bags to Manda. "I'll get the details later, okay?" With a sexy laugh, she grabbed Bay's left hand and Jake's right, and dragged both men off to the bedroom.

Manda watched them go, but her mind was on Montana, and a forlorn little girl who'd lost her mother. A little girl who had treated Manda as a friend, not a freak.

* * *

Daci lay perfectly still on the hard, wooden door in the middle of the big bed. She looked so damned tiny. Her eyes were wide and Deacon not only sensed her fear, he could smell it. Fear, and something more.

She was aroused, too, and that didn't help him one bit, because his damned cock was way too aware of her scent. Whether it was from Anton's touch or his own, her body had reacted and he could tell she was totally pissed off about it. In the meantime, Anton was off to find either Adam or Logan to take a look at her, now that she was awake. It was up to Deacon to keep her still and help her relax until they could move her safely off of the flat surface and onto the bed.

Which would be a hell of a lot easier if only he could relax.

"Are you comfortable?" Dumb question. Of course she wasn't comfortable. She couldn't move her legs and she was still lying on that stupid door. There really wasn't anything he could do until one of the guys got here and . . .

"I'm fine, considering." She took a deep breath. "What was Mr. Cheval talking about? Do the others really want to kill me? Why does being my mother's daughter make me valuable?"

Deacon scooted his chair closer and took her hand. "Your mother was a very special woman, but that's all I can say for now. Don't worry. I won't let anyone hurt you."

He wouldn't either. No matter how much Adam might hate her for what her father had done, Deacon knew he'd do whatever it took to protect Daci from the man's anger. She wasn't guilty just because her father was a bastard.

Daci frowned. "I don't understand. My mother was a lab technician. That's all. She was Romany . . . you know, Romanian. She was killed in a car accident when I was little."

"Who raised you? Bosworth?"

She shook her head. "No. Another lady who worked in

the lab took me in. I was never formally adopted. My mother was an illegal. My father never legally acknowledged me, so I sort of slipped through the cracks. I think he paid for my upkeep and he did pay for my college. I was a biology major. Sometimes he came to see me at school."

"Why were you watching us?"

She looked away. "My father was all I had. We were beginning to get to know each other as adults when he was killed. He told me you were killers, that you could change into wolves. That you killed without remorse."

Deacon shook his head. He ignored her comment about their ability to shift. "Anton said your father died of a stroke. One thing I've learned about that man is he doesn't lie. Why do you think your father was murdered?"

"He was involved in a bunch of secret stuff. Most of it had to do with learning more about shapeshifters. A lot of his work, I never understood, even with all my education. He told me if he ever died suddenly, it would be because he was murdered. He made me promise I would find out who killed him."

Deacon leaned forward and rested his chin on his steepled fingertips. "I asked Anton . . . Mr. Cheval. He said Bosworth was found on his front porch wearing his robe and pajamas. There wasn't a mark on him, and the autopsy showed he'd had a massive stroke. It wasn't murder, Daci. It was a natural death."

"I don't believe you, or the autopsy results." She tried to sit up. Deacon leaned over the bed and pressed down on her shoulders. She felt so damned fragile beneath his big, clumsy hands that it scared him to touch her. "Stay put," he said. "Logan and Adam both insisted you need to lie still."

Daci glared at him, but she didn't try to move. He didn't take his hands off her shoulders, either.

"Who the hell are Logan and Adam? Why should I listen to them?"

Deacon grinned. Even lying here partially paralyzed, she had spirit. He fought a powerful desire to lower his head just enough to kiss her. "They're our healers. Trust me, they're good," he said. He focused on her eyes and hoped he could convince her of the truth. "They're the ones who saved your life, and your ability to walk. You'd better play nice with them."

She frowned, but he felt her shoulders relax beneath his fingers. "They didn't operate on me, did they?"

Deacon sat down on the bed beside her. He released his grip on her shoulders, but took one of her small hands in his big mitts. He played with her fingers while he talked to her. She didn't try and pull away.

"They both have the ability to reach inside your body with their minds. Adam saw the damage to your spine. You had a couple of fractured vertebrae that were pressing on your spinal cord. He repaired the bones, but said he couldn't do anything about the bruising. That's why you need to lie still. To let it heal."

"I don't understand."

She looked lost and confused and it broke Deacon's heart. "You don't need to," he said. "Don't worry. It will all come clear to you in time. Why don't you think about your mom and what made her special. It's the same thing that makes you special."

She took a deep breath. "I had to promise never to tell her secrets—the things that she could do—especially to my father. She could tell what I was thinking, just like Mr. Cheval does, and I know she could do other unusual things, though I'm not sure exactly what. It was all a huge secret. I think she was afraid if my father knew how different she was, he would put her in a cage, the way he did that girl who was part wolf. I've never forgotten that girl. He did terrible things to her, but he said he had to. That he was trying to help her."

Deacon shook his head. "He wasn't, you know. Everything he did was to satisfy his own curiosity, but you don't need to worry about that now. You need to be still and get better."

Her eyelids flickered and he knew she must be exhausted. "Will you stay with me?"

"I promise." But he wasn't sure if she even heard him as her eyes slipped shut and her slim body relaxed into sleep.

Chapter 10

Three days later, when Deacon slipped quietly into the kitchen and grabbed a cold beer out of the refrigerator, he paused and glanced out the window. For a moment he just listened to the now familiar sounds—voices nearby, bird song from a vine twisting its way around the front porch, the hum of the refrigerator, and the soft whisper of wind through the trees.

He felt such a powerful sense of connection to this place, to these people. He'd only been here a few days, but already it was more of a home than any place he'd ever lived. Of course, when you'd been on the streets from the time you were fourteen, any bed you got to sleep in for more than one night had to feel good.

Just as any friends you kept for more than a few weeks had to feel like family. Jazzy and Logan, and now all the Chanku he'd met here in Montana . . . they were all family.

He was beginning to feel so comfortable here that it terrified him. Good things never lasted. Deacon glanced into the big dining room where Anton and Stefan sat with their mates and two couples he didn't know. One of the women must be Manda, the one Daci remembered. Strangers or not, he knew they'd soon be part of his extended pack, and that sense of upcoming familiarity gave him the courage to walk into the room and introduce himself.

Anton glanced up and smiled. "Ah, Deacon. Meet our friends from Maine. Jacob Trent and his mate, Shannon Murphy." He pointed to the couple sitting together on the small love seat at his right. Deacon shook hands with the man, nodded to the woman. Damn, she was so beautiful she took his breath, and he could tell from the twinkle in her eyes that she wasn't at all the fragile type.

No, fragile described the slim blond woman sitting beside the big man to Anton's left. "This is Baylor Quinn and his mate, Manda. You know Manda's brother, Adam."

So this was Manda. Deacon shook hands with Baylor. When he turned to acknowledge Manda, she quickly stood up and wrapped her arms around him in a tight hug.

He hugged her back, surprised.

"Thank you for watching over Daci," she said.

"It's nothing. She's . . ."

"She's important to me. I don't know if you know my past, but she was very sweet and she was one of the few people who never treated me as a freak. I can't wait to see her. I really hope she remembers me."

Deacon shrugged. "Staying with Daci's no chore. She's mentioned you, so I know she remembers." He knew Manda had been caught between shifts for most of her life, but it was hard to imagine this tall, beautiful woman as any kind of a freak.

Anton laughed, and Deacon knew immediately he'd been inside his head. "You'd be surprised, son. Manda's life was an absolute nightmare. Do you think Daci's up to a visit now?"

Deacon jerked his head around and stared at Anton. No man had called him "son" before. The casual term had a deep, almost visceral effect on him. He cleared his throat to cover his reaction and turned back to Manda. "She was sleeping when I left her with Eve. I'm headed back there now. She's got more feeling in her feet and legs, and she was able to stand today. How about I let you know as soon as she awakens?"

"That would be wonderful." Manda sat down beside her mate. They immediately clasped hands, and he caught himself staring at the comfortable way they sat so close together. The way they touched. What would that be like? To know love. To find the perfect mate?

"I hope my brother's being nice to her," Manda said. "I love him more than you can imagine, but I've decided Adam can be a real pain in the butt at times."

Deacon laughed. "He's coming around. He was determined to hate Daci when he found out who her father was, but when she started talking about you in such glowing terms, he had to change his mind. I don't think he does that easily."

Manda shook her head. The movement sent her long, blond hair flying. "Adam is a very steady man. He kept me sane for so many years, merely with the power of his mind. We'd never met, much less had any idea we were related, and twins, no less, but we were able to communicate over impossibly long distances. I often wondered if he was a figment of my imagination, but even in my wildest fantasies, I couldn't have come up with someone as unique as Adam."

Deacon would like to have stayed as Manda talked about her amazing mental relationship with her brother through the long years of her captivity. Hearing her story from Daci first and now from Manda herself gave him a fascinating view into the minds of two entirely different, yet strongly connected women.

But he sensed Daci's call. Without actually hearing her voice, he knew she wanted him near. Smiling, he left the conversation and returned to the beautiful young woman who actually seemed to need him.

* * *

"Deacon. Hello. She's doing so much better." Eve stood up and touched Daci's hand. "You'll be walking before long. Your strength is returning faster than any of us expected." She smiled at Deacon and left. He slipped easily into the chair beside Daci's bed.

It had only been three days since her fall, but already Daci was noticeably stronger. The feeling was back in the lower half of her body. She could stand with help, and she was able to use the bathroom on her own as long as someone helped her get there. Most important, the fear was gone from her eyes. Now, she actually seemed happy to see him.

He noticed she was scratching at her arms as if she might have a rash, and it made him smile. He remembered that itchy feeling as his body made the subtle change from human to Chanku. The pills Anton was slipping into her food must be having their desired effect.

"Is Manda finally here?" Daci scratched a spot on her wrist.

Deacon nodded. "Yep, and she's gorgeous. She can't wait to see you. Can I call her in now?"

Daci shook her head. "No! I look awful! I'm a mess and my skin is so dry and itchy . . ."

Deacon laughed. "You're perfect. But I'll get you a washcloth and a hairbrush if you want. And some skin lotion."

"What I really want is a bath." She blushed and looked away. "You'd have to help me. This bathroom just has a shower. I don't think I can stand that long by myself yet."

"Help you take a shower?" Deacon's skin flushed hot and then cold. He forgot all about her itchy skin and what it meant.

"Please? I asked Logan if it was okay, and he said as long as I had someone help me."

"Why didn't you ask Eve? I mean, not that I don't want to, but I . . ."

"I did. She said she wasn't sure if she was strong enough and thought I'd be safer with you or one of the other men." She glanced at him out of the corner of her eye. "I can't ask any of the other guys. I don't know them as well as I know you."

Was she flirting with him?

He gave up, sighed, and nodded. The last thing he wanted was another man seeing her naked. "Sure," he said, as if it was something he did all the time. "I'll do whatever you want."

She smiled and he felt his heart rate jump up a notch or more. As she pulled the blankets back and slowly swung her feet over the side of the bed, it suddenly hit him why he felt such a powerful attraction to her today, even stronger than he had before.

Her scent had changed. Now instead of merely attractive, it was a powerful aphrodisiac. Deacon recognized it for what it was, the scent of a female Chanku nearing her heat. Did Daci even know?

How could she? She had no idea she was Chanku. No idea Anton had been giving her the nutrients in her food for the past three days. Was she ready to shift? Was that the reason her scent had altered? The reason she was recovering so much faster?

The reason he was suddenly hard as a post and wondering how he was going to help her shower without her realizing exactly what effect she was having on him?

She knew he would have carried her, but Daci really wanted to walk the short distance to the bathroom. She still couldn't believe what they were doing, that she'd actually coerced this gorgeous man into helping her shower.

She had asked Eve, and Eve had suggested she ask Deacon. Was Eve matchmaking? No matter. This was exactly what Daci had dreamed about, wasn't it? Deacon had one arm around her waist and held her elbow with his other hand. His body was so big next to hers. He was warm and strong and he smelled so good that she had butterflies in her belly, just being this close to him.

And she was walking okay, too, placing one foot carefully in front of the other. It was absolutely wonderful, standing and walking, all wrapped up in Deacon's arms.

It was weird, too, but she felt drawn to him on so many levels. As each day passed, she'd felt a stronger attraction, well beyond appreciation for his care.

Of course, the fact he was gorgeous and smart and attentive to her every need might have something to do with it, but she'd gotten to know him better than she'd ever known any guy in her life. They'd talked about lots of things, and he'd hardly left her side since she'd been hurt. While the others had checked in on her and everyone had introduced themselves, only Deacon and Eve had actually spent the time sitting by her bed so she wouldn't be alone.

Eve was really nice, but Deacon was the one she wanted close. He was the one she thought of at night when everyone figured she was sleeping. He was the one who ran beside her in those strange, almost hallucinogenic dreams she'd been having.

Nothing here had gone as she would have expected. She no longer thought of any of these people as killers. In fact, she thought of Deacon in far more intimate terms. So intimate she'd been hiding her thoughts, just in case he could read her mind. She'd absolutely die of embarrassment if Deacon knew what she was thinking.

She hadn't seen any of them shift, though they certainly had unusual abilities. They reminded her of her mom. Mom had always known what she was thinking, but then, she was Romany. Maybe these people were part Romany, too. Maybe that's all it was, and they weren't really shapeshifters.

Maybe her father had been wrong.

The mind reading though . . . was it an ability that grew

in some people as they got older? Over the past day, she'd discovered herself slipping in and out of Deacon's thoughts as easily as if she were listening to a radio station . . . just as Mr. Cheval had said.

She'd be mortified if he knew what . . . no. She already knew he felt the same way. Why should she be embarrassed? Why shouldn't she just go for it . . . and see what happened?

She loved what she'd heard Deacon thinking—it was all about her. He was attracted to her and seemed to want her every bit as much as she wanted him . . . but did he know how she felt? Was he reading her thoughts as easily as she read his?

Deacon paused at the doorway to the bathroom and looked down into her upturned face. "Yes," he said, without any preamble at all. "I hear every word spinning through that gorgeous head of yours, and I want you even more, but we can't even think about it until you're completely well."

"Oh." Blushing, she continued on into the bathroom. How much else did he know about her? Wasn't there any way to block her crazy mind? She thought she'd kept her thoughts to herself, but now that she knew he could read her, it felt like every private thought she'd ever had was spilling out of her head!

And on top of that, she suddenly had to pee and Eve was gone and she wanted to curl up in a ball and hide.

Deacon laughed. Daci raised her head and glared at him. "What's so funny?"

"I'll help you to the toilet and I promise to leave the room and not peek."

Mortified, she nodded. He did as he said he would. When she was done, she was able to stand up by hanging on to a towel rack before she called him back in.

He helped her stand beside the shower while he adjusted the spray and water temperature. She saw his shoulders rise and fall as he took a deep breath and turned toward her.

"Daci, I know you're in my head, so you know how much I want you. You're still not completely healed, so we can't have sex yet, but that doesn't mean I don't want to look at you, or touch . . . or get naked with you."

She blinked her eyes, shocked all the way to her toes. She hadn't really thought this through at all, how he would actually help her in the shower. She hadn't thought of the fact he'd be naked, too. "Oh." She was still blinking wildly when he helped her pull the nightgown over her head. Before she had time to think about being naked in front of him, he was kicking off his sandals and slipping out of his jeans. The T-shirt came off over his head and he slipped the shower door open as if the two of them together, naked, was the most natural thing in the world.

Now that sensation was returning to her lower body, she realized this was natural. This was exactly why she'd been lying awake at night, why she'd talked him into helping her bathe.

Shameless didn't even come close to describing the way she was acting, but even so, it felt perfect. So why couldn't she stop blushing?

Deacon stepped into the shower first and reached for her hands. Carefully she lifted her foot over the low lip of the shower. She really needed to watch where her feet were going, but he was naked and aroused and she wanted to look.

Obviously, Deacon had a lot more self-control than she did. He held her steady as she stepped entirely inside. Then he supported her until she could sit on the molded seat at the end of the shower stall.

Her eyes were perfectly level with his groin, and his long, thick penis hovered right in front of her nose.

This time his laughter sounded a strained. "I hadn't thought about that."

She didn't say a word. She couldn't. All she could do was stare. His penis was long and fat and partially erect and there was a shroud of skin covering the end that she hadn't expected. It took her a moment to realize he looked different because he wasn't circumcised, the first uncut male she'd ever seen in real life . . . not that she'd seen very many naked men. Deacon was absolutely fascinating.

He was also getting bigger. His penis slowly gained in length and girth, turning dark as it filled with blood, rising up until it was almost touching his belly. The loose skin stretched back to expose the swollen, red tip. A drop of white fluid covered the narrow slit at the end, hanging there like a small, shimmering pearl.

She swallowed, laughed, and all the nervous tension went out of her. "It looks as if part of you is thinking about it now."

"Ignore it. I'm going to." He reached for the shower spray and pulled the nozzle free. The hose was long enough for him to hold it over Daci and soak her hair and body.

Easier said than done, she thought, as she shampooed her hair. Not with him so close to her mouth and some little demon reminding her she'd never once taken a man in her mouth.

Deacon rinsed her hair with the shower sprayer, which forced her to shut her eyes. She got her raging libido under control and washed carefully with the soft cloth he handed to her, but she gave him a look when it was time to wash between her legs. He turned his back without her having to ask.

His butt was just as gorgeous as his front. There wasn't an ounce of fat on Deacon. His body was long and lanky with the promise of more weight as he got older, but for now it was all angles and planes and tautly sculpted muscle.

His skin was unusually fair. He'd told her he'd gotten

his nickname because he looked like an old-time preacher with his tall, gaunt build, dark hair and thin, pale, angular face.

It was a beautiful face, as far as Daci was concerned. A serious, masculine face and a perfect body, and she wanted him so much she ached.

He soaped up and rinsed off as well, and then he carefully placed the shower head back in the holder. The water beat down on both of them, filling the shower stall with steam. Slowly Deacon knelt in front of her. Water streamed down his face and his hair clung to his cheeks and throat. He rested his big hands on top of her thighs.

"Good Lord, Daci, I want you, too. We can't make love, but will you let me taste you? I promise to be careful."

She had no words. His dark amber eyes were level with hers, the need in them every bit as powerful as what she felt. She nodded.

He grinned. His smile destroyed the appearance of the grim ascetic, and he looked like a boy for a moment, a young man without cares, without the tragic history Daci had been so shocked to hear.

Did he know the others had shared his past with her?

The question was forgotten as Deacon lowered his mouth to her belly and kissed the soft swell above her thighs. The water cascaded over both of them as he carefully moved her legs apart and dipped lower. He nuzzled the thick tangle of her dark pubic hair and then lapped at her sex with the flat of his tongue. She bit back a cry of pure, unadulterated pleasure.

Her feeling had definitely come back to that part of her body. Daci shivered and curled her fingers against the slick fiberglass seat when Deacon used his long fingers to separate her folds. He found her clit and sucked gently, sending more shivers up her spine.

She moaned when his fingers brushed the opening of her channel and she felt two of them slide deep inside. The combination of long fingers penetrating and his soft lips suckling took her to the edge in a heartbeat.

Then, without any warning at all, Daci fell into Deacon's thoughts. She tasted her own flavors and they were intoxicating on a tongue that was not her own. She felt the clench and clasp of inner muscles tightening around fingers that were Deacon's not hers. She knew his excitement, the fact he hovered on the brink of orgasm merely from the taste of her, the feel of her rippling muscles, the scent of her arousal.

Intense, overwhelming, mind-blowing sensation built higher, stronger. Daci's thoughts looped over and around Deacon's into a single, shared experience. Awareness intensified, perception increased, the scents and flavors of wet, needy flesh, of hot, pounding water, of the pressure of an engorged cock and aching balls, of rippling muscles and clenching sheath . . . growing, expanding, exploding into orgasm.

His fingers thrust deep inside her sex, his lips tightened around her clit. Daci heard him growl against her needy flesh. His free hand slipped down between them and he grabbed his erect penis in his fist. His arm jerked in time with her pulsing body as he stroked himself. Groaning, he joined Daci's climax. Her body shuddered and her knees gripped his broad shoulders as his body bucked with each jerk of his hand.

She felt the hot jets of his ejaculate hitting the backs of her legs, like bursts of molten lava against her suddenly chilled flesh. His muscles tensed, rock hard between her thighs, until finally he relaxed against her, perfectly still except for the harsh sound of his breathing.

Panting as if she'd run a mile, Daci leaned forward and rested her cheek on his shoulder. "Oh. My." It was all she could say between gasps for air.

She felt his body shudder. When he pulled away and sat back on his heels, he was laughing. "Works for me." He stood up on shaking legs and grabbed the shower head once again. The water was growing cooler as he hosed off the backs of her legs and aimed the spray between her thighs.

She shrieked and slammed her legs together. Laughing, she covered her face with her hands. "I don't think the doctor would approve," she said, when she finally caught her breath.

Deacon carefully finished hosing her off, rinsed himself, and turned off the tap. "You're probably right, but damn, girl." He grabbed a towel and dried her as she sat. Daci felt so loose-limbed and relaxed she merely held up one arm, and then the other for the towel.

He helped her out of the shower, grabbed a clean nightgown for her and slipped it over her head. Then he put his own clothes back on. Daci sat on the closed toilet seat, combed out her wet hair and braided it in one long, thick braid.

Neither of them said another word about what they'd done.

They didn't have to. Her body still throbbed with the final vestiges of orgasm and her breasts were sensitive to the soft brush of the nightgown. When Deacon helped her back to the bed, his touch was gentle as before, but somehow more intimate.

Whatever was growing between them had taken a powerful leap to an entirely new level. Smiling to herself, Daci let Deacon pull the covers up over her legs and fluff her pillows behind her. She watched him with a new appreciation, a new sense of who he was, and what he was coming to mean to her.

The quest she'd undertaken in her father's name slipped quietly to the back of her mind.

Chapter 11

Deacon was running a comb through his tangled hair and getting ready to go after Manda when there was a soft knock on Daci's open bedroom door. An absolutely gorgeous blonde Daci'd never seen in her life stuck her head around the corner and smiled.

Daci frowned and glanced back at Deacon. He grinned at her and shrugged his shoulders.

"Who are . . . ?"

"I didn't think you'd recognize me, but I know you, Daci. I'm Manda."

"Manda? From the lab? But . . ." She grabbed Deacon's hand and held on for dear life. "You were . . . you can't be the same . . . you were . . ." Speechless, she just stared.

Manda laughed. "Oh, honey, you have no idea." She walked into Daci's room and leaned over to give her a hug.

Daci burst into totally unexpected tears. "But you're beautiful." She grabbed the tissue Deacon shoved into her hand, wiped her eyes, and thought about crawling under the bed to hide. "I'm sorry . . . it's just that, I remember you from when I was little, and you looked . . . you were . . ." She shook her head and tried to clear her mind of the old images of Manda. "Now you're absolutely gorgeous."

"Thank you. So are you." Manda sat down on the edge of the bed and held on to both of Daci's hands. "I wondered if I'd ever see you again, after your mom died and Bosworth wouldn't let you come back anymore. I've wondered about you for years."

"Me too. I mean I was so afraid you were still trapped in that horrible cage and they were still doing awful things to you." Daci's voice cracked as old memories flashed into her mind. "I hated him for that. When he wouldn't let you go free, I hated him, but I was just a little kid. There was nothing I could do."

"I know. I did get away from the lab, finally. Not until after your father died, but I was still a freak. Then Bay rescued me." She glanced over her shoulder at the tall, dark-haired man waiting in the doorway. "Sweetheart, come and meet Daci. She knew me before, and we were friends."

"Manda's mentioned you, Daci. It's good to meet you." He nodded at her, but his smile was for Manda. He stood beside her, his entire demeanor protective, with his hand placed firmly on her slim shoulder.

Deacon seemed fascinated by their hands, by the obvious intimacy between Manda and her mate. He turned back toward Daci and caught her watching him. There was a serious gleam in his amber eyes.

She smiled, felt the color rise in her face and looked away.

Then she slipped her hands free of Manda's gentle grasp and rubbed at her arms. "I'm sorry. They've been so itchy. It must be the dry air, or something I'm allergic to."

Manda glanced at Deacon, and than leaned back against Bay's solid thigh. She tilted her head up and smiled at him. "Sweetheart? Why don't you go and get Anton? Maybe Logan and Adam, too."

Her mate left without saying a word.

Daci scratched a red streak on her arm. "Is something wrong?"

Manda shook her head. "No, Daci. Things are all wonderful. It's just that I want Anton here when I explain what happened to me. Why I was so deformed when you knew me, and why I'm not anymore."

Logan was actually sort of surprised when Adam trailed after him as he followed Anton down the hallway to Daci's room. Adam had avoided the girl as much as possible since her fall. Logan figured it was only Adam's curiosity about her medical condition that brought him back to her room.

That, and his desire to protect his sister. Adam would probably never get past the guilt he felt over not being able to help Manda for all those years when Bosworth held her prisoner, which Logan thought was pretty stupid. Adam hadn't even known if Manda was real, much less that she was his twin.

Keisha remained in the kitchen. She hadn't made an issue of it, but it was more than obvious she disagreed with Anton's decision to give Daci the nutrients without telling the girl what was going on. The other women agreed with Keisha, but they hadn't hesitated to speak their minds. Hopefully, it would all blow over soon, because the tension wasn't helping anyone's mood. Only Eve had kept quiet, but then she was with Daci every day and probably didn't want to get involved.

Logan's ears still burned after Jazzy had let him have it. She was barely civil to Anton, even though they were all guests in his house. The women didn't seem to understand the need for secrecy, all hung up the way they were on personal choice and control issues.

He wondered if he'd ever figure them out.

"Probably not." Anton chuckled and slapped him on

the shoulder. "Just be thankful they love us in spite of our blundering methods."

Logan paused outside Daci's closed door. "Why didn't you tell Daci what you were doing? What she is?"

Anton shrugged. "I didn't trust her. I still don't, really. She is, for all intents and purposes, her father's daughter. We caught her spying on us, and I'm still not sure why. There was nothing to stop her from going to the press and disclosing our existence, if, for no other reason, than revenge, but at the same time, I had to make sure. Without the nutrients, we'd never know if she was Chanku or not."

"So what's changed now?" Adam obviously still didn't trust Daci one bit.

"Deacon."

"I don't get it." Anton could be so cryptic at times. Logan reached for the door. "What's Deacon got to do with it?"

"Daci loves him. He loves her. She won't betray the man she loves."

With that, Anton grabbed the handle and pushed the door open. Logan stared at him for a minute. The man could be so damned arrogant, as if he never made a mistake. What would it be like, to have that kind of confidence?

Shaking his head, Logan followed Adam and Anton into Daci's room.

She'd been so focused on Manda, Daci hadn't realized her bedroom was filling up. Deacon was still there, and Manda sat on the edge of the bed. Bay, her mate, had returned. Eve and Jazzy had slipped in quietly at some point, and even Mei and Oliver were in the room.

Another couple she'd never met leaned against the wall, and when Adam walked in with Logan and Anton right behind him, there was hardly room for anyone else.

Daci gripped Deacon's hand and stared beyond Manda at all the others. "What's going on? Why is everyone here?" She scratched at her itchy arms and scooted closer to Deacon. There was the oddest sensation, as if she could actually hear the heartbeats of the people around her, as if her hearing had gone ultrasensitive.

Her nose definitely had. She picked up the various scents of men and women in what seemed to be a collective state of arousal. What was it with these people?

At least she could be thankful they weren't naked.

Deacon squeezed her fingers. Anton stepped forward. The easygoing smile he generally wore was nowhere to be seen. Instead, he looked serious, almost angry for some reason.

"Manda was going to tell her story," he said. "We all wanted to hear it." His hand stroked Manda's long, blond hair and she turned and smiled at him. Adam stepped up and took her hand, raised her fingers to his lips and kissed them.

"It's ultimately your choice," he said.

Manda smiled at Adam and then at Daci. "I know."

None of this made sense. Daci bit her lips and kept her mouth shut.

"No one knew my whole story, until recently, and that includes me." Manda still clung to Adam's hand, but her other hand was securely wrapped in her mate's, as if she needed both men for their strength.

"Adam and I are twins. We were taken from our mother at birth and adopted out to two different families. We never even knew the other existed, though each of us had always had a strong sense of loss we could never really define. I ended up in Tibet with missionary parents. For the first years of my life, things were pretty normal. Then my mother and father were brutally murdered when I was twelve. My entire life changed that night."

She glanced over her shoulder at her husband. He nodded. Manda took a deep breath and looked directly at Daci. The gleam in her amber eyes was unsettling, to say the least. "The morning after my parents were killed, the people of the village who found me were terrified. I was no longer a pretty little girl with long, blond hair. Somehow, overnight, I had changed into a monster. I had patches of dark fur and twisted legs, horrible, sharp teeth and a stubby tail. They thought I was a demon, cursed by God. I believed them. There was no other explanation."

Daci nodded. "I remember you that way, but you weren't scary. Not really. You were sad."

Manda nodded and brushed tears out of her eyes. "I was very sad when you knew me." She sighed and stared blankly over Daci's head as she spoke. "A congressman from America was visiting the area and took me home with him. I called him Papa B, but I had no idea who he really was. He kept me for twenty-five years at various secret labs, but I spent most of that time in a cage in the laboratory where you saw me. I thought he was going to rescue me, but I was treated as nothing more than a lab animal with privileges." She shrugged and her sigh was audible in the silent room. "I had a television and they would give me paper and crayons. My hands were so misshapen I couldn't hold anything smaller, like a pen or pencil, but that's how I learned to read and write and do math. Watching children's shows on TV and writing with crayons. My whole connection to the world outside was through the TV . . . that and the times I got to spend playing with you."

Daci nodded and glanced at Deacon. "They never let her out when my father was around, but if my mother was working, Manda could come out of her cage and we'd play." She turned back to Manda. "I remember you calling him Papa B. What happened? Why did you turn into that creature? Did it have something to do with my father's obsession with shapeshifters?"

"Yes, it did. He had heard reports of creatures able to shift from human to wolf. When he found me, he figured I was proof of the rumors, but he could never make me shift one way or the other, despite putting me through all kinds of horrible experiments. His goal was to breed an army of shapeshifters and I was a huge disappointment." Manda's voice cracked.

"Sweetheart, you don't need to . . ." Even Bay's voice sounded ragged.

"Yes. I do." Manda smiled up at her mate, then looked directly at Daci. "He tried mating me with both men and wolves. I was still a child, but he didn't care. Obviously, I didn't get pregnant despite his attempts. It became an obsession for him. He searched for more shapeshifters for the rest of his life."

Daci knew her father was obsessed, that he had done bad things, but rape? Rape a child? That would make him a monster. She couldn't accept that. She wouldn't.

She forced Manda's horrible accusations out of her thoughts, wrapped her arms around herself and shivered. "But you? What happened to you?"

Manda glanced at Anton. "I was . . . I am, a shapeshifter. I'm part of an ancient race called Chanku that we believe originated somewhere on the Himalayan steppes. With the proper nutrition, a small gland in our brains matures and gives us the ability to change into wolves."

A direct lightning strike couldn't have shocked her more. Daci stared at Manda. Her words seemed to reverberate in her mind. *Shapeshifter . . . change into wolves.*

For some reason, Manda looked over at Mei and Oliver, standing quietly across the room. "Or, sometimes into other creatures besides wolves. I shifted as a result of fear when I saw my parents murdered, but I wasn't old enough, or possibly hadn't had enough of the right nutrients, to shift completely. When you knew me, I was trapped, halfway between human and wolf. I remained that way, caught in a freakish hell for all those years your father kept me prisoner."

Manda's soft voice faded into the roar of blood rushing in her ears. A lifetime of questions in search of answers spooled across Daci's brain. Trembling, she looked around the room, no longer seeing the new friends she'd made, the young man who had cared for her.

Shapeshifters. All of them . . . So many things her father had said finally made sense. His obsession wasn't because he was crazy . . . it was because he was right, but no one believed him. She wasn't crazy, either, out there watching these people for so many cold and lonely nights. She'd wasn't!

"Everything my father believed . . . it was all true. He was right!" She twisted around, her eyes flashing from one face to the next before focusing once again on Manda. "All those years when people told him he was crazy, he wasn't. It's not just you, is it? It's you, too." She looked at Anton. "And you, Adam. And Logan." Her head spun as her eyes blazed from one person to the other. People she'd begun to think of as friends. How stupid she'd been! What a fool, to trust any of them. "All of you? Are all of you the same?"

She turned to Deacon and saw the hurt in his eyes when she tugged her hand free, but it didn't matter. He'd lied to her and suddenly her world was spinning, all that she'd known and believed whirling and twisting out of control. "You, too? You're one of them? Did one of you kill him?" She scooted away, back toward the head of the bed and her mind spun as she looked at each and every person crowded into her room. Her nostrils were filled with their scent, her ears vibrated with the sound of their hearts beating, their lungs working. "Did one of you kill my father? Why won't anyone answer me?"

All those years she'd tried to win her father's love and now, now when she'd finally proved he was right, it was too late . . . much too late.

"Stop it, Daciana. Stop now!" Anton stepped forward and touched Manda's shoulder. She trembled visibly, shaking like a leaf in the wind. "Your father was not murdered. He died of a stroke. As I told you before, we do not mourn him. The bastard deserved to die, for his cruelty toward

Manda, for the attempts he made on the lives of our packmates, for the threat he posed to every single one of us."

His words cut into her like a knife. She'd hated Bosworth a lot of the time herself, but that was her right. He was her father. Anton had no right to feel that way. None of them did. "I knew it," she cried. "You're all the same."

"Yeah, Daci, we are." Disgust dripped from every word as Deacon shoved himself away from the bed. Away from her. "But, ya know what's funny? So are you, Daci. And so was your mother."

She sat back as if she'd been slapped. He was lying. He had to be lying.

Without a backward glance, Deacon pushed his long frame away from the bed and stormed out of the room. The rest of them quietly followed. No one would meet her gaze. Not one of them looked at her on their way out, until only Adam and Anton remained. Even Manda had gone without another word, wrapped in her mate's protective arms, sobbing quietly. So what? Manda was one of them, too.

"Well, Anton. That went well, don't you think?" Adam glared at Daciana with a look of pure contempt. Then he, too, spun around and stalked out of the room.

"I'm not wrong about people very often." Anton spoke very quietly, without any inflection at all. His dark amber eyes seemed to bore through flesh and bone as he stared at her. "But when I am, I really fuck things up royally." He turned his back on her and wrapped his fingers around the door handle. "We shall have to decide what to do with you. It's obvious you can't be set free, not with the information you have. Certainly not with your abilities, or your immense reservoir of hatred."

Just before he shut the door behind him, Anton glanced back at her one more time. "In case you hadn't noticed, the windows on this room are barred. The door will be locked and your meals brought to you. You'll have plenty of time to think about your birthright, about your mother and your father—one of whom lived honorably, the other who was dishonorable in all ways possible. You have a choice of the one whose footsteps you follow. I would suggest you choose the more honorable path."

Daci couldn't speak. If she could have, she had no idea what she'd say in the face of such overwhelming disgust. He looked her over with utter contempt. Daci shivered, frightened and ashamed beneath the full brunt of his scorn.

"While you're choosing your path," he said, speaking so softly she had to strain to hear him, "think of the young man who loves you. At least, he was beginning to love you. I imagine that's all changed now."

He closed the door quietly but his anger remained. It filled the room, a seething, living entity fueled by disdain and disappointment. Daci heard the sharp clang of the bolt sliding into position. Heard the hollow sound of herself swallowing.

For the first time in days, she was entirely alone.

Well . . . not exactly. Memories of her mother and father filled the room. And memories of Manda, of the pathetic creature her father systematically tortured for twenty-five long years.

"Yet I defended him. Why?" She stared at the wall opposite her bed, but saw only Deacon's disappointment. His disgust.

Well, she'd earned it, hadn't she? What did Anton mean by that? *The young man who loves you.* Obviously, he didn't know what he was talking about. Deacon didn't love her. He couldn't.

She wasn't worth loving. Her father had proved that much.

When she closed her eyes, Anton's words filled her head. *Choose the more honorable path.* Not her father's. She'd been so alone when her mother died. The lab technician who raised her provided a bed and meals and made sure she went to school, but there'd been no love lost between them. She'd tried so hard to win her father's love before he died.

He was all she'd had, but she'd never really had him. He certainly hadn't wanted her.

Of course, if he'd known his only daughter was a shapeshifter, he might have cared.

Would she have ended up in a cage, just like Manda?

Had her mother truly been a shapeshifter? Had she been able to turn into a wolf? Was that why she'd cared so much about Manda . . . because she'd understood the young girl's plight?

Questions beat at Daci's brain. Questions without answers, until her head hurt from the pressure. Did Deacon really love her, or had she totally destroyed his feelings for her? Was he one of them? Was *she* really one of them? And what of Manda?

She'd never thought of herself as a cruel person. Never, yet she'd terribly hurt the people who had only been good to her. Better, more loving, than her own father. Why? How could she have been so mean?

The hours passed and light faded. The shadows crossed her room and eventually filled it up, until Daci sat alone in the semidarkness, her mind still seething with recriminations, lost in a mounting tide of despair.

Anton had been right about one thing. She had more than enough time to think, locked alone in her room. No matter how she looked at what she'd done, what she'd said, there was no way to excuse her behavior.

She'd been wrong. Dead wrong. And there was absolutely no way she could see to make things right, ever again.

A sharp click snapped her gaze toward the door. The knob turned and she felt the shift in air currents as the door slowly opened. Manda slipped into the room and quietly shut the door behind her. She raised her head and glared at Daci. Gone was the timid blonde, the woman who'd been a victim for so many years. She wasn't crying anymore. Now she just looked pissed.

"Manda? I'm so sorry. I . . ." Daci swallowed back her apology. It was much too late for that. "Why are you here?"

Chapter 12

Manda stared at her for a moment, almost as if she wasn't quite sure what she was doing in Daci's room. Then she walked across the floor and sat on the edge of the bed. She looked down at her hands for a moment. When she raised her head, she didn't meet Daci's gaze.

"Manda, I . . ."

Manda shook her head, one short, sharp jerk of her chin. "I came to tell you that I'll set you free if you want to go. Anton locking you in here was wrong." She took a deep breath. "He may hate me, and I know Bay will be furious, but I spent my life as a prisoner. I won't have any part of holding you against your will, no matter what the consequences of freeing you are. I can't be part of this."

Daci opened her mouth to reply, but the bedroom door opened again. Deacon, Jazzy, and Logan slipped into the room.

"Manda? What are you doing here?" Deacon touched Manda's shoulder, but his eyes were on Daci.

Manda shrugged. "I came to set her free. Anton has no right to hold her prisoner."

Jazzy plopped down on the bed beside Daci and Manda. "That's why we're here, too." She turned to Daci. "I don't agree with what you said and the fact you can give us up to the authorities scares the shit out of me, but I don't believe in holding you against your will. It's not right."

Stunned, Daci looked from one person to the next. All of them, here in her room, willing to risk Anton Cheval's anger? "Why?" she said, shaking her head. "Anton will never forgive you. I don't understand."

Deacon took her hand. He stared at their linked fingers for a moment, and then lifted his head and gazed directly into her eyes. "Even though I don't like what you said earlier, I love you, Daci. I know you think I hardly know you, but I've been in your head. I know who you are, even if you're not exactly sure. Locking you away, especially when you're ready to make your first shift, is just wrong."

Manda nodded. "That's it exactly. I've been there. I can't be part of keeping another Chanku imprisoned. I won't do it."

Jazzy got up and stood beside Logan. She wrapped her fingers around his and smiled. "I was a prisoner, too, only my jailer was my pimp. This whole thing—being Chanku—is new to us, Daci. We don't know the rules, but we know the difference between right and wrong. Locking you up is just wrong." She looked up at Logan, standing tall and serious beside her.

His eyes were on Jazzy when he spoke. "We think you're ready to make your first shift. We've decided to help you through it. Anton will have to agree we're right, once you're fully one of us, but even if he doesn't . . ." He took a deep breath and turned his gaze on Daci. "We have to live with our choices, and we choose to help one of our own, not lock you up."

A shiver raced along Daci's spine. Deacon had said it earlier, that she was one of them. She'd hardly dared believe him. "Are you sure I . . . ?"

Deacon nodded. "Logan saw the inside of your brain, remember? He was the first one to recognize the part of you that makes you shift. Anton's made sure you've been getting the nutrients you need."

She shook her head. "I haven't been taking any pills or anything like that."

"He's been putting the stuff in your food without telling you." Deacon shook his head. "That's just wrong."

"That's another thing." Manda stood up and slapped her hands down on her slim hips. "He gave you no choice. I know Keisha is upset about it. So are all the other females. Most of the men don't seem to understand that they're taking away our choice when they give us the nutrients without telling us what the pills do. We're not even human after taking them! I'm not saying that being Chanku is bad—just the opposite. It's wonderful, but whether or not you embrace your birthright should be your choice, not Anton's. It's wrong and we won't stand for it. What's even worse, Anton's given you what you need to shift, and now he's got you locked up in here so you can't run free."

A soft knock on the door silenced everyone. Daci squeezed Deacon's hand and they all stared at the door as it slowly opened.

Keisha and Xandi stepped into the room. Eve was right behind them. Then Mei crowded in, followed by Shannon Murphy. Daci hadn't even met her yet, though she'd been in Daci's room when she'd had her meltdown.

Shannon looked around at all the faces and grinned. Then she went straight to the bed, leaned over and gave Daci a big hug. "Looks like we're all in this together, eh, girls?"

Manda hugged Shannon and laughed. "The guys are going to be so pissed."

"Hey," Logan said, laughing. "Not all the guys. I'm here."

"Me, too." Once again, Deacon squeezed Daci's hand. "Do you think she's ready?"

Keisha walked around to the far side of the bed and touched Daci's forehead. Her fingertips felt cool against her skin. After a moment, Keisha looked up and smiled. "Oh, yeah. She's ready." Without another word, she untied the silky sarong she wore and let it fall to the floor in a swirl of pale blue silk.

Daci knew her eyes must be as large as saucers, but Keisha looked like a primitive queen, her body so ripe and beautiful Daci couldn't stop staring. She was rounded and soft, her breasts and hips full, her skin as smooth and perfect as dark chocolate.

The shuffle of fabric dragged her eyes away from Keisha. Everyone else in the room, including Deacon, had stripped off their clothing as well. Daci grabbed Deacon's hand and stared. What the hell were they doing?

He grinned at her, and before she could object, tugged her nightgown over her head. Daci flung her hands across her breasts, though she had to admit she felt silly, covering herself when everyone else was naked.

"Link with me." Deacon didn't give her time to blush. He spoke so sternly she did exactly as he instructed without taking time to think. "Get into my head. Do what I do."

She fell into his thoughts, tumbling headfirst into his mind as if she were Alice stumbling down the rabbit hole.

At first, the myriad images terrified her, a kaleidoscope of color and light, sound and scent.

Then they made absolutely perfect sense. It was so simple. So very, very simple.

Without warning, Daci was looking down from her perch in the middle of the bed, mesmerized by a pack of wolves. They circled the bed while she sat there blinking at the change in the light, the difference in perception.

Awestruck, she lifted her right hand, only it wasn't a hand any longer. It was a paw. A big, broad, hairy paw, tipped with sleek, black nails. Her fur was dark gray with silvery tips, the pads on the bottoms of her feet thick as leather and black as night.

All the air rushed out of her lungs. She felt light-headed, dizzy, and disoriented, her mind was spinning, her heart pounding. *What'd happened? How . . . ?*

Keisha's soft laughter echoed in her mind. It took Daci a moment to figure out which wolf she was. There, the dark brown one with fiery highlights glinting in the overhead light. She sat while the others moved, staring at Daci with her long tongue lolling from her mouth, framed in sharp, white teeth.

You are truly one of us, Daci. Just as your mother must have been so many years ago. Come. The men are with the babies. They think Xandi and I are running alone tonight. We'd rather you ran with us.

Deacon?

I'm here. Are you okay? The big dark gray wolf reared up and placed his paws on the edge of the bed. *Come with us.*

As if she moved within one of her dreams, Daci followed the pack of wolves out of her room and across the hallway to another bedroom. There was a large glass door that opened on to a deck.

The door had been left open, and each of them raced through the gap. Surprised that she actually recognized them now, Daci watched as Jazzy and Logan, then Manda, Shannon, and Xandi raced out onto the deck and leapt to the meadow below. Eve was right behind them.

Mei and Keisha hung back, as if waiting for Daci to make the leap. She did, side by side with Deacon. Then she paused in the meadow below the deck with all the others, and watched as Keisha arced over the railing.

Only Mei remained. But she wasn't a wolf anymore. Blinking in shock, Daci sat back on her haunches as a beautiful snow leopard practically flew off the deck with such power and grace that she actually sailed right over Deacon and Daci's heads.

Show-off! Keisha's mental voice cut through the pack's silent laughter.

The leopard snorted, and then it was once again a wolf. Daci trotted close and touched noses with Mei. *How?*

My primary shape is the snow leopard, but then I can't communicate with the rest of you as wolves. No way am I going to miss out on all the chatter tonight!

Mei took off at a full run. The rest of them followed, streaming out across the dark meadow, headed for the forest.

The night was magical. Daci lived the dream that had haunted her for so long. The scents, the small sounds, the whispers of movement along the trail. As she ran, knowledge spilled into her mind, words from Keisha and the others, as well as instincts coming to life from some deep well of Chanku knowledge that must have been freed by the shift.

She understood her ability to control her fertility and knew how to release an egg should she want a child. Her heat was upon her, and that explained so many of her sexual urges, the arousal she'd had so much trouble controlling. Was her scent the reason Deacon was attracted? Maybe that was all it was, the fact he was male and she was a bitch in heat.

She'd need to think on that one for a while. Anton couldn't be right. Deacon couldn't possibly love her.

More information flooded her mind. She knew she could only become pregnant in the form of the wolf, now that she had finally shifted. Knew that her body was impervious to human diseases, that cancer and viruses and even the common cold were no longer a threat.

But it was Keisha who explained the mating bond. The link so powerful, so all-consuming, that it could only occur when she finally chose her mate and he took her as a wolf, their bodies connected physically and mentally in a merge so complete it could be broken only in death.

Xandi described their unique pack structure—a matriarchal society where the alpha bitch ruled in a powerful partnership with the male. The male alpha might have the cunning and the physical strength, but he usually deferred to his mate. He might not always like it, but he accepted, on a level beyond conscious thought, that her strength ran deep and true, that her choices were for the pack, for their young, for their future. In this way their society as a whole found its strength.

Keisha's thoughts slipped into Daci's mind with perfect clarity. *Tonight was a perfect example,* she said. *Anton is our leader and he has the right to order your confinement, but it's my right and duty as the pack's alpha bitch to question his decision, and to countermand it if I disagree.* She glanced at Daci and her amber eyes sparkled. *Obviously, I disagree. He'll accept my decision whether he likes it or not.*

Wide-eyed, Daci followed Keisha and the others, with one thought uppermost in her mind—Keisha must be one tough bitch, if she was so willing to go against Anton Cheval! Deacon ran steadily behind her, but she was hardly aware of his presence. The thought of Keisha facing up to Anton amazed her. The fact she'd stood up to him for Daci, especially after the terrible things Daci had said, was almost too much to comprehend.

Her mind felt crammed full of new experiences, of unexpected sensations, but most of all, with the innate knowledge that she suddenly had a family where before there'd been no one.

A family she could never betray. A family her father had persecuted. How could she have aligned herself with him, when he was so obviously wrong?

Because he was your father, and you wanted his love. Deacon's soft voice slipped into her mind.

Will you forgive me? I feel so stupid. I'm not sure what I was thinking.

You were still thinking as a human. As Bosworth's daughter. Tonight, you're thinking as Chanku. You are your mother's daughter, Daci. You've shed your human self.

He stopped. Daci paused beside him.

You'll never be the same again, Daci. Please forgive us for taking that choice away from you. Keisha's right. We should have discussed it with you first.

She shook her head, aware it was a very unwolflike gesture. *What's done is done. I need to go back and apologize to everyone. I feel like such a fool.*

You're not a fool. Never a fool, sweetheart.

Suddenly Xandi's thoughts filled her mind. *Game. Just ahead. Daci, you and Deacon circle to the left and come in around the pond. We'll approach from the far side.*

Daci followed Deacon, shocked when the instinct to slip through the scrubby willows at the water's edge in absolute silence governed her amazing body. She crept stealthily around the pond. A young buck stood with his front feet in the shallow water. He drank slowly. Then he raised his head and snorted.

Setting her human self aside, Daci exploded out of the willows. The buck reared back. Daci's jaws closed around his throat, but she missed the solid killing bite her instincts told her she wanted. Jazzy shot in from the right at almost the same time and clamped her jaws higher on the animal's throat, just beneath his jaw. The weight of the two wolves took the animal to the ground.

The other females crowded in. The kill was quick, though not as neat as Daci knew it should have been. She still had so much to learn, but hunger ruled her now. Immersed in her new reality as wolf, she tore into the soft belly, ripping through hide and skin. Her blood ran hot with the scent of the kill and the taste of warm meat. She gorged herself, feasting with the other females in a frenzy of snarling lips and bared teeth, their ears flat against their broad skulls.

Logan and Deacon circled for a few minutes, snarling and growling until the mood shifted and the bloodlust cooled. Then they moved into the seething pack and found their places at the rapidly cooling body.

Later, when the buck had been reduced to a scattered carcass of skin and bloodied bones, the pack began to disperse. Keisha touched her nose to Daci's flank. *Xandi and I have to go back. The babies need us.* She snorted. *And we need them. We've discovered our milk comes in heavier when we've made a kill and gorged ourselves. You've done well, Daci. The others will accept you, once you come to them. I'll talk to Anton and tell him what we've done.*

There's no need.

Daci spun around. The wolves near the carcass all turned in the same direction. A huge black wolf stalked out of the forest. It didn't stop until it reached Daci and Keisha.

Daci felt her legs begin to tremble the moment she recognized Anton. She leaned close to Deacon. He stood beside her without any sense of fear at all. Jazzy and Logan moved closer to stand next to them. Manda crowded close and then pushed out in front to face the wolf.

It was my idea to set her free, she said.

But we all agreed. Logan faced Anton as well. Soon the others stood beside and behind them.

Anton looked at Keisha first. Then he gazed directly into Daci's eyes. She felt his mind touch hers, but there was no sense of what he thought or felt. He looked absolutely regal, standing there in front of her with all the others facing him.

Then, without responding to either Manda or Logan,

he spun around and trotted back into the woods. Keisha turned to Daci. *Don't worry. Everything will be fine. I'm going with him.*

She and Xandi trotted after Anton. The others followed, until only Daci and Deacon remained in the quiet meadow. The scent of blood and death from their kill still lingered. The amazing rush, the sense she'd finally found her place in the world, had been dulled by Anton's appearance, the reminder of what she'd said, what the others had done on her behalf.

Deacon was the first to shift. Daci followed, hesitant now that so many truths had been revealed. The night was cool and she wrapped her arms around her naked body. "What now?"

"Do you still hate us?" Deacon smiled at her, but his hands stayed at his sides.

Daci raised her head and gazed steadily into his amber eyes. "I can't believe I defended my father. He doesn't deserve my loyalty. He never showed me any compassion, never loved me as he should have. He was obsessed. Maybe he was insane." She shook her head. "I feel so stupid. So many things make sense now. They didn't before. Even my mother. She was always such a mystery to me. Now, it's like my entire sense of reality has shifted."

"That's because you shifted." He touched her chin, lifted her face so that she couldn't avoid the light in his amber eyes. "I do love you, Daci. Make love with me. Here, now." He touched her shoulders. His fingertips lightly traced the curve of her arms all the way to her wrists. He linked their hands.

She shook her head. "I don't know if I love you, Deacon. I don't know anything, anymore. I think I do, but so much has happened. I can't mate with you. Not as a wolf. I understand the permanence of that now, and I'm not ready. It's all too new."

He leaned over and touched his forehead to hers. "I'm

not ready for the mating bond, either, though I have a feeling it will happen, and it will happen with you . . . when we're both ready. My first shift happened this week, remember? Make love to me, as a woman loves a man. If I don't have you right now, I think I might explode."

His voice cracked. She wasn't sure if it was laughter or a sob, but when she looked up he was smiling.

"I really can't face Anton with a boner, Daci. Have pity on me!"

Laughter burst out of her. She threw her arms around his slim waist and buried her face against his chest. "You idiot. Of course. But I have to run first. I'm not ready to face Anton at all. Not yet."

She shifted and spun around in one, flowing motion, as if she'd done this all her life. Then she realized she had—for years, in her dreams. Those amazing dreams that finally, after so long, made sense.

Deacon shifted and followed. Daci felt his sharp teeth as he nipped her flank. She kicked into a higher gear until they were flying across the ground, feet barely touching the hard-packed earth, tails aloft like flags in the wind.

Daci had never felt so free. She ran from her mother's death, from her father's betrayal. From all the years she'd lived with people who didn't care for her beyond the money her father sent them to keep her.

She ran from everything that had shaped her, that had formed her into the young woman she'd become, and in the process she realized she was no longer racing away from her past.

No. With Deacon behind her, Daciana Lupei raced forward, into her future.

Chapter 13

Keisha left Anton and nursed their daughter the moment they returned from their run. Then she put Lily back to bed, showered and wrapped herself in a pale blue sarong. She found her mate leaning against the railing on the back deck. He'd put on a pair of worn Levis and a soft, black sweater, so unlike his usual dark slacks and white shirt. His dark hair was still wet from his shower, his feet were bare. She stood behind him, studying the long, lean lines of his body until her eyes settled on the frayed hems of his jeans and the soft dusting of dark hair across the tops of his feet.

She'd always loved looking at his long, narrow feet. There was something inherently sexy about a man's bare feet, in the touch of vulnerability combined with the strength to carry him upright. She thought of how she could make his toes curl when she went down on him. How it felt when he ran his toes along her bare leg during sex.

How very much she loved him.

"Why, Keisha?" Anton turned around with his arms folded over his chest. There was no condemnation in his eyes. Only curiosity. A need to understand.

"Two things." She stopped a couple of feet away from him and gazed into his dark, troubled eyes. "It was wrong to give her the nutrients without her permission. You took away her choice. You know how I feel about that. How the other women feel, but you chose to act without considering our very real distaste for what you did. That was wrong, and I have a right to my anger."

He blinked, but said nothing.

Keisha clasped her hands together in front of her waist. She didn't want to hurt him, but he needed and wanted the truth. "Ultimately," she said, "it was Manda. She was held against her will for too many years to allow it to happen to anyone else. Your decision harmed Manda more than it hurt Daci. It awakened all her old pain, her fears. You didn't see what was so patently obvious in Manda, and you wouldn't listen to my arguments. We had no choice but to act."

She sighed and shook her head. "Manda didn't even think to come to you. She was devastated by your decision to lock Daci in the room. She still is."

"Logan and Jazzy?"

"They're young and idealistic, and they believe in total freedom of the spirit. They were shocked when you locked Daci up, even though they were totally disgusted by her reaction when she learned the truth about us. You took away the chance for them to have a part in the sentence you decreed. You took away their choice."

"And Deacon?"

Keisha smiled. "Ah, you were right about Deacon. He loves her, in spite of the hateful things she said. It just took him awhile to come around, to get past his hurt."

"But I was wrong where it mattered, wasn't I?" He held his arms out to her, and Keisha flowed into his embrace. He smiled ruefully, dipped his head and gently kissed her mouth. "Arrogance triumphs again, eh? I am so sorry. Keisha, my love, will you forgive me?"

She raised up on her toes and kissed him back. Her tongue traced the seam of his lips and slipped through, into the welcoming warmth of his mouth. *There's nothing for me to forgive, you fool. I love you in spite of yourself.*

He broke the kiss, threw back his head and laughed. "No wonder I love you. No one else would have me."

"There is that," she said, "though you'll also need to ask Daci's forgiveness. It's her trust we need. Her loyalty." She wrapped her fingers in his and tugged. "Lily's asleep. Make love to me before she wakes."

He gripped Keisha's hand as if it were a lifeline, and followed her toward the bedroom. Xandi and Stefan met them in the hallway, and it was as if there'd never been any anger, never a disagreement of something so vital as the freedom and rights of one of their own.

"She is one of ours, isn't she?" Anton's words slipped out, as if he'd not really meant to say them aloud.

Keisha and Xandi nodded. Keisha paused with her hand on the bedroom door. "Of course she is. Now that she's shifted, she understands what she couldn't before."

Stefan threw an arm over Anton's shoulders. "Sometimes, bud, you're too damned smart for your own good. She needed the nutrients to understand the truth, but it was too dangerous to tell her the truth until after she'd had them. Where do we draw the line?"

"Somewhere in the middle, I imagine." Xandi linked her arm in Anton's and winked at Keisha.

Stefan nodded in agreement. "The babies are both asleep and it's been too long since we've all been together. Forget about Daci and Bosworth and all that crap. Let's get naked together and fuck."

Chuckling, Anton followed Keisha into the bedroom. "I have always admired your subtlety, Stef."

"Isn't he great?" Xandi slipped free of Anton's arm, grabbed her mate's hand and tugged him through the door. She glanced toward the empty portable crib. "Where's Lily?"

"Back in her own room. We've decided to try it again." Anton turned to Keisha and his eyes were filled with love and regret.

Keisha tried to smile, but it wasn't easy. She still wasn't comfortable with their daughter out of her sight. She'd never forget the last time they'd moved Lily into her own room and intruders had almost succeeded in taking her.

Never again, my love. Never again.

Keisha nodded and forced her tense muscles to relax. Anton slipped the sweater over his head and she dropped her sarong to the floor in a swirl of pale blue silk. Xandi's sweats followed, and Stefan had his shirt and pants off before Anton stepped out of his worn jeans.

"I like the look." Xandi gestured toward the faded jeans lying in a heap on the floor. "It's a new one for you, isn't it?"

Anton glanced at the pants and then took a long look at Xandi's slim, naked body. "It's the closest I could come to sackcloth. I figured ashes were overkill."

They were all laughing at his dry comment when he threw an arm around Keisha and another around Xandi and tumbled the two women into bed. Stefan followed and they slipped into the familiar patterns of longtime lovers. Stefan knelt between Keisha's thighs and dipped his head. She arched her back and moaned with the first light brush of his tongue between her legs. Xandi knelt above her. Tilting her head back, Keisha swept her tongue through Xandi's sleek folds and lost herself in the flavors and textures of the other woman as Stefan took her closer and closer to climax.

Anton sat back on his heels and watched with a feeling in his chest that bordered on pain. He loved these three so powerfully that it frightened him. Tonight, he'd almost blown it. Had blown it, actually, until saner heads prevailed.

Thank goodness for the three young kids who'd come to him to learn the ways of the Chanku. In this particular instance, the roles of teacher and student had been reversed. They'd taught him a powerful lesson—one he'd not soon forget.

He stroked Stefan's back, running his fingers along the

row of vertebrae all the way to the dark crease of his lover's perfect ass. Stefan shivered from his touch, but he never lost his rhythm as he licked and sucked between Keisha's thighs.

Anton could have forgone contact altogether. Watching Stefan make love to Keisha as she practically devoured Xandi had him hovering on the edge of climax.

But he knew it could be even better. Grabbing the lubricant off the bedside table, he coated his fingers and spread the clear gel between Stefan's sleek buttocks. Anton heard him moan. Keisha gasped, most likely from the vibration of Stefan's lips, so Anton did it again.

This time, when he reached the taut puckered ring, Anton pressed and swirled his fingertip, slowly working his way beyond the tight muscle. One finger, then two, and finally a third, pressing and retreating, twisting slowly in and out, finding and then matching Stefan's own rhythm until the four of them moved in a coordinated dance of bodies and mouths.

He slipped a condom over his erect penis and pressed against the softened muscle. Stefan gasped when Anton finally slipped through the tight ring. The gasp became a long, low moan of pleasure when Anton slowly pushed forward, driving as deep inside as his cock would go.

Finally, when his balls pressed tightly against Stefan's rounded sac, he withdrew every bit as slowly. Once again, he searched for and found the rhythm of the other three. Opening his thoughts, he linked with Stefan, Keisha, and Xandi, sharing the sensation of deep thrust and slow withdrawal, of heat and pressure, of clenching muscles and profound pleasure.

Stefan's thoughts collided with his, the dark pain yet even more powerful bliss of full penetration, the knowledge it was the man he loved more than any other who fucked him so completely. Anton reached around Stef's slim waist and wrapped his gel-covered fingers around his lover's cock. Thrusting his hips harder now, slamming into Stefan with enough force to drive him forward into Keisha, Anton took control. Harder, faster, until the stimulation was almost too great to bear. Only then, still afraid of what he would find, Anton opened his thoughts wide to the three beneath him.

He found only love. Love and acceptance, the honest knowledge that all of them were fallible, yet each of them acted out of love.

It was a powerful message. One he needed to hear. Keisha's thoughts spilled over him, her rising excitement, the taste of Xandi's fluids and soft, welcoming folds, the love she felt for Stefan and his mate, but most of all for Anton. Her amazing, mystical lover, a man capable of great failures as well as sublime achievements, a man who always, eventually, did the right thing.

It was her steadfast belief in him that took him over the edge. Not the tight clench of Stefan's rectum around his sheathed cock, not the sight of Keisha's tongue circling the tiny nubbin of Xandi's swollen clitoris or the shared tastes and sensations as Stefan drove his tongue deep inside Keisha's sex.

No, it was her belief in him, her honesty, her unyielding and unforgiving love. A shock of pure sensation raced from his balls to his cock and back again. He grabbed Stefan's shaft in both hands, squeezing and jerking up and down its length as if he stroked himself.

Stefan cried out and climaxed with his face and fingers buried between Keisha's thighs. Anton threw his head back and groaned, but his hips continued their in-and-out thrusting as if he no longer controlled his own body.

Passion exploded as Keisha and Xandi reached climax together. Their shared orgasm blossomed in Anton's mind and he tasted Xandi's bittersweet cream, felt her clenching, rippling muscles around Keisha's fingers, lips, and tongue.

His hands were slick with Stefan's ejaculate, his body

covered in sweat. Tendrils of hair clung to his face and neck, his legs trembled and his chest heaved with each breath he took.

The thought drifted through his mind between one heartbeat and the next, that there was no subterfuge in sex this open, this earthy. No ego, no agenda. There was only pure, honest love. Love without barriers or boundaries, without secrets.

He wanted to weep for the beauty of their love, but laughter won. The ultimate answers were always so simple. Why the fuck did he always have to make things so difficult? Anton wrapped his arms tightly around Stefan and collapsed beside him with his cock still firmly planted in Stefan's backside. Xandi and Keisha sprawled in a limp tangle, their sated bodies rippling with pleasure.

When Anton shared his epiphany, they all lay together, laughing as one, loving as one. Once again, Keisha, Xandi, and Stefan's pure unquestioning love had shown him the way.

Honesty. It was all about honesty.

Deacon led her to a secluded glade with a small creek that emptied into a shallow pond. Here the air was fresh, far from the scent of blood and the questions that lingered. Grasses grew thick and lush near the waters' edge, and the cool night air carried the perfume of cedar and fir.

He shifted first. When Daci rose to stand on two legs, she felt like some sort of mystical goddess meeting her warrior in the dark forest. None of this seemed real. After so many dreams, the entire evening was magic, another figment of her overactive imagination.

Yet the hand Deacon held out to her was real, solid and strong. His fair skin glowed in the pale moonlight. Her night vision was much stronger now, after her shift, and she took a moment to admire his unearthly male beauty. Finally she wrapped her fingers in his and he tugged her close.

Daci's legs were stronger. The last vestiges of her injury had disappeared with her shift and she stepped toward Deacon with a new confidence.

For the first time since her mother's death, Daci realized she was no longer alone. Not only Deacon, but so many others had stood up for her tonight. Even Anton Cheval appeared to have acquiesced . . . but then, she couldn't imagine anyone going against Keisha's wishes. The sense of family gave her a new confidence, a sense of herself that was powerful yet still feminine.

Deacon pulled her closer, and her breasts pressed against the hard line of his chest. She felt his heart beating, felt his strong cock rising against her belly, heard the soft cadence of his breathing. She raised her head. He was smiling at her.

Daci stood on her toes to kiss him, but he still had to bend down before their mouths could meet. How strange, that their bodies were closer in size when they ran as wolves, as if their four-legged form gave them a physical equality not matched as humans.

She'd have to ask the others about that, sometime. Now, though, all she wanted was Deacon. Daci reached up and wrapped both arms around his neck.

Laughing, he lifted her. Two broad palms beneath her buttocks brought her close. She wrapped her legs around his narrow hips and felt the hard ridge of his erection pressing against her sex. Locking her heels together at the small of his back, she held them close together.

"It's real, isn't it? I really am a wolf." Merely saying it made her giggle. Touching him like this made her hot. He'd said she'd be horny after shifting.

She'd had no idea. Her body quivered with need. Her sex pulsed, pressed against his cock. She wanted him inside. Filling her, thrusting hard and fast until she screamed with pleasure.

"It's real." He lifted her just a fraction, enough that the length of his cock slid along the wet corridor of her sex.

She tightened her thighs around his hips and pressed closer against him.

"I can't take much more, Daci." He tilted his head and kissed her. His fingers dug into her cheeks and one pressed against her puckered anus. She'd never been touched there before by any man. The sensation sent nervous shivers up her spine. He wouldn't take her there, would he? Not their first time . . .

Deacon laughed. "No, not the first time. Maybe not even the second, but before long, I will take you in every way that's possible . . . just as you'll take me. I promise you that."

She unhooked her ankles and let her feet slip to the ground, but when Daci went to her knees and touched him, Deacon backed out of her reach.

"No. Not this time. This time we do it my way." Grinning, he knelt in front of her and ran his hands over her body, stroking her from breast to thighs. His touch sent shivers over her arms and legs. Her sex reacted with a rush of creamy moisture. She tilted her hips forward, reaching for more of his touch.

Deacon ran one long finger between her legs, brushed her clit lightly, then slipped between her damp folds. She grabbed his arm with both hands, cried out as her body jerked at the intrusive touch. He stroked her again, penetrated again and she climaxed without any warning at all. Doubling over his arm, Daci clung to him as he continued fucking her with just one finger.

Tears ran down her face. Her body quivered and jerked in response to each thrust. She'd never been so sensitive. Never reacted so violently. Never wanted so much.

Scrambling away from him, she lay back in the cold grass and spread her legs. Even the damp, icy grass couldn't cool her desire, not now, when her body was hot and need was a living, breathing entity coursing through her veins. She raised her knees and stroked one finger between her legs, as wanton an invitation as any she could make.

"More, Deacon. I need all of you. Don't tease me anymore."

He quickly moved between her thighs and took his cock in his fist. Stroking slowly, he held it against her swollen lips. She raised up on her elbows to look at him. He was huge. His glans was broad and thick, slick with a steady stream of white fluid escaping from the narrow slit at the top. His foreskin framed the end like a cowl, stretched tightly just behind the plum-shaped head, and the fat length of his cock was ridged with veins.

Daci's breath caught in her throat. She wasn't a virgin, though not all that experienced, either. One or two misguided attempts at sex with boys who didn't have a clue, and a couple of pathetic dates that never should have ended up in bed didn't come close to preparing her for Deacon's monster.

Not for his sexual confidence, either. She wondered how many women he'd been with. How many different things he'd tried. If he'd find her lacking . . .

"Never, Daci." He dragged the slick head between the folds of her sex and then swirled the damp tip over her clit. "You're amazing. You're beautiful and mysterious and I have never wanted any man or woman the way I want you."

She knew her eyes were as big as saucers. "You've been with a man?"

He laughed. "Most recently with Logan." Then he took a deep breath and lost the smile. "I was a prostitute, Daci. I told you I've been on the streets since I was fourteen. How else do you think I survived? I fucked whoever wanted me for money and the only ones willing to pay were men. It was a job. A very dangerous job, but it was all I knew. I had no idea how good sex with a woman could be until I ended up in Jazzy and Logan's bed. I know it's going to be even better with you."

"Jazzy *and* Logan?" Her first thought was that she should be jealous, except all she could think about was putting herself into the mix. She'd never been with a woman, but the fantasy of two gorgeous men, their bodies slick with sweat as they writhed together . . . that was one that always got her off.

Picturing Deacon and Logan . . . oh, my. "Next time, invite me along, too." She grinned and arched her hips. Deacon pressed forward, slowly. He was bigger than anyone she'd ever been with, and her body tensed.

"Relax. I promise to go slow. I'll try not to hurt you." Pressing forward, then retreating, and then moving forward again a fraction of an inch at a time, he slowly forced his way inside. Her pussy burned as it stretched to accommodate his size.

He rolled his hips slowly, carefully, and went a little deeper. When he was only halfway in, Daci already felt full. She looked up at Deacon and blinked away tears. So far, this was not nearly as much fun as she'd expected.

He withdrew and she wanted to cry. "Aren't you going to . . . ?"

"Shush. This will work. Trust me. Lie back and close your eyes." He leaned down and put his mouth where his cock had been. It felt like heaven. Daci lay back down in the cool grass and shut her eyes.

His tongue soothed her tender flesh, and then suddenly he was licking her deeper than she'd ever felt before. Swirling against her inner walls, teasing her clit, lapping and licking as if she were a feast and he was a starving man . . . or wolf?

Jerking her head up with eyes wide open, Daci looked into Deacon's amber eyes and shrieked. "What are you doing?"

He raised his wolven head and yipped, and then he was Deacon again. Laughing, he crawled up and over her until his cock was nestled against her soaked and sensitive sex. This time, when he pressed forward, his thick cock slipped all the way in, stretching her slick channel without any pain at all.

Wet and ready and fighting back giggles, Daci raised her knees and lifted her hips to meet his thrusts. She'd never felt this before, the powerful penetration only a big man could achieve, driving deep inside until the pressure and pleasure verged on pain.

He angled his hips so the top side of his cock slipped over her clit on every thrust. Then he dipped his head and suckled first one nipple and then the other between his lips.

Daci's fingers dug into the thick grass and she clung to the wiry roots as Deacon took her higher than she'd gone before. Her body burned with arousal, hovering on the knife-edge of orgasm.

And when she reached the pinnacle, when her body thrashed beneath his and her moans filled the night, he thrust harder, deeper, and took her higher yet. Tears covered her cheeks and she gasped for air, trapped in a spiral of physical sensation she'd never imagined existed.

His cock brushed the mouth of her womb on every inward thrust and her body trembled in response, clinging to Deacon with muscles designed to hold him deep inside, to wring every ounce of pleasure from his body.

He wrapped his arms around her and leaned back on his heels, lifting Daci with him. She wrapped her legs around his waist and felt him slide even deeper inside.

Without any warning at all, Daci was no longer alone. Deacon filled her thoughts, sharing the sensation of her rippling muscles grasping his cock, the contrasting softness of her breasts against his chest and their tightly pebbled nipples drawn tight with desire, the deep, pulsing pressure as his own orgasm drew near.

Sharing sensations, this totally unexpected ability to experience all the pleasures of sex through Deacon's body as well as her own, left her breathless, yet energized beyond belief. She sensed her approaching climax as if a storm hurtled closer and closer, as if the air around them had been sucked away and only she and Deacon existed, two entities alone in a world of sensation.

Her body jerked, her muscles spasmed and held him tight. Deacon cried out and thrust deep, three, then four more times before he finally slowed with a convulsive gasp. His chest billowed in and out with each breath he took.

Daci merely burst into tears. Again.

"Did I hurt you? Sweetheart, I'm so sorry . . . I didn't mean to . . ." He brushed her hair back and kissed her damp cheeks and her lips. His cock still pulsed inside her and she knew her body was filled to bursting with the hot streams of his seed, but she wanted more. She wanted all of him.

Carefully, she opened her thoughts and let him feel her joy, her need, her amazing elation over what they'd shared. She wasn't ready to bond with him yet, but there was no doubt in her mind—she never wanted this feeling to end.

Forever? She hardly knew him. She loved him. She wanted him for all time.

He'd proved himself in so many ways. He'd cared for her while she was paralyzed. Had stood up to Anton, the pack's alpha male. He cared enough to disagree with her, to force her to see what was right. He made love to her more beautifully than she'd ever been loved before.

He loved her in spite of her stupidity and her misguided loyalties and all her mistakes. Deacon loved her . . . and she suddenly realized, she didn't even know his real name.

She'd have to ask him. Later. Now, though, nestling against Deacon's chest with his strong arms wrapped around her waist and his thick cock still buried deep inside, Daci totally relaxed, at peace for the first time in forever.

Chapter 14

Anton and Stefan were sitting together on the back deck when Deacon and Daci trotted across the dew-damp meadow in the pale light of early dawn. Pink and lavender light reflected off a few clouds floating high above the mountains, but the sun hadn't yet crested the peaks.

Daci's heart rate jumped into overdrive when she saw the two men, and fear slowed her steps. What would Anton say? What would he do?

We were right and he was wrong, Daci. There's no need to worry. Just relax.

She glanced at Deacon trotting beside her and felt her confidence return. So much had changed tonight. She'd done more than embrace her Chanku birthright. She felt as if she'd embarked on an entirely new life, complete with a new family, one that loved and supported her in spite of herself.

Deacon shifted when he reached the deck. Daci did the same. Naked, sweaty, and probably reeking of sex, she should have felt embarrassed to face the pack's leader and his closest friend.

Instead, she felt empowered. Deacon took her hand and the two of them stood across the broad expanse of deck, waiting to see what Anton would do.

He stood up and smiled at both of them. Stefan reached for a pair of sweatpants and a shimmering length of pale blue fabric. "Here." Stefan handed the pants to Deacon, the sarong to Daci. "It's a good time to talk while everyone's sleeping, but it's always easier with pants on . . . or one of these things." He shrugged as Deacon slipped the sweats on and Daci took the fabric and wrapped it around herself. "I don't know how you girls figure those things out," he muttered. Then he grinned, turned away and kissed Anton full on the mouth.

Daci grabbed Deacon's hand as, without another word, Stefan flipped a salute to the two of them, grabbed his coffee cup and headed into the house.

"Sit down a moment with me, please?" Anton waved them toward the chair Stefan had vacated and pulled another one up beside it. "Relax. I'm the one who should be nervous, not you."

Daci kept her mouth shut, but when she looked at Deacon, he was smiling.

"I owe you an apology, Daci. My mate often has cause to point out the error of my ways, but this is the first time my entire pack has united against me. I'd be angry, except they were right." He reached for Daci's hand and folded her chilled fingers in his warm grasp. "I should never have given you the nutrients without explaining what they were and the permanent impact they would have on your body. It's a conundrum, though. Without the nutrients, you would not have understood what you were capable of becoming, yet knowing your history, I couldn't trust you enough to tell you the truth. Still, I took away your choice, and for that I apologize. I'm not sorry I did it, but I will admit I was wrong."

Daci laughed. She couldn't help it. Keisha had said her mate was arrogant but she loved him in spite of himself. Suddenly her comment made perfect sense. "You had every right not to trust me," she said. "I was here, after all, to prove you existed, to prove that my father wasn't crazy. Well, I've proved you existed, but I've discovered my father wasn't just a little crazy, he was most likely criminally insane. He would have to be, to have done the things he did to Manda, to have pursued all of you so ruthlessly over the years. I apologize, too, Anton, but for even more. I'm so sorry I was rude to all of you. None of you deserved the horrible things I said or the accusations I made. I was wrong."

"Thank you." Anton squeezed her fingers and carefully replaced her hand in Deacon's grasp.

Deacon wrapped his long fingers around hers and held her tightly. "We need to get some sleep, Anton. It's been a long night." He stood up and held his hand out to the wizard. "I hope you understand that what we did, what happened, wasn't about you . . . it was all about Daci."

Anton took Deacon's hand and smiled. "That's another thing Keisha keeps telling me, that it's not all about me. Now I've got you telling me the same thing. That probably means I should pay attention."

Anton's smile wavered. He shoved his hands in his back pockets and gazed off toward the sun-kissed mountains. "When we first heard you were coming, all I could think of was how wonderful it would be to teach young Chanku about their heritage, about this amazing birthright we've all, for whatever reason or another, been blessed with. Things didn't work out as I planned. You and your mates succeeded in teaching me more than I could ever hope to teach you." He turned back and gazed intently at both of them. "I am proud to call you friends, and hopefully, packmates."

Daci stood up, but Anton halted them as they turned to leave. "Daci, I know you still have questions about your father. If you and Deacon don't mind a trip to Colorado, I think you should meet Ulrich Mason. He was the last man to see Milton Bosworth alive. Ulrich can tell you exactly what happened. I don't want you to have to wonder exactly how your father died."

"Ulrich Mason? He's the one Deacon said his friends are staying with. I'd like to meet him." She nodded. "Very much."

"Good. That's settled, then." He touched her hair with his fingertips in an oddly familiar gesture, and sighed. "I was reminded of something very important tonight. It's all about honesty, Daci. Yours and ours. Mine." He leaned over and kissed her on the forehead. Then he shook Deacon's hand. "Take care, son. It's been a very long night. All of us need to get some sleep."

They left Anton standing by himself on the deck, staring off toward the dark forest. He looked lonely and a little bit lost, as if this lesson had not come easily.

Deacon grabbed Daci's hand and they went into the house together. She glanced up at the tall, young man by her side, the one who had shown her what love was all about, and grinned. "He's not scary at all," she said, knowing it was true. "He's just like a regular guy. A really nice, regular guy."

Deacon didn't say a word. He was smiling, though. Smiling as if all was right with his world.

Part II

Chapter 15

He followed his bitch across the sunny ridge and thought how they would appear to the casual observer—two healthy wolves running free in a sanctuary dedicated to the preservation of the species. No one would realize just how far removed they were from the creatures brought here for care.

They paused near a large outcropping of granite and scanned the horizon using all their senses. Sight, sound, scent . . . as well as that other sense, the one they couldn't explain, the one that warned them when danger was near. Assured of privacy, they shifted.

In less than a heartbeat, a naked man and woman stood in place of the wolves. The two of them found a flat spot of rock where they sat, leaning close together in the warm, afternoon sun. They'd run far this afternoon and it felt good to soak up the warmth of the sun and the heat from the stone, after sneaking off by themselves. The week had been filled with their three young guests from San Francisco—they'd needed this time alone.

Ulrich Mason nuzzled his mate's blond hair. "The exuberance of youth is entertaining, my love, but it's exhausting as hell. It's a good thing they're still a little too intimidated by us to expect intimacy. I'm not sure if I could handle their level of energy in the sack."

Laughing softly, Millie wrapped her arms around Ric's neck and leaned her head against his shoulder. "I agree, but it's fun to think about those firm, young bodies."

He laughed and nuzzled her shoulder. "There's nothing wrong with this body of yours." He nipped the nape of her neck between his teeth, and laved the bite with this tongue. He loved everything about this woman.

"I'm glad they're here." She tilted her head back, freeing her throat to his kisses. "They're a lot of help with the sanctuary, but even beyond that, they bring a new sense of life to the place."

"I think you just like looking at those beautiful young men."

Millie laughed. "There is that."

"You're free to go to them, you know." He tipped her chin up with his fingertips. "We are Chanku. There's no fault in your finding sexual satisfaction with someone besides me. To be honest, I hate knowing you've never been with anyone other than me and the man who was Manda and Adam's father."

She turned and nibbled his fingertips. "And when do you think I would find time for this sexual exploration you keep insisting I pursue?"

He laughed softly. "You make time, my love. What better chance than now, while we've got two young men staying with us . . . not to mention a beautiful young woman? I know you've never been with a woman before . . . and I know Beth is interested."

Millie sighed. "I know. And I am interested, too, believe me. I just don't know how to—"

"Look. There they are." Ric lowered his voice and pointed to the clearing beneath their perch on the sunny hillside.

Three wolves, two dark brown, the third a lighter golden shade, raced across the small meadow. They shifted as one. Two young men stood, tall and slim, one on either side of a slender young woman with dark olive skin.

She kissed them both, lingering over her embrace with Nick, her mate. Then, as if she remembered Matt, the taller of the two, was still there, she turned and linked her fingers in his.

With a smile, he slowly pulled his hand free.

Millie squeezed Ric's arm and strained to listen.

"I'm going back," Matt said. Laughing, he leaned over and kissed Beth and then Nick. "I won't wait up, so come in quietly if you're late. I'll be in my own room."

He turned away and shifted, but in that brief moment when his back was turned to the others, a look of infinite sadness crossed his beautiful face.

Within moments, the three of them were gone. Matt going one way, Nick and Beth another.

Millie turned to her mate and sighed. "I feel bad for him, Ric. They do their best to include him, but they're so newly mated all they really need or want is each other. He's so lonely, and he's not aggressive enough to take what he wants. Not like the other young Chanku males I've seen."

Ric stroked his fingers through her hair. "You could help him with that, you know."

"Ri-ic!" She pretended to punch him.

He turned away, laughing. "You could. He needs a woman to give him confidence, someone nurturing and sexy. You'd be the perfect teacher."

"Right. The only Chanku female who never sleeps with anyone but her mate. Like I'd know how to teach him about sex? I don't think so." This time she connected when she punched his shoulder.

"Okay. I give . . . but trust me, m'love. There's someone out there for him, somewhere. He just needs to find her. "

"Like you found me?" Millie tilted her chin and grinned at Ric. "What took you so damned long?"

Laughing, he tumbled her off their low-lying rock and onto the ground, twisting so that she landed atop him in the pine needles. "It only took me, uhm . . . thirty, forty years? I needed all those years of training to be able to keep up with you, insatiable wench!"

"Insatiable? I'll show you insatiable."

It was such a simple thing for Millie to raise her hips and slide down on the solid length of his erection. Clasping muscles encased him and sent shivers racing along his spine. He almost climaxed from the mere joy of penetration, the slide of hot, feminine flesh along the length of his cock. Her muscles rippled around his shaft and her fingers curled against his chest.

They both sighed when she settled her hips into the curve of his groin. He felt the press of his glans against her womb, the tight little knot of her cervix, a place he'd always thought so mystical within a woman. The source of her being, the magical place where new life grew.

For some reason, this time he thought of the children he might have created with Millie, but that would never happen.

They'd found each other too late. Though she might look and act much younger than her years, Millie, as a Chanku bitch, dealt with an aging reproductive system just like any human female.

At least she'd discovered her own children, Manda and Adam, the twins she'd given birth to so long ago, though she hadn't been the one to raise them. It pained him as much as it did Millie, that her babies had been taken from her before she even saw them. Adopted separately, they'd only recently found each other—and their mother.

Ric knew she would have been a wonderful mother if she'd been able to keep her babies. She had such a loving, nurturing soul. The regret would always be with her, that her life had taken such a brutal turn from what should have been. That her children's lives were not as they should have been. Regrets . . . there was nothing to be done about old regrets, beyond living their lives now, in the best possible way.

This way.

He wrapped his big hands around her firm breasts and gently pinched her nipples. Then he raised his hips, sliding even deeper inside her. Laughing with the pure joy of the moment, Millie arched her back and caught the perfect rhythm that would take both of them over the top.

Matt Rodgers leaned against a fallen pine at the top of the ridge and tossed pebbles over the edge into a small pond. Despite what he'd told Nick and Beth, he really wasn't ready to head back to the cabin. Instead, he watched the pack of wild, soon-to-be relocated wolves running in their pen in the valley below. They followed the fence line across from the pond, forever searching for escape and the freedom that was currently denied them.

After a week at the Colorado High Mountain wolf sanctuary, he knew exactly how they felt. Except the wolves would be set free once they were strong and healthy. Free to hunt and run, to find mates among their own kind, to live out their lives as the fierce, wild creatures they were meant to be.

He'd just go on as he was, forever the odd man out. Hell, Nick had Beth, Logan had Jazzy . . . even the old guy, Ulrich, had Millie, and she was one hot lady. There must be something to the Chanku physiology that kept them looking young, because Millie didn't look any older than Tala, and Tala was definitely hot.

Even Ulrich looked like a young guy, or he would if not for that white hair of his. Weird, though, that when he shifted he was a dark wolf. But, whatever color, he had his mate and she loved him.

What really brought Matt down, though, was that Deacon had called just this morning to tell him all about a female he'd met named Daci. Hard to believe it, but even the Deac had found someone who loved him, and he'd barely been in Montana for a week!

Everyone here was so damned nice, Matt hated to complain, especially when he wasn't even sure what he wanted. He'd envied Mik and AJ their amazing bond, and at the same time wondered if he'd ever find a woman like Tala. Was he gay or bi? Hell, now that he knew he was Chanku, did it matter?

Mik didn't think so. He'd told Matt he'd always considered himself gay, at least until he met Tala. He'd laughed when he said a confused sexual identity was all part of being Chanku, mainly because sex with anyone, male or female, was good. Matt couldn't quite find the humor in it, even when AJ had agreed. AJ hadn't even blinked when he admitted he'd usually choose sex with another guy over a woman . . . unless it was Tala, of course.

Matt grinned and tossed another pebble into the pond. He aimed for a golden leaf floating near the center. The rock missed it by mere inches, but the ripples set the leaf to swaying.

Now that he knew Tala, he'd have to agree with AJ. She was one hot lady, and every bit as sweet as she was sexy. The best thing about her, though, was that she loved both her men equally, just as they loved her. As far as Matt was concerned, their threesome was a perfect relationship.

He watched the ripples spread across the surface of the pond until they lapped against the edge on one side and joggled the cattails on the other. Ripples, spreading out from the center and bouncing off the shore. Those ripples made more ripples, and more . . . a reminder why he didn't want to say anything to anyone. He really hated making waves, but finding a woman who liked being with two men . . . wow!

That really would be the ideal situation . . . a guy who loved him and a woman who didn't mind sharing. He'd hoped for a while it might be Beth and Nick, but they were so wound up in each other there really wasn't room for him.

Besides, Beth had some weird issues. He wasn't sure he could handle life with a control freak, and she definitely liked taking charge, whether she was in or out of bed.

Of course, it wasn't like he was the world's greatest lover. He knew what felt good for him, but what did a woman really want? He never had the feeling Beth was as satisfied after they'd had sex as she was when she'd been with Nick, or even Mik or AJ.

Maybe it was all about experience, of which he had very little. Hell, most of his sexual training had been giving guys head in public restrooms for cash, or dropping his pants for the ones who wanted to shove it up his ass. He'd reached a point where it didn't matter, really. Not as long as he had enough money to keep himself alive.

That was all that had counted, after all. Back then, before he knew he was Chanku.

"I'll be fine, Ric. Hurry now. You need to go. It'll be a good experience for the kids, especially if they end up working for Pack Dynamics. Someone's got to find that little girl." Millie touched his cheek and forced him to look into her beautiful amber eyes.

He blocked his thoughts, hiding the elation that filled him. He'd been trying to figure out how to get her to spend some time with other men, but the last thing he wanted was to make it obvious. Now, with the perfect young man available . . .

"I don't want to leave you here alone," he said, mentally crossing his fingers and shoring up his mental walls. "I wish you could come."

"You know I can't leave the sanctuary. We're short-handed as it is." Her eyes sparkled with tears. "You're wasting time. That little girl has been missing for almost twenty-four hours. It's cold at night and she's got to be terrified."

"I know, but I really don't want you alone. There've been too many attacks against our kind." He sighed, as if the idea had just come to him. "Matt will stay here. I'll take Nick and Beth." He kissed her and nibbled at her lush mouth. "I'll feel better if Matt's with you in case you need anything."

Slowly, Millie turned her head and stared at Ric. Before she could say anything, he leaned over again and kissed her hard. "I need to go. Now. The helicopter will be here in just a few minutes." He picked up the phone and called Nick.

"Right," he said, when Nick answered. "Mik, Tala, and AJ are already in the Black Hills—Tala's the handler so she'll stay in human form. Mik and AJ will be wolves for the duration. Same with you and Beth, so you don't need to pack anything beyond a set of clothes in case we end up driving home. You can shift to human once we're well away from the site. We'll be searching for a six-year-old girl who wandered away from the family campground. Tell Matt I want him to stay here and keep an eye on Millie."

Ric disconnected the phone and checked his travel bag. The helicopter was due any time and the flight shouldn't take more than a couple hours. Already his heart was pounding from the rush of adrenaline slamming into his system. He'd founded Pack Dynamics with just this sort of job in mind all those years ago. Lucien Stone might be its new leader, but it was still Ric's baby and he couldn't wait to get going on the assignment.

Working in teams with highly trained wolves had been

a cover that paid off handsomely over the years. They'd had a string of successful rescues and covert assignments from a government unaware of the true identities—or species—represented by the Pack Dynamics teams.

Of course, the fact their wolves had human intelligence was a big factor in their success, something the government didn't need to know.

Stuffing a few extra items into the bag he kept prepared for emergencies, Ulrich managed a quick glance at Millie. She looked as if she were a million miles away, but she had a pensive smile on her face.

He slipped quietly into her thoughts and quickly backed out. She was thinking of Matt and the lost, lonely look on the young man's face. *Good.*

The heavy *thump, thump, thump* of a helicopter flying in to the sanctuary's landing area echoed through the cabin. "We need to go. I love you, Millie. I've got my cell phone if you need to reach me and I promise I'll be home as soon as I can."

"Be careful. Find that little girl." She cupped the side of his face with her palm, kissed him hard and fast and stepped away. "I love you, too." Then she grinned at him. "And don't you think for a second I don't know why you left Matt here for me. I promise to do my best."

Laughing, he swatted her on her perfectly shaped ass. "No doubts at all, m'love." He kissed her again, grabbed his bag and headed out the door. Immediately, he picked up Nick and Beth's thoughts. They were waiting at the landing pad, already in wolf form. He sensed their excitement about the upcoming trip, even from this distance.

Jogging over the short trail through the forest, Ulrich sensed Matt's thoughts as well. As expected, Matt accepted the fact he'd not been chosen, accepted being left behind. Dealing with a true beta Chanku was unusual to say the least, especially in their unusual society of mostly alpha males.

Ulrich reached out, connected. *Watch over my mate, Matthew. There is nothing more important to me than Millie's safety and happiness. She's your responsibility while I'm gone. You will care for her, in all ways. Promise me you'll do whatever she asks of you.*

I promise.

Go to her now. I don't want her left alone at any time. With all that's happened in Montana, I can't assume we're entirely safe here.

Yes, sir. I'll take care of her.

Good. He severed the link as he approached the waiting helicopter, but an image of Millie and Matt filled his mind. He glanced back toward the house and whispered, "You've got no idea what you're in for, m'boy."

Two wolves waited patiently beside the landing pad. Ulrich snapped leashes and collars on both Nick and Beth under the watchful eye of the pilot and led them onto the helicopter. As they lifted off, he took one last glance in the direction of Millie's cabin, and grinned. *No, Matt . . . you've got no idea at all.*

Chapter 16

Millie sensed Matt at the front door within minutes after the sound of the helicopter faded over the mountains. She paused a moment, thought ruefully of strangling her mate, and then finally opened the door.

Matt stood there like a lost boy, all six-foot-three of him, looking as if he wanted to be anywhere else rather than her front porch. His brown hair was shaggy and hung in his eyes. His big hands sort of dangled at his sides, as if he didn't quite know what to do with them. Millie knew he was at least twenty-five, but he could have passed easily for sixteen.

An absolutely breathtakingly beautiful sixteen.

He was young and gorgeous, and so obviously uncomfortable he broke her heart. "Hi, Matt. Come on in." She held the door open. He stepped into her small cabin, his eyes still staring at his feet, at the floor, anywhere but at Millie.

"I guess Ulrich sort of forced you into the job as my bodyguard slash babysitter for the next couple of days. I hope you don't mind. Can I get you something to drink?"

He shook his head, glanced up at her, looked back at

the floor. "I don't mind. Really. Is there anything in particular you want me to do?" This time he raised his chin and glanced at her. Then he looked down again.

"I really want you to relax." She laughed. "You're making me nervous!"

"I'm sorry. It's just . . . I just . . ." He shrugged and looked at her with a slight smile. "I'm not used to going anywhere without the others. I've always been kind of shy, and . . ."

"I know." Millie grabbed his hand and dragged him over to the couch. She sat down beside him. He scooted away, far enough that their legs wouldn't touch. "Me, too," she said. "Ric is always with me and I feel sort of lost when he's away."

His chin snapped up. "You do? Really?"

She nodded. "I do. I've lived here my whole life, right on this mountain. I've hardly been anywhere and I haven't met all that many people. I've only been to San Francisco once, when I went with Ric. That's where you're from, isn't it?"

"Yeah. That's where I lived my whole life. I'd never been in an airplane or even seen mountains like these until we came here last week."

"Your life's changed a lot in a very short time, hasn't it? What did you do before you learned you were Chanku?"

"Nothing, really."

He stared back at the floor. She tried to see what he was thinking, but found only a dark swirl of misery without form or substance.

She touched his knee and he flinched. "Matt? What's wrong? Do I make you nervous?"

He nodded. "Kind of."

"Why? I'd never do anything to hurt you."

"I know," he mumbled.

Millie had to strain to hear him. This was not going to

be easy. The role of seductress wasn't one she'd ever pictured herself playing. "I need to go check on the pens in the upper meadows. Would you mind going with me?"

He raised his head, obviously relieved to have something concrete to do. "Sure. Do you want to take the Jeep?"

"I'd rather shift and run. The wolves recognize me in that form, and I can get a better feel for their general health and well-being. Just stay close to me. They're a little intimidated by a strange male."

This time he actually laughed. "I doubt they're afraid of me, Millie. I'm not very scary."

"If you say so." She stood up and slipped her sweatshirt over her head.

Matt blinked nervously. He took a deep breath, as if trying to calm himself before he slipped off his shoes and began to undress. Millie noticed he kept his eyes averted.

Millie let her gaze wander. She'd never really paid much attention to Matt's body when they shifted. Now she wondered why. He tugged his shirt over his head and her mouth went dry. He was long and lean with a swimmer's build. Broad shoulders, narrow waist, long, slim legs still covered by his worn Levis.

His skin was smooth and tan, his nipples like dark copper coins against the curve of a surprisingly muscular chest. A dark line of hair ran from his navel and disappeared beneath his waistband.

Millie quickly untied her hiking boots and slipped them off, then tugged at her jeans, but she kept her eyes on Matt. He unzipped his jeans and shoved them, along with his knit boxer shorts, down over his lean hips.

The dark trail from his navel disappeared into the silky swirl of his pubic hair. His cock was huge, even in its flaccid state, resting against perfectly formed balls. Millie curled her fingers against her palms to keep from reaching out to cup him, to hold their warm weight in her palm.

She'd been with two men in her fifty-eight years. The young cowboy who'd fathered Adam and Amanda, and many years later, Ulrich Mason. She'd hardly looked at the other Chanku when they shifted, though Ulrich had often encouraged her to be more open to sex with them.

She wasn't interested. All those years she'd been alone, she'd not found anyone she wanted. Now that she had Ric, there was no need.

But Ric wasn't here and he'd asked her to try and help Matt gain more confidence. Not that she expected to turn a beta personality into an alpha, but if she could help him just a little . . .

Who am I kidding? She almost laughed out loud. His body fascinated her, his personality drew her. Matt's obvious shyness, his loneliness, his need for someone to care called out to her nurturing soul, but it wouldn't work if he didn't find her at least a little bit attractive. Though she still looked like a woman in her thirties, Millie knew she was old enough to be his mother. Would that repulse him, or would the increased sexual need of the Chanku be enough to get his attention?

Maybe after they ran. Running always had an amazing effect on her sex drive. It certainly had a powerful effect on Ric's, and the other guys' as well. Biting back a smile, Millie waited by the door while Matt carefully folded his clothing and left the pile stacked neatly on the couch. He still didn't look at her. Instead he shifted.

A beautiful golden brown wolf with a dark ruff around his neck waited patiently while she opened the door. With a flourish, she waved him outside, followed him and closed the door behind her. Then she shifted and led the young male into the forest.

* * *

He knew she was naked, knew she waited by the door for him, still in her human form so that she'd be able to shut the door behind them when they left. He was not going to look. He couldn't look, not when it was just the two of them. He'd seen plenty when they'd shifted over the past week, when he could admire Millie without anybody noticing. She had an absolutely gorgeous body. He knew that if he looked now, he'd have such a boner he wouldn't be able to walk, much less run.

Just thinking about her made him ache. Beth was pretty, but Millie epitomized sensuality. She was kind and loving, so darned nice he wanted to crawl into her lap and lay his head against her breasts, which would have been pretty stupid for a guy his age. On top of her personality, she was sleek and strong with a mature body that looked fantastic even in her old flannel shirts and jeans. Naked, she was . . . she was . . . .*oh, shit.*

Thank goodness she opened the door! He raced out and didn't even wait. He couldn't, or she'd know how horny he was. It didn't matter. She caught up with him before he even reached the trail, passed him by and raced on ahead.

Her scent led him, but when he tried to draw closer, she ran faster. Within seconds they were flying down the narrow trail, racing as if the devil chased them.

Maybe he did. What Matt felt for the female racing ahead of him couldn't be right. Wasn't acceptable. She was Ulrich's mate and his job was to watch over her, not fuck her silly out here in the woods.

Which was all he could think of. The hot slide of his cock between slick folds of feminine flesh, the clench and pull of powerful muscles, milking him, wanting him. What would it feel like, to actually be wanted by a woman?

He knew what it was like to have men desire him. With his looks, he'd always had lots of male attention. They liked the tall, slim guys who looked younger than their years.

When he'd been on the streets, passing as a teen had kept a steady line of customers ready to pay him for his services.

When he was eighteen, he'd looked twelve. When he was twenty, he'd passed for fourteen, but that's when his parents discovered the source of his extra income and kicked him out of the house. He'd left without a backward glance. He doubted he'd been missed. Once they had their own twin girls, they'd lost interest in the odd son they'd adopted.

He'd never been a good fit with them, anyway.

Of course, he hadn't known then that he wasn't really human, and they hadn't known it either. What would they think if they saw him now, racing on four legs through a Colorado forest, his wolven body a perfect example of power and cunning?

Well, maybe not perfect, but a damned good facsimile. With an extra burst of strength, Matt caught up to Millie just as she entered the wide service road. Without giving himself time to even consider what he was doing or why he did it, he nipped her shoulder and then raced beside her. He wouldn't do anything she didn't want him to, but there was no reason not to enjoy the fantasy.

They reached the pens in the upper valley just as the sun slipped behind the mountains. The sanctuary employees would be gone for the day, but Millie always checked to make sure everyone had been fed, that water was available, and the wolves were okay.

As their numbers had begun to increase after so many years hovering on the brink of extinction, wolves had suffered terribly. Bouncing off and back on the endangered list had weakened their levels of protection, and she'd had more injured animals to deal with than before. More wounded wolves, some caught by illegal traps, others poisoned as ranchers and farmers were emboldened by the ever-changing policies. It sickened her, but she did her best to heal the ones that eventually ended up at the sanctuary.

Thank goodness there were still people out there who cared enough to risk injury in order to bring the wounded, suffering animals to her.

With her mind focused totally on the caged animals waiting desperately to regain their freedom, she'd almost forgotten the young wolf shadowing her every move. When she paused to check one older male recovering from an injured leg, Millie was almost overcome by the powerful scent of aroused male beside her.

She studied the wolf on the other side of the fence, yet she was more aware of Matthew standing mere inches away. He waited patiently while she appeared to ignore him, and hoped he didn't recognize her body's response to his arousal.

She moved on to the next pen, and then the next, checking the inhabitants as she did each day. Matt followed silently beside her, watching quietly. She'd never been able to completely understand her wild brethren, not the way Anton Cheval seemed able to do, but she could pick up their mental images and any sense of major discomfort or emotional stress as long as she was in her wolven form.

Tonight, all was calm. They wondered about the male beside her, but he was different enough that they didn't recognize him as a threat. They disliked being penned, but she soothed them as best she could. There were some that would never be freed again—those too old or infirm to survive in the wild. Others, though, once recovered, would be returned to areas where they would be as safe as was possible for a wolf.

She understood, though. It was better to run free and risk death than survive in safety behind a wire fence. Hopefully, both government and public policy would eventually tilt in their favor and they would regain what little protection they'd had. She shook her head, dismayed by the short-sightedness of man. When would people understand that all species had a necessary place in the scheme of things, if mankind itself was to survive?

Sighing, she reached the last of the pens, relieved to see that all was well. She turned away from her caged brethren and the service road and followed a trail that led deeper into the forest. Hunger gnawed at her belly. She glanced at Matt. His head came up and he watched her. *I'm hungry,* she said. *Let's hunt.*

Before he could reply, she whirled away and raced down the trail, weaving through thick underbrush that almost obscured the narrow track. Matt stayed right on her tail. When she neared the meadow that was her destination, he slowed as she did. When she picked up the scent of rabbit, he paused beside her and then slowly cut off to the right.

She went in from the left. There were six rabbits nibbling away at the short grass, easily visible even in the evening's dark shadows.

Two of them weren't fast enough to escape. Millie fed, as did Matt. She wiped her muzzle on the grass and then trotted to the small creek at the edge of the meadow where she drank her fill of the cool water. Matt followed and did the same.

Her body thrummed with arousal, the deep, gut-clenching need that always followed a run and successful hunt. She knew that the moment she shifted it would become a living, breathing entity, frantically seeking release.

Would Matt feel the same?

There was only one way to find out. Standing beside the creek, Millie shifted. Her body was on fire, her breasts already sensitive, her nipples beaded with arousal. Without conscious thought, she slipped two fingers between her legs and found her clit, swollen and slippery with her cream. Softly massaging the hard little nub, Millie threw her head back and groaned.

A soft whine caught her attention. She glanced at the golden brown wolf sitting close beside her. He watched her, panting softly, tongue lolling, eyes narrowed to dark slits and ears pressed flat against his broad skull. His bright red penis extended from his furred sheath, balanced by the hard knot at its base.

"Shift," she said, rubbing her fingers slowly between her legs. Without intending it, she realized her voice sounded soft and throaty, thrumming with sexual command.

Matt shifted. He rose to his full height and towered over her, almost as tall as Ric, though not nearly so massive. His lean body reminded her of her cowboy, the one who'd taken her virginity so many years ago. The one who'd left her pregnant with twins and gone away before either of them knew she carried the babies who would grow up to be Adam and Amanda.

So many years ago. Another lifetime, but one that had led her here, to this meadow high in the Colorado mountains. To this one spot with a very lonely young man, who watched her now, wary and uneasy, yet aroused every bit as much as she was.

"It's okay, you know." She smiled and stepped close to him, surprised at how easy it was to take the initiative with a beta male like Matt. This was what Ulrich had hoped for, this ability to take the lead. Though there was nothing she didn't enjoy with her mate, she knew she generally lacked the aggressive approach of most Chanku females.

Of course, with an alpha male like Ulrich, it wasn't necessary that she show aggression. Still, she knew he wanted her to be comfortable with her own sexuality, comfortable finding release with someone besides him.

With someone like Matt. Feeling empowered, Millie gently ran her fingers across his smooth chest, even though she ached to fall to her knees and take that long, lovely cock between her lips.

There was no need to rush. She intended to enjoy this time with Matt as much as she possibly could . . . and with any luck, he would enjoy it as well. She moved her fingers slowly over his well-defined pectorals, fascinated by the bunch and ripple of muscle beneath her fingertips. She sighed, knowing full well her breath tickled across his chest. "Ulrich understands what it's like after a run," she said. "To want so much. To need so badly."

Matt's heart thundered beneath her touch, pounding even harder than her own.

"He made me promise to do whatever you asked . . ." Matt's voice trailed off, as if he didn't really believe this was quite what her mate actually had in mind.

"Ah," she said, and it was just a whisper. "So I have to ask you?" She trailed her fingers vertically down the length of his chest, swept them around his navel and then rested them just above the dark thatch of hair at his groin. His cock bobbed in response.

"I . . ." He cleared his throat. Nodded his head in two short, sharp jerks.

She noticed his hands, fingers clenched tightly into fists as if he forced himself not to touch her without permission. It made her smile, knowing someone this young, this perfect, had to fight for control in her presence. It was unbelievably empowering. Gaining confidence, Millie tilted her head, looked him in the eye and grinned.

"What if I tell you that you have to take the first step? That I give you permission to do what you want with me, and I do mean anything you want with me, but it has to be your idea?"

He groaned. She traced the line above his dark pubic

hair, weaving a trail from hipbone to hipbone. A small drop of white fluid bubbled from the slit in his erect cock. Millie ached to touch it, to lean over and lick it off of him, but this was too much fun, this sense of power, the illicit joy that came from teasing a beautiful young man while knowing what was to come.

"Millie . . . I . . ." He cleared his throat and then grabbed her wrist in both hands, stopping her exploration of his abdomen.

She raised her head and looked directly into his dark amber eyes, studying the almost frantic level of arousal he barely contained.

"Millie, I have way too many ideas and you might not like them."

"Try me." It was barely a whisper. Had he heard?

"Here? Now?"

He touched her hair, trailing his fingers through the tangled strands. Did he see the gray? Would that bother him, those gray hairs mixed with the blond?

"Wherever you like," she said. She leaned close and kissed his chest. Then she licked him, just over his left nipple. He tasted of salt, of young man. Of carnal need. "Whatever you like."

"I want anything you want. Whatever you're willing to do with me, I want it. Wherever you want, any way . . . I . . ." There was an almost childish desperation in his voice. As if he feared saying something wrong, doing something that might make her change her mind.

He was absolutely charming. He was sex personified, a temptation she didn't need to avoid. One, instead, that she was welcome to taste. Invited to devour in any way she wanted. A deep thrill of excitement lifted her level of arousal even higher.

"Follow me." Millie turned away and shifted. Matt followed. Her scent as the she-wolf must be making him crazy, but the barn wasn't far. As much as she wanted release, the night was cool and the mattress she and Ulrich had hidden in the old barn at the far end of the service road was a lot more comfortable than damp grass on a cool night.

Chapter 17

The door was ajar, but it was pitch-black inside. Millie slipped through, ahead of Matt. He followed, blocked her way and told her to stay put. Considering his usual laid-back attitude, this intense protectiveness of his was a pleasant surprise. He'd definitely taken Ulrich's instructions to heart. She watched him while he carefully circled the interior, sniffing and listening as he checked for intruders, and made certain it was safe.

Millie waited to shift until Matt rose from four to two feet. She found the kerosene lantern near the door with a box of matches on the shelf next to it. Once it was lit, the lantern threw off just enough light to keep them from stumbling into things.

"I didn't know this barn was out here." Matt stood in the center and looked around the vast interior space. The pale light threw flickering shadows that accented the cut of his muscles, the darkness between his legs. He was still hard, even bigger than he'd been earlier.

"Not many do." Millie glanced around the familiar interior. "It's part of the old ranch, the one where I grew up. We occasionally use it for storage. Mostly it's just a place for bats and other critters." She laughed. "And sex.

There's a comfortable mattress over there . . ." She pointed to a dark corner, where one of the stalls had been cleaned and lined with fresh straw.

He ignored the direction she pointed. His attention focused entirely on her. Millie bit back a grin. He was staring at her breasts.

"Did you come here when you were little?"

She shook her head, smiling. "Not all that much, but it's a special place to me. Something happened here I'll never forget."

"What was that?"

He'd moved closer, almost within reach. Already inflamed to a fever pitch, her body reacted. She felt a single tear run down the inside of her thigh. Could he sense her arousal? Did he have any idea how much she wanted him?

"What happened here, Millie?"

Snapped out of her sensual daydreams, she looked up at him. "I lost my virginity here. I was twenty years old. He was a cowboy, just wandering through, but he was so damned sexy."

"Here? In this barn." Matt looked around, as if trying to imagine a younger Millie, her first time.

"Yep." She took a step closer and looked up at him. "He looked a lot like you, only his hair was blond. He was tall and lean, but very strong. He knew how to touch a woman. He showed me things about myself even I didn't know." She traced the line of his chest again, just as she'd done earlier. She heard him swallow, felt the thundering beat of his heart as, once again, he responded to her.

He reached for her. His fingers trembled. "I wish I knew those things . . . how to touch a woman. How to make her feel as good as she makes me feel. I want to touch you."

"Wherever you like." She smiled at him, feeling her power, his need, the strength of the link growing between them. "In any way you want. I'm yours for tonight, Matt. I'd love to be the one to show you . . . everything."

He groaned and suddenly she was wrapped in his arms, pressed tightly against heat and hard muscle. His cock rose between them, long and hot against her belly. Her breasts flattened against his chest and she felt his heart beating, thundering in counterpoint to her own.

He lifted her as if she weighed nothing and marched across the open floor toward the dark corner, to the stall with the mattress she and Ric had moved in here a few weeks ago. When Matt released her legs, she let herself sag and dropped slowly to her knees in the thick straw. His hands rested on her shoulders. She raised her head and looked up at him. "Tell me what you like, Matt, and I'll do the same for you."

He nodded. She heard him swallow, felt him brace his legs, preparing himself. "Just touch me, Millie. With your hands. With your mouth."

His big body trembled when she cupped his warm testicles in her palm. His sac was warm and heavy, the orbs inside the wrinkled skin two perfect egg shapes filling her hand. His sac tightened and drew close to his body when she stroked the hard length of his cock with her other hand. He groaned and thrust his hips forward, inviting her touch. When she circled the broad, plum-shaped head of his penis with her tongue, the sound he made was more of a whimper.

A single drop of white fluid leaked from the narrow slit on his cock. Millie lapped it up with the very tip of her tongue. His taste was different than Ric's, sweeter. More appeared, a thicker drop, and she sucked it into her mouth, savoring the flavor as she twirled the tip of her tongue in the narrow slit. Her fingers stayed busy, rolling his hard balls inside their wrinkled sac, stroking the heavily veined length of his shaft.

"Shit. Ya gotta stop. I'm gonna come, Millie. I don't want this to end yet."

She slipped him out of her mouth and blew a cool breath across the tip. "It won't. I want you to come. The first time will take the edge off and you'll last longer when we do it again. Go ahead. Let go . . . then it's your turn. I'll tell you exactly what I want."

She dipped her head and sucked him between her lips, tongued the ridge on the underside of his glans, licked her way across the broad flare. She loved the feel of him there, so silky soft and sweet with the taste of his seed. Licking and suckling her way over the surface, she slipped the very tip of her tongue back into his leaking slit, licking up every drop she could find. He thrust his hips forward. His cock slipped deeper into her mouth.

Softly kneading his balls in her hand, she felt the tightening in his groin that preceded ejaculation, knew he hovered on the brink of orgasm.

Hollowing her cheeks with the strength of her suction, she drew him deep inside her mouth. He was so big she couldn't avoid scraping the sensitive sides of his cock with her teeth. He shuddered in response, obviously turned on even more by the threat of pain.

She turned his sac loose and grabbed his taut buttocks in both hands. His glutes quivered in her grasp. She sensed his struggle for control, knew he fought the powerful urge to come.

No way in hell could she ignore a challenge like that.

Smiling around her mouthful of erect cock, Millie walked her fingers across his butt and slipped them into the dark crevice between his cheeks. She found the tight little pucker of his ass and rimmed it with one finger, sucking harder on his cock, pressing deeper with her finger.

He was slick with sweat and it only took the slightest pressure to breach his tight opening, to slip beyond the ring of muscle. He arched against her mouth as she pressed deep. She backed away until only the head of his cock was between her lips, and she held him in place with teeth and tongue while her finger probed, searched, and finally found the tiny round gland inside him, the one that took all choice of whether or not he was ready to climax entirely out of Matt's control.

She rubbed firmly against it and his body jerked. He cried out a colorful litany of curses as orgasm slammed into him. Millie sucked and swallowed the thick jets of his seed while her finger kept up a relentless massage. His climax went on and on, until he curled over her body, his hips jerking in response to her touch, his cock still a solid presence between her lips.

Finally she pulled her finger free and released his cock from her mouth. She gave him one long, sweeping lick from balls to tip. He collapsed into the clean straw and flopped down on his back. It took him a long time before he could suck in enough air to speak.

"You're trying to kill me, aren't you?"

Millie ran her finger down his chest. "Not yet," she said.

Matt groaned. "That's what I was afraid you were going to say. You're definitely going to kill me."

Millie laughed and wiped her mouth with the back of her hand. "Oh, no. Just getting you warmed up. We still have more lessons."

Matt propped himself up on one elbow and grinned at her. "Lessons? I'd forgotten this was supposed to be purely educational. What are you going to teach me, Ms. West?"

"Everything I love." She crawled toward him on hands and knees, feeling younger than she'd felt in years. "Everything you need to know to make a woman happy."

He sobered then, and glanced away. "I don't know much. I've only been with a couple of women. Beth. Our friend Jazzy Blue. I'm a queer whore from San Francisco. Not a good place to learn to please a woman. Guys don't require a lot of finesse."

"You might once have been a prostitute, Matt. Not anymore. You're not a queer whore. You're Chanku. Sex is the most powerful drive we have. Stronger than the need to eat, the need to sleep . . . You'd be surprised to learn how many of our kind whored to survive."

He looked away, staring into the darkness. "Actually, considering the number of guys I fucked without protection, I'm surprised I have survived."

"You know Chanku can't get AIDs or other STDs, don't you? You can't catch them, can't pass them on." She touched the side of his face. "You were meant to live, Matt. Just as I'm meant to teach you whatever I can. Here, tonight. Don't be ashamed because you've never had an opportunity. That's what we have now. An opportunity. For me to show you things . . . and maybe for you to show me."

He laughed, but there wasn't much humor in the sound. "What can I show you? You're beautiful and you're so damned sexy you make me ache."

"I'm also a woman in my fifties who has only been with two men my entire life. My cowboy, and Ulrich Mason." She paused a moment for dramatic effect. "There was a long, long dry spell in between."

Obviously surprised, he raised his head and stared at her. "No shit? That's all? Just the two? I thought all Chanku had sex with anyone around."

She shrugged. "Who else is around? I haven't known for very long that I am Chanku, and my upbringing was such that . . . Well, let's just say that before I knew who and what I was, it really wasn't an option. Now, it's just me and Ric here, and when we've been with the others, there's always been so much going on, the opportunity hasn't arisen."

She scooted closer, leaned over and kissed him lightly on the mouth. Then she backed away before he could follow through with more. She wrapped her fingers around his thick erection. "Looks like opportunity is rising right now."

He laughed, but there was a strangled quality to the sound. "What do you like, Millie? Tell me what you want." He curled his lanky body around and sat up, facing her.

She felt a shiver along her spine when she looked at him. His hair fell in light brown tangles across his forehead. His eyes were dark amber jewels, his lips parted, still damp from her kiss. As she watched, he ran his tongue along his lower lip and then drew it between his teeth.

She imagined those lips, that tongue, those teeth, all working together to bring her to climax. Tasting her. Instead of saying the words out loud, she used her mind to show him.

It was so much easier, showing him things she still had a hard time saying.

He grinned and moved aside. Millie crawled through the straw to the mattress that was covered in a clean fitted sheet and rolled over on her back. Matt knelt between her legs and gazed down at her, as if he'd never looked this closely at a woman before.

"I haven't," he said, obviously reading her. "Never . . . not like this. Until now." He lifted her buttocks and adjusted her long legs so that they hung over his shoulders, leaving her exposed and vulnerable. Then he stared at her, as if studying all her folds and crevices. He parted her outer lips with his fingers and swirled one fingertip around the sensitive inner folds.

Millie sighed when he dipped inside, slowly burying his finger all the way to his knuckle. She felt the tip of it curl against her inner walls. Her muscles clenched, holding him.

"I feel that." He grinned at her like a little kid with a new toy. "Where's your clit? I hear Beth and Jazzy talking about clits all the time."

"Here." She touched herself, rolling back the small, protective hood and exposing her clitoris. "This is where I'm most sensitive. You have to touch it gently at first, but the more turned on I get, the harder you can rub it." She grinned at him. "Or suck it. I love when it gets sucked."

"Really?"

He lifted her up and leaned close. She felt the tip of his tongue, the warmth of his saliva as he moistened the sensitive bud. He licked her, slowly running his tongue between her folds, circling her clit, even sucking her labia into his mouth. Then he placed his lips around her clit and gently sucked. The suction of his mouth drew an unexpected groan from between her lips. Her arousal had grown exponentially since they'd run.

"Does that feel good?" He raised his head and left her wanting. Her vaginal muscles rippled and clenched, desperate for more touching.

"Don't. Stop." She hadn't meant to growl, but at least it got his attention.

Laughing, Matt lowered his head between her legs. He touched her with more confidence, now that he knew she was aroused. That he had been the one to bring her to this point.

He used his mouth on her, licking and sucking, but it wasn't enough. "I need more, Matt. Use your hands, too. Your fingers. I need to feel you inside me."

He didn't answer, but she felt the thickness of his thumb at her vaginal opening, and then, unexpectedly, the pressure of his middle finger against her bottom. Her tissues were dry, but before she could speak, he'd moistened his fingers with saliva and once again pressed against her tight anal ring.

Penetration was almost enough to take her over the top. She shivered from the burn of entry, the amazing sensation of his long, thick finger sliding deep inside. He filled her with thumb and forefinger, his big hands wrapping around her two openings, pressing deeper, thumb and finger bending until they met, pressing one against the other through the thin membrane separating her two passages.

Filled to bursting, she arched against his hand, against his mouth, and he replied by wrapping his lips around her clit and suckling it as if it were a nipple. Hard pulls that had her crying out as her body bucked and writhed beneath his touch.

With tongue and lips, teeth and fingers, he took her to the precipice. He held her there as he played her body, stroked her so completely she burned for release, then with one final tug at her clit, sent her tumbling over the edge.

She convulsed around him, coming hard and fast, her body gripped in the heat of sensation, in the touch and feel of a man who'd never touched her before. Her vaginal muscles grabbed his thumb, rippling over the bony length while her sphincter spasmed and clutched his finger. Sobbing, she tried to wrench away from him, but he held her as she'd held him. Gently he stroked her sensitive tissues until she cried out again and shuddered in yet another powerful climax.

He didn't let her rest. Empowered now by her reaction, it was obvious he had no intention of stopping. He pulled his fingers free of her clenching muscles, carefully slipped her legs from his shoulders and parted her knees. When he knelt between her thighs, she wasn't sure if she could take anymore, not now, while her body still trembled and her vaginal muscles spasmed in undulating waves.

He was big, his erect penis easily as long as Ulrich's, but thicker and heavier. When he pressed the silky glans against her vaginal lips, she whimpered, unable to form a coherent thought, much less speak.

"Millie, if you want me to stop, I will. Just tell me." He looked down at her with so much need in his amber eyes, so much desire, she couldn't have turned him away even if she'd wanted to.

Still gasping for breath, she merely opened her thighs to him, touched her swollen lips and parted them to give him entrance.

"All right!" He grinned at her and eased his way inside. She felt her muscles shift and adjust to his larger girth, felt the burning, tugging sensation as he entered her. He was careful, obviously aware of his size and the tightness of their fit. It took long moments before the soft curl of his pubic hair pressed against her mons, until she felt the tickle of his heavy sac where it brushed her buttocks.

He was in, filling her completely, hard as a post and ready to go, but he kept perfectly still, giving her time to adjust to his length and girth. His arms trembled as he held his body above hers, and she thought of a racehorse at the starting gate. The image almost made her laugh, but she caught herself and thought better of it. Instead, she lifted her hips and forced him even deeper. That was all he needed to turn loose. His hips went into motion, thrusting hard and fast into her welcoming body.

Ric was right. There was something utterly amazing about the exuberance and energy of youth . . . and his technique wasn't bad, either.

Had she ever been this young? Ever felt as free as the young man who covered her now? She'd been raised by an abusive uncle whose perverse punishments had taken their toll, pregnant at twenty by a man who left her, bereft when her babies were taken away. Since then, she'd lived her life in a vacuum, avoiding relationships, working at the sanctuary all those long, empty years.

It had been her sanctuary as much as that of the wolves. A place to avoid the complications of a world that had treated her so badly. Until she'd met Lisa Quinn and Tinker McClintock, until she'd been discovered by Anton Cheval . . . until the moment she'd met Ulrich Mason.

A man generous enough to want her to experience this, here and now, with a man less than half her age. She looked up at Matt. His eyes were closed, his jaw clenched as he methodically thrust and retreated, filling her on every stroke.

She lifted her hips, forcing him even deeper. He opened his eyes and grinned at her. Then he reared up and sat back on his heels, lifting Millie with him. She wrapped her legs around his lean waist and met him hard and fast. His long cock rubbed over her clit on every thrust. Her climax rose, building on the heat and friction of each solid penetration.

She opened her thoughts, tried to connect with him as she did with Ulrich, but it took her a moment to find the link, to recognize Matt's mental signature. There! She found him, felt his disbelief that the woman he'd lusted after all week had actually taken him into her body. That she actually seemed to like what they did together, seemed to like him.

Oh, Matt . . . you're gorgeous and kind and smart. You're a wonderful lover. You just need to believe in yourself.

His laughter settled just above her heart. *With you, Millie, I think I can believe almost anything.*

Then words disappeared and there was only sensation. His sensations, coupled with hers. The tight clasp of her muscles around his cock, the heat building in his testicles, the coil of pending orgasm tightening at the base of his spine. She felt it all as if she were the one with the huge cock, as if her balls ached and her body shivered on the edge of climax.

Without even thinking, she leaned closer and caught his nipple between her teeth, biting hard enough to make him jerk in surprise. He pressed his chest against her mouth and cursed. She held him between her teeth, tonguing the tip while his fingers dug into her hips and his cock plowed deep inside her cunt.

Orgasm slammed into her, into Matt. She felt the sting of her teeth on him, the clench of her muscles holding his cock and then sensation overwhelmed her, both hers and Matt's, confusing her synapses, pulling her into an unimaginable maelstrom of pleasure and pain.

Sensation took on a life of its own, a visual montage of color and sound, of hearts thundering in syncopated rhythm, blood racing through veins and arteries, air rushing in and out of straining lungs. Their skin glowed pale beneath the golden light of the kerosene lamp and hair hung in dark sweaty tangles, while their shadows slumped together against the old barn walls, merged into a single entity wrapped in the final pulses of orgasm.

Long moments later, Millie raised her forehead off of Matt's chest. His cock still pulsed inside her, her muscles still clenched and rippled around him. He was staring at her with a soft smile and a rather bemused expression on his face.

"Okay," she said, running her fingers through the sweat beading his chest. "That was good."

"Just good?"

Laughing, she leaned over and butted him with her head. "So far past good, I'm not even going to try and describe it."

"Ah," he said, rolling her to one side but making sure they remained connected. "I would imagine 'indescribably good' isn't bad for a first lesson."

She touched the side of his face with her fingers and felt his cock jerk inside her. He was already growing hard again. "Not bad at all for a first lesson. When you're ready for lesson number two . . ."

"Oh, I'm ready," he said. He rolled Millie to her back and settled once again between her thighs. "What now, Ms. West?"

Chapter 18

Ulrich set the phone back on the table. Millie hadn't answered, so he'd left a message. He hoped she and Matt were somewhere together, though if he was going to be perfectly honest, he'd rather she was here in South Dakota with him.

Actually, he didn't care where he was, as long as Millie was by his side, but some things couldn't be helped—like the fact his cock was hard as a post, his balls ached and his body vibrated with arousal, the deep, soul-searing need that followed a shift or a successful hunt.

He poured himself a glass of whiskey and added a couple of ice cubes in deference to the unexpected heat of this late fall afternoon. Maybe they'd help cool his raging libido, along with his body temperature. Sipping at the chilled drink, he wandered outside to the private veranda and stared at the snow-capped mountains in the distance. The others should be knocking on his door any moment. He swirled the amber liquid over the cubes, took another sip, and wondered.

Had they followed his orders?

He chuckled. Asking young Chanku to abstain from sex after a run was bad enough, asking them to remain celibate after an emotionally charged day such as they'd just had was downright sadistic, especially when there was really no reason to give such a command. No reason beyond showing them how much better it could be, if they were willing to delay gratification.

Not that they were required to listen to him anymore. No, Luc was their boss, now, but Ric had given the command as much to test his own authority as their ability to follow orders.

Foolish, probably, but he'd been in such high spirits after they'd so quickly found that little girl, he'd acted without really thinking.

So often, these things, these horrible searches for lost or missing children, did not go well.

Ric heard a soft tapping. He walked back inside and opened the door between the adjoining rooms to Mik, AJ, Tala, and the new kids, Beth and Nick. Freshly showered and comfortably dressed, they wandered in as he held the door wide. All but Tala had been in wolf form since they'd first stepped into the helicopters that had rushed them to the staging grounds for the rescue. Now that they were far enough from the site of the search and would be driving the rental cars that would take them home, they were finally free to walk as humans again.

Tomorrow, Tala and her boys would head back to San Francisco while he took Beth and Nick home to Colorado. Tonight, they were all his, though to be perfectly honest, he accepted the fact the five of them would head back to their beds without him tonight.

Mik and AJ each gave Ric a high five, Nick bumped knuckles. Tala threw her arms around his neck and hugged him so hard he almost choked. Beth waited quietly off to one side, but she had a huge grin on her face.

As she should.

As soon as Tala set him free, Ulrich slipped an arm around Beth's tiny waist and gave her a hug. He toasted her with his glass. "To the star of the hour! Beth, this would not have ended so happily without your brilliant sleuthing."

Her mate laughed and kissed the top of her head. Beth blushed a deep red. "I didn't do anything one of you guys wouldn't have thought of."

"Not true." AJ shook his head. "I was so frustrated when we couldn't find that child's scent. I was sure we'd lost her. I didn't think she could survive more than one night in the woods, even if that."

Mik nodded and hugged Tala close against his body. "I never would have thought to search the minds of the rangers. What made you go there?"

"Yeah." Tala touched Beth's arm. "And why that guy? He seemed okay. I didn't pick up anything unusual from him at all."

Beth shrugged as they all followed Ulrich through the main room and out to the broad veranda. He'd found a duplex-styled suite of rooms for the night with a small deck off the side he'd chosen. The youngsters had taken the larger set of rooms, though he imagined they'd end up all crowded into one of the king-size beds. If he'd been their age, he knew that's where he'd be headed.

He envied them their closeness, the fact they knew they'd not sleep alone tonight. Was that why he'd asked them to abstain? He chuckled. Anton's need to control everything must be wearing off on him.

"What was it, Beth?" Mik took her hand. "What made you search that guy's thoughts the way you did?"

"I sensed he wasn't being honest." She glanced at Nick, her mate, then down at her toes. "Sometimes I can tell when someone is lying. I could do that even before I knew I was Chanku. He was too eager to help, too quick to let us know what areas had been thoroughly searched. That made me uneasy, so I tried to see what he was thinking. It's easier when I'm the wolf. I could see him digging out a small cave, covering it with branches. The girl's image was clear in his mind, but she had that gag over her mouth and her hands were tied. She looked terrified."

"She was." Ulrich poured wine and handed a glass to Beth and one to Tala. The guys each grabbed a cold beer out of the ice chest he'd set out for them. "She'll need a lot of therapy, a lot of love, to get through such a horrible experience, but at least she'll have that chance . . . because of you, Beth."

He caught Beth's shy glance and nodded. "Yes. Because of you. Okay, guys, dinner'll be here in about five minutes. I ordered steaks all around. Hope that's okay."

"Great. I'm starved." Mik gave AJ a sideways glance. "For a lot more than food."

The others all laughed. Ulrich sensed the underlying strain and bit back a grin.

"Yeah," AJ asked. "What's with the 'abstain until we talk' bullshit?"

"Bullshit?" Ulrich slapped a hand to his heart. "Me?" Laughing, he perched on the railing. "I wanted you bastards to suffer a little like I am. I won't get home to Millie until tomorrow. Why the hell should you all get your rocks off?"

"That's it?" AJ laughed. "That's the only reason? You son of a—"

Ulrich shook his head. "Seriously? I knew, after the successful rescue, you'd all be higher than kites. You'd normally have come back, hit the showers and then fucked like bunnies. No finesse, just screwing to ease the tension. I want more for all of you tonight. Tonight should be special. I want you to think about today. About the fact we saved a little girl's life because one of us . . . Beth, here . . . had the audacity to think outside the box. She searched the mind of a totally improbable suspect and found an innocent little girl who will now have the chance to grow up and have a wonderful life."

He held the glass up and looked at the amber liquid inside. His mind whirled with a kaleidoscope of memories. The time he'd been kidnapped and held prisoner by Milton Bosworth, the weekend of Tia and Luc's wedding, when the Montana pack's plane was hijacked and they'd gone down in a swamp not all that far from here, up in North Dakota . . . So many times they'd been in danger, yet each time they'd been saved by others of their kind.

He looked at the five young people and acknowledged the power in this group. Amazing power. He wanted them to feel it, too. "Tonight," he said, still staring into his glass, "when you go back to your room and you come together, when you blend your bodies and your minds, I want you to do it with the awareness that we are a good and powerful people. That we really can make miracles happen. That, because of all of you, we made one happen today."

The silence that followed was broken by a loud knock on the door. "Looks like dinner's here," he said, ending the moment. "I'll turn you loose as soon as you eat."

Mik laughed and jabbed AJ in the ribs. "Then we can finally go fuck like bunnies, eh?"

Shaking his head, loving them all as if they were his own, Ric opened the door and helped the deliveryman carry their meal into the room.

Millie wasn't certain how they ended up back in the cabin Matt shared with Beth and Nick. She'd lost track of time out in the old barn. And somewhere along the line, they'd both lost track of any inhibitions either of them might have had.

Ulrich was, by far, the better lover with all his years of experience, but as he'd said before, there was a lot to be said for the exuberance of youth.

And the stamina. Millie rolled to her back and stretched, feeling like a well-sated cat. She ached where she'd not realized she had muscles. Felt twinges that, by tomorrow, would probably need more than a few aspirin to loosen up.

Unbelievably, when she heard the shower shut off, she felt herself growing aroused once again. After a couple of minutes, the door opened and Matt stood there, silhouetted by the bright lights in the bathroom. A damp towel was slung loosely around his slim hips and his wet hair clung to his cheeks and forehead.

Already his demeanor had changed. The way he stood, the way he walked. The confidence in his voice. Ulrich had certainly known what he was talking about . . . and the thought fluttered through her mind, that maybe she had changed as well.

"I was hoping you'd still be awake."

"Oh?" Millie rolled to one side and propped herself up on one elbow. "Aren't you tired?"

He shook his head. "I thought I would be. Probably should be. It's the middle of the night, but . . ."

"Have we covered all our lessons?" She rubbed one finger across her lower lip and wished he'd lose the towel.

Matt sauntered slowly across the small space between the bed and the bathroom door. He leaned over and crawled up on the bed, hovering over her on all fours. "I'm not sure," he said. "I'd sure hate to flunk the final."

Laughing, Millie reached up and tugged one corner of the towel. It came loose and she pulled it off his hips. His cock hung down, engorged with blood, too heavy to rise up against his belly. She touched the full weight of his ball sac, stroked the wrinkled flesh and rolled the hard orbs inside between her fingers.

Matt groaned, but he managed to hold perfectly still. Millie scooted over just far enough to slip her head between his knees. His smooth glans brushed her lips. She traced the edge of the flare with her tongue, licked the dampness from his slit. He arched his back and thrust his hips forward, but she drew away, licking softly instead of taking him in her mouth.

"Come over me," she said, but he was moving before the words were spoken. With his knees at either side of her head and his cock hanging over her mouth, he was perfectly placed to put his mouth between her legs.

She tried to ignore the way his tongue felt against her sex and concentrated instead on the taste and texture of his cock. She reached over her head and grabbed his buttocks, stroking his muscular cheeks and reaching for the sensitive puckered ring between them. She licked the full length of his shaft along the underside, and finally drew it between her lips. Teasing him with her fingers, suckling hard and using teeth and tongue and lips, Millie lost herself in the flavors of only the third lover she'd ever known.

If they hadn't been screwing for at least the past eight hours, Matt didn't think he'd be able to last more then ten seconds in Millie's mouth. She had a way of using her tongue and teeth on him that was unreal.

He usually preferred men . . . hell, a guy was more comfortable with what he knew, right? And generally he'd been the one doing the sucking, but right now, with his face buried between a woman's legs and her flavors and her mouth turning him into a shivering wreck, he realized there was a lot to be said for sex with a woman.

Definitely a lot to be said with an older woman, one who didn't hesitate to say what she wanted or to try anything a guy wanted. Matt figured he'd probably never make it to heaven, but this day and night with Millie West had been damned close.

Beth was good, but she was Nick's. He liked her a lot, even when she got so bossy after mating with Nick, but he always knew he was there as a friend, not a lover. Of course, Millie had her mate, too, but right now it was just the two of them, and a guy could dream, couldn't he?

It might not be love, but it was a damned good substitute.

He tried to remember the things she'd told him, the way she wanted to be licked and sucked, but it was almost impossible, with his mind all caught up with the wet heat of her mouth, the sharp scrape of her teeth, and the way her fingers gently rolled and rubbed his balls.

And if she wasn't careful with that soft fingertip rubbing his asshole, she was going to get a mouthful before she expected it. He'd always been extra sensitive there. He buried his face in her soft folds and tried to lose himself in her flavors, but she sucked really hard and he almost lost it. He raised his head and looked down and back, beneath his belly. He caught Millie's eye when she raised her head and grinned around her mouthful of his cock. *You're playing with me, aren't you?*

Laughter whispered through his mind. He put his mouth against her just as her fingers slipped over his butt and she pressed against his ass again. He groaned with her clit between his lips.

Nice. I like that. Vibrations are very nice . . .

Great . . . she liked it and now he knew she was going to make him pay. Her finger circled his ass, slipping in the moisture left from his bath. If she slipped inside, he was going to lose it, just embarrass the hell out of himself right there if she—

Oh shit.

Like that?

He couldn't answer, not and hang on to whatever threads of sanity she might have left him. Her finger went deeper, her lips practically crawled along his dick and he felt it, the curl of heat from his spine to his balls, the shock of pleasure so intense it hurt. He stabbed his tongue deep and then pursed his lips down around her swollen clit, struggling to keep his own climax at bay while he took Millie over the edge.

It must have worked. She screamed and arched her hips up, clamping her thighs against the sides of his head, pressing her sex against his mouth. She took his cock deep, then deeper still, and he was fucking her mouth, going hard and fast. She took all of him, the whole frickin' thing going down her throat, while she kept one hand on his balls and the other with that one finger stabbing deep inside his ass.

He didn't want to drown her, but it was too late and she wouldn't turn him loose. He felt the first jerking spasm of his climax, his ejaculate shooting out while her throat muscles worked around him, swallowing his seed. Milking him, she nursed each drop while his muscles screamed and his legs quivered.

It seemed to take forever before his brain cleared enough for him to realize he was still conscious, but there was no way he could hold himself up any longer. Carefully, hoping he didn't crush her, Matt rolled to one side and his cock slipped slowly out of her mouth. Millie turned around on the bed and grinned at him with a twinkle in her bright amber eyes, and if he hadn't known her real age, he would have thought she was a mischievous teenager, intent on getting him into trouble.

He leaned over and kissed the smear of white off her lips, tasting himself, tasting Millie. His body thrummed with the last tremors of another amazing climax. A stray thought intruded, dragging him back to reality, and he wondered what it would be like, going back to life with Nick and Beth.

Wondered if he could go back, after experiencing this.

"I'm going to miss you, Millie."

Frowning, she touched his cheek and ran her fingers to

his chin, along his jawbone. "Why? Are you going somewhere?"

He shook his head. "Ulrich should be home tomorrow. You got his message."

"Oh, Matt! Don't you understand? Ric is the reason you and I have had such a wonderful night. I never would have had the nerve to approach you without his push. He asked you to stay behind so we could be together." She kissed him. "We both needed this. He recognized it. Just because Ric's coming home doesn't mean we can't be together again. I think he's hoping you'll join us."

"Oh." What else could he say? He hadn't thought that was even an option. Folding his hands behind his head and grinning like an idiot, Matt lay back beside Millie.

"I can't believe you'd think I won't want to do this again." She leaned over and kissed him.

He kissed her back, running his tongue over the full swell of her lower lip, slipping between to trace the edge of her teeth. She sighed and kissed him again. Then she curled up next to him and wrapped her fingers around his flaccid cock.

He lay there, his body warmed by her slight shape, his heart beating a slow and steady tattoo. He thought about the soft touch of her hands on his cock, about the night they'd spent together, the chance of other nights beyond this one.

Her fingers tightened just a bit and his cock began to stir. He sighed and ran his fingers through Millie's tangled hair. Her even breaths against his chest told him she slept. As good as her touch felt, his body relaxed. Instead of waking up for another round, he slowly drifted off to sleep.

Chapter 19

Dinner was over and it was growing late. They'd stacked the plates on a tray outside the door and tossed what few leftovers there'd been in the trash. Ulrich cleaned up the beer cans and wineglasses while the kids policed the rest of the area. Within minutes, his room looked good as new.

He was almost sorry they were so efficient because he hated to see them go. They were funny and smart and every one of them was sexy as hell, but he was especially close to Mik and AJ. Those two were like the sons he'd never had. He'd known both of them since they were barely in their twenties, two young toughs who'd ended up in prison for crimes of which they were questionably guilty.

From the first time he'd met them, he'd known they were Chanku.

It didn't always happen that way, but he'd recognized it in the two of them and, with a little help from some very important people in government, he'd managed to get them out of prison early. The discretion and skill of Pack Dynamics had saved more than one career over the years, and those markers he hung on to came in handy at times.

Rescuing Mik and AJ from prison had been one of those times. They'd never once disappointed him. Tala had been a surprise addition to the boys' previously homosexual bond—a little spitfire with enough love in her heart for both men.

He glanced at Nick and Beth, and caught Beth looking his way. She smiled and then grabbed Tala's hand. Nick saluted him.

Ric frowned. Something was going on here, but he wasn't certain what . . .

Tala kissed Mik and then AJ. Beth planted one on Nick. The guys grinned at Ric and headed for the door.

The two women stayed put.

"What's going on?" Ric looked from one young woman to the next.

Tala shrugged. "We're staying. You can go with the guys or stay with us." She flashed him a cheeky grin.

"If you're smart, you'll choose us." Beth, usually so quiet, had a broad smile and a calculating look in her eye.

"I don't get it." Not that he didn't want to, but two young, beautiful women choosing him over three sexy studs didn't compute.

Tala crossed the room and touched his right arm. When she looked up at him with those beautiful almond-shaped eyes of hers, he felt his heart stutter and then move into overdrive.

"Mik and AJ were really looking forward to spending some quality time with Nick. You know where their preferences lie. Beth and I love the guys, but once in a while it's nice to do something different for a change."

Beth was suddenly beside him, stroking his left arm. "We thought, since Millie's not here . . ."

"And she's probably spent the day doing her best to wear poor Matt to a frazzle . . ." Tala had a huge grin on her face.

"That you wouldn't mind if we spent the night here . . . with you."

Ulrich decided Beth wasn't nearly as shy as she appeared. In fact, right now she looked more like a sloe-eyed, olive-skinned temptress in blue jeans, a princess right out of *Tales from the Arabian Nights*.

"With me, eh? Chasing the senior circuit?" Ulrich shook his head, well aware these two young women had already scented his arousal, and knew they had him where they wanted him, right in the palms of their pretty little hands.

"Cut it out, Boss." Tala trailed her fingers along his arm until she had his hand. "You've been pulling that old guy stuff as long as I've known you, but you look younger than either Mik or AJ."

Beth grabbed his other hand. "Besides, we want a guy with some experience." She palmed the bulge beneath his zipper. He felt the heat of her hand all the way through the fabric and knew he'd lost an argument he really didn't want to win.

Of course, that was one of the things he loved about this business . . . you never quite knew what to expect next.

Tala had said she'd wondered what kind of lover Ulrich Mason was as long as she'd known him, but when she'd suggested staying with him tonight, Beth had hesitated.

She'd only been with an older man once, and it wasn't by choice. The night her stepfather raped her was a nightmare she'd never erase, but for some strange reason, she'd felt drawn to Ulrich from the start. She wasn't sure why, beyond his innate kindness and his obvious adoration of his mate.

Of course, since he was Chanku he didn't look forty, much less his real age. She'd been shocked to find out how old he was. Most men in their sixties seemed ancient, but even with his white hair, Ulrich Mason was hot. His sexy grin, beautiful body, and natural sense of authority merely added to the package.

In fact, his authority, his alpha male status within the pack, affected her more than she'd realized. The way he acted, the power behind his soft voice, all of that was a turn-on as far as Beth was concerned. It was also a challenge. He obviously had more sexual experience than any of the others, especially Nick. The other guys deferred to him, acknowledging his status as this pack's alpha. The loved him, obviously, but they respected his power even more.

She got off on the power, the sense of leadership that was such a natural part of him. It was impossible to imagine Nick ever having that same air about him, that self-assurance, unless, of course, it came from her. It never hurt to learn from the master . . . and with a little help, Nick would eventually gain more confidence.

Maybe even sooner than she'd expected.

Ric poured her and Tala another glass of wine. What looked like whiskey went into his own glass. Beth and Tala sat on the couch while Ulrich leaned against a table in the small sitting area. He dressed like the younger guys, in faded jeans and a cotton shirt with the sleeves rolled back on his forearms. His feet were bare, crossed at the ankles. He sipped his drink and watched them.

Beth glanced at Tala. Tala just smiled and touched the rim of her wineglass to Beth's, which told her absolutely nothing. She wished she knew more about the culture of being Chanku. She felt sometimes like she was playing a game with only part of the pieces and none of the rules.

"I hope you realize how much you young ladies honor me with your request." Ulrich tipped his head to each of them. "Which means, of course, that I can't disappoint either of you. It's been a long time since I've been with more than one partner." He glanced away, as if thinking of times long past.

Tala finished her wine, stood up and slipped her blouse over her head. "How about we take all the worry out of your hands. Trust me, Ulrich. You and I both know that I know exactly what I'm doing."

Beth giggled. Tala made no secret of her past as a prostitute. She wasn't the least bit ashamed of it. "I'm glad one of us does," she said, playing the shy ingénue while sliding the straps of her tank top over her shoulders. "I'm actually here to learn from the masters."

Tala was already out of her jeans by the time Beth got hers off. Ulrich was still dressed, but he watched them with an appreciative gleam in his eyes.

"Put the drink down, big guy." Tala grabbed the glass out of his hand and set it on the table. Then she began to unbutton his shirt. As tiny as she was, she had to reach up to do the top button. Ulrich didn't lean over a bit to help her.

Instead, he widened his stance so Tala could move closer, and placed his hands, palms down, on the table behind him. Naked, Beth got down on her knees beside Tala and undid the snap to his jeans. As Tala slipped his shirt down over his broad shoulders, Beth slowly lowered the zipper, one set of teeth at a time.

She expected to see underwear, but as the placket separated, it bared a dark tangle of silky pubic hair and the powerful bulge of an engorged cock. Beth shoved his jeans down carefully, just enough to expose his entire package, but not far enough to set him free of the fabric holding the head of his cock against his left leg.

A tight coil in her belly spread out at the sight, heating her sex like warm butter melting between her legs. She bit her lips to keep from planting a kiss on the strong curve of his trapped shaft. He was bigger than Nick, with all the muscle and strength of a mature man, yet intimidating at the same time. She wasn't sure why he scared her, but he did. It made her hot. She felt like her pussy was melting.

Tala stood beside Beth and ran her fingers along Ulrich's veined length, stroking him softly with just her fingertips. Beth glanced at Tala and then tugged Ulrich's jeans down far enough to free him.

Tala wrapped her small hands around him and stroked his full length a couple of times. Then she bent forward and slipped the plum-shaped head between her lips. Beth reached both hands between Ulrich's legs and caught the heavy weight of his testicles in her palms. While Tala suckled him, Beth lifted his sac to one side and, with her cheek pressed against Tala's, ran her tongue over the egg-shaped globes, suckling first one and then the other between her lips.

Ulrich groaned, the first sound he'd made since she'd tugged his zipper down. Beth glanced up. His head was thrown back, his eyes closed. His jaw was clenched tight.

"I think he likes this," she said, nudging Tala's hip with her shoulder.

"Oh yeah." Ulrich's voice was a harsh whisper. "He likes this a lot."

"Good." Tala took one last lick of his cock and stepped back. "Get those clothes off now."

Comfortable to follow Tala's lead for now, Beth released him as well and sat back on her heels while Ulrich slipped the shirt off his arms and shoved the jeans down his long legs. Naked, he made her think of an avenging angel with his perfect body and the thick strands of white hair curling around his ears and covering the nape of his neck. The hair around his navel was mostly dark blond, growing darker as it trailed to his groin.

He leaned over suddenly and scooped Tala up in his arms, carried her across the room and deposited her on the bed. She sat up, giggling when he turned and reached for Beth. She felt a brief flash of fear, but she covered it well. Laughing, she tried to evade him, but he was fast and his arms were long.

Within seconds, she lay beside Tala.

Ulrich stood over them, looking down. "Let's do this my way."

Beth glanced at Tala. This wasn't exactly what they'd planned. Tala just shrugged and stretched out beside Beth, arching her body like a cat in heat.

Ulrich crawled across the bed until he was between Tala's thighs. The mattress dipped when he leaned down and licked her, running his tongue between her legs and then settling on her clit.

Beth raised up and leaned on one elbow to watch, growing wetter by the moment. The two of them looked so gorgeous together, lying close enough beside her to touch. Tala was so tiny, barely five feet tall, and she looked like a fragile doll with a man as big as Ulrich between her legs. She whimpered and grabbed at the bedcovers while Ulrich nibbled and sucked between her legs. Beth thought he was going to bring her friend to climax, but Tala was still whimpering that needy little sound when he sat back on his heels. His chin and lips were slick and shiny, his attention now focused on Beth.

He crawled over Tala and knelt between Beth's legs. She felt the heat of his big body, the tickle of hair where his calves brushed her legs. She fought an involuntary shudder and forced herself to relax.

This was not her stepfather. This was a man she trusted. A man who wanted only to give her pleasure. Instead of using his mouth on her, he took his cock in his fist and rubbed between her wet folds with the broad head. Over and over, up and down and across her clit and labia as she grew slick with her fluids and his.

She closed her eyes and lifted her hips, caught on the edge of climax without enough contact to send her over the top. Damn, why couldn't he just shove it inside! Her sex rippled with need, her muscles clasped at nothing, when all she wanted was the length and width of his cock as far inside as he could go. Instead, he kept teasing her, holding her there, ever so close to the edge.

Close, but not over. As she hovered, panting, unsatisfied, on the brink of that dark precipice, he stopped.

Beth's eyes flew open. Ulrich straddled both of them now, one leg trapping Beth's left thigh, the other holding Tala's right. His genitals rested atop their legs. The heat of his balls and the hot length of his cock branded Beth's flesh.

He was bigger than Nick. Heavier. Hotter. More forceful. He buried his fingers deep inside her sex. She swung her head wildly as Tala cried out beside her. Ulrich's fingers pleasured her as well. Beth groaned as the rough, callused fingers scraped painfully over her sensitive clit, leaving shivers of absolute pleasure in their wake. The weight of his body trapped her, the clasp of his legs held her close against Tala so that neither woman could so much as wiggle.

Fear sparked through her, and for a moment she flashed back on that horrible night, the night her stepfather had raped her. She felt her muscles begin to tighten, knew her heart raced, but Ulrich's steady touch seemed to soothe away her fear.

Beth looked up, directly into his dark amber eyes. He watched her. Then he smiled and traced a gentle line from her breasts to her navel, as if reminding her he would never hurt her. Beth began to relax once again as arousal overwhelmed her memories.

He didn't know. He couldn't, but somehow he'd noticed her fear and he'd done his best to soothe it. She hadn't expected that . . . not at all.

Rocking slightly, Ulrich used his hands to pleasure both of them. Thick fingers slowly filled Beth. She closed her eyes and groaned as his thumb traced the curve of her clit, but it wasn't enough. Not nearly enough. She had to touch him. Her body was on fire, her fingers shaking as she reached for Ulrich's cock.

She felt Tala's hand. Both women clasped his shaft, but he was so big Beth could only wrap her fingers partway around his heavily veined girth.

She flashed once again on that other man, that other time. Her stepfather, forcing her down on the bed, ripping her cotton gown off her sixteen-year-old body, forcing his big penis into her virgin hole, tearing into her while she screamed and thrashed, and . . .

Beth forced the terror of that night back into the private recesses of her soul. Instead she focused on Ulrich, on the hot flesh beneath her palm. She stroked him, aware of Tala's hand leading hers, the two of them sliding up and down his shaft, flowing with his rhythm . . . flowing into his thoughts. Holding him like this, the two of them together opened a link into the sensual images filling Ulrich's mind.

Beth became Ulrich, his big hands buried deep in soft, wet women, their rippling vaginal muscles clasping his fingers with surprising strength. She felt slim, muscular legs held tightly between masculine thighs, scented the rich aroma of arousal, of clean, feminine sweat, and the floral perfume of soap and shampoo from the shower.

She knew how his ball sac felt, resting on smooth legs, and she felt the shivers that coursed along his spine with both Beth and Tala's fingers stroking his shaft. Their touch was perfect and it was killing him.

Beth grinned, and with the shared thought, both she and Tala stroked him harder, faster. When Tala felt the first drops of pre-ejaculate, Beth looped her hand down, over the broad flair of his glans to fill her palm with the sticky fluid. Tala did the same, and they worked him now, hand over hand, finding a rhythm that transferred to his fingers thrusting harder, faster, deeper inside their bodies.

Tala screamed. She bowed her back and fought Ulrich's weight holding them both. Arching into his touch, grabbing his wrist with both hands as he took her over the edge, her thoughts and feelings exploding in Beth's skull.

Beth cried out when orgasm claimed her. Deep, pulsing rivers of sensation held her in stasis. Lips parted, she arched her back with a long cry of completion. Her body shuddered and she curled into Ulrich's thrusting hand, the thick penetration of his fingers, the continual pressure of his thumb against her clit.

Amazing, unbelievable, unexpected pleasure, but hovering at the edge of her mind was the dark memory, the one that wouldn't leave her alone. Her demon refused to retreat, and she knew there was only one way to shove it back into the dark.

Rolling to one side, still trapped beneath Ulrich's heavy thigh, she wrapped both hands around his cock and managed to twist herself close enough to draw his hot length between her lips.

Beth knew when his body jerked in surprise that he hadn't expected her mouth, hadn't known she would think beyond her own pleasure at the height of climax. Suckling hard, cheeks hollowing with the strength of each pull, she took him deep inside her mouth.

Tala pulled free beside her, and between the two of them they forced him back on the bed, laid him out like a pagan sacrifice, and took control.

Holy shit. He hadn't expected this. Hovering on the edge of orgasm, his body primed to explode, he'd been thoroughly enjoying the sense of absolute control over two beautiful young women. There was nothing he loved more than feeling their lithe bodies climax around him, knowing they were completely lost in sensation while he still mastered his own body's reactions.

Now Beth straddled his chest and clasped her knees

against his ribs while she sucked his whole damned cock down that pretty throat. Her pussy was hot and wet against him and he felt the tiny flutter of her muscles as they eased down from orgasm.

When he raised his head, all he could see was her perfect little heart-shaped ass. She leaned forward as she worked him with her mouth. The tilt of her body exposed the pink petals of her sex, all slick and creamy with her fluids. It separated her perfectly shaped cheeks and showed off the tight little rosebud of her ass. The sight made him even harder.

Tala had scooted down between his legs and forced them apart. He felt her nose nuzzling the underside of his balls, and her fingers slipping beneath his butt, lifting his ass.

He hadn't done anything remotely this wild in years. Two gorgeous women, both doing as they desired to please him. Control was slipping fast, but he didn't want this to end . . . not yet! Then Tala's lips fastened on his scrotal sac, her tongue licked hot flames over his perineum and she slowly, carefully drew both his balls into her mouth at once.

Her tongue separated the two, circled one and then the other . . . and then she sucked him hard and deep against the hot, wet walls of her mouth.

His world exploded. He forgot about pride and control, forgot dignity and his age and his standing within the pack. He knew only sensation, nothing but scalding mouths and curling tongues, feminine scents, stroking fingers and clenching legs. Lightning streaked from his tailbone to his balls, his cock jerked between Beth's lips and he felt the first streams of his seed spurting down her throat.

He tried to pull out but she sucked him harder, deeper, and he gave in to sensation, gave up all semblance of control and turned himself free to their keeping. His fingers clawed at the soft bedding, his back arched and he lifted Beth with the power of his cry, a harsh, guttural curse that seemed to give her amazing mouth even more strength to drain him dry.

All the while, Tala suckled his balls and her tongue worked his sac. She held him in her mouth while her hands grasped his buttocks and squeezed the taut muscles. Her sharp nails dug stinging furrows into his willing flesh.

He'd be marked for sure. The thought almost made him laugh out loud, but he couldn't. Not the way he was struggling just to draw breath!

He couldn't recall coming so hard, not in a long, long time. He thought of Millie and his love for her, of the wonderful yet comfortable sex they had. So good in its own way, so perfect for the two of them, but it was nothing like this. Now, his body wilted against the bed, wrung out, depleted—replete. Beth still straddled his chest, his cock, still trapped in the warm cavern of her mouth, was loosing tumescence. Tala lay between his thighs. Her hot breath tickled his ball sac, still damp from her mouth and tongue.

He felt like he should say something . . . anything, but by the time words came to him, Beth had rolled to one side and slept, snuggled against his shoulder with her hair tangled across his lower jaw. Tala had shifted, and now a she-wolf snored softly from the spot where she lay all curled up between his legs. Her fur tickled the insides of his thighs and made him think of other things they could do together.

Later. If he ever caught his breath. If his heart ever slowed its thundering beat. Damn . . . he grinned at the ceiling as he brushed Beth's hair off his chin and out of his mouth.

No fool worse than an old fool. . . . But he didn't feel very old. No, he didn't feel old at all. He hadn't realized how much he missed having other Chanku around, how much he missed the variety of sex with more than one partner, though the partner who mattered to him the most wasn't here. He wished Millie was curled up beside him . . . except Millie was with Matt, and he was with Beth and Tala, and tomorrow all of them would finally go to their respective homes.

Of course, Beth was going with him. And Nicholas. And now that Millie had Matt, she might be more inclined to experiment with the others.

Dreaming of the possibilities, basking in the reality, Ulrich finally drifted off to sleep.

Chapter 20

The phone rang, but when Millie reached for it, the table was in the wrong place and there was a large body draped across hers, holding her down.

She'd forgotten. This wasn't her bed and that wasn't Ric.

Matt raised his head, stretched across her and answered the phone. He frowned and then blushed a dark red. Silently, he handed the phone to Millie as she struggled to come fully awake.

Anton Cheval?

By the time she ended the call, Millie was blushing more furiously than Matt.

"How'd he know to find you here?"

She snorted and flopped back on the pillow. "Anton knows everything. Haven't you figured that out?"

Matt shook his head. "I've never met him."

"You will. By the way, he approves most heartily of what we've been up to." Stretching, she sat up and rubbed her eyes. "I need a shower, but I think I'll head back to my own cabin and take one there." She leaned over and kissed him. "Come over in a bit and I'll make you breakfast."

"Isn't Ulrich due home today?" Matt threw the covers

back, exposing the fact he had more on his mind than bacon and eggs.

Millie had to bite back the giggles. He was beautiful, and any shyness she might have felt just a day ago over waking up in bed with a man who was not her mate seemed to have totally disappeared. Ric had been right, as usual. She leaned over and kissed the silky tip of Matt's penis. "He is," she said, licking her way around the crown and testing the narrow slit in the end with the tip of her tongue.

Matt closed his eyes and tilted his head back as she tasted him. "Don't you think he'd mind finding me in his house, eating breakfast?"

She liked the fact his voice sounded strained. "Well, by the time he gets home, you'll probably be having lunch. No, I doubt he'll mind." She raised her head, looked into Matt's questioning eyes, and sighed. "Actually, he's going to have more on his mind than whether or not there's an extra man at the table. Anton called to tell me your friend Deacon and his girlfriend Daci are coming in a couple days. Daci wants to know how her father died. Ric was the last one to see him."

"Why do you look so upset?"

She looked away, out the window at the tall trees beyond. "Because even Anton doesn't know exactly how Milton Bosworth died."

"And?"

"Ric killed him."

"Matt? They're here." It was almost dark. Millie had been out on the porch, waiting impatiently for the past couple hours. Matt was inside, glued to a football game on TV, but he wandered out as the car pulled into the drive.

Beth was riding shotgun while Ric drove the rental. Nick crawled out of the back, looking like he wasn't quite awake, but he grinned and waved at Matt as his buddy bounded down the steps to help with their bags.

Ric slipped into Millie's embrace as if he'd been gone for weeks, but it was obvious he sensed a problem almost immediately.

"Millie?"

"We need to talk."

Ric nodded and then, with his arm still around her waist, turned to the kids. "Go ahead and get a shower. Be back here in half an hour. The food'll taste better if I can't smell your rotten hides."

"You too, old man." Nick saluted and they grabbed their bags and headed down the trail to their cabin.

Millie raised one eyebrow and grinned at Ric. "Looks like the young are no longer intimidated by the old alpha."

He laughed, threw his bag over his shoulder and followed Millie into the cabin. "That happens after you've shared one too many bodily fluids."

"You and Nick?" Millie stopped him. She wanted to see his face when he answered. The idea of two men together had always turned her on. The image of Ric with one of their young guests . . .

But he was shaking his head. "No. Beth and Tala. They just about killed me last night. How'd things go with Matt?"

Millie giggled. "There are no words to describe . . ."

"But I imagine you'll think of some." Ric stepped through the open door and tossed his bag on the floor. "So what's up? Why do we need to talk?"

Millie handed him a glass of good whiskey, neat, and shoved his bag to one side. "Anton called. There's a young lady coming to visit. She wants to know how her father died."

Ulrich nodded. "Bosworth's daughter. Anton told me that's who was spying on them. Turns out she's Chanku."

"She thinks you were only with her father when he died. She doesn't know the truth."

"That is the truth, Millie. I was with him. Of course, I also helped rush the process."

"What are you going to tell Daciana? That you killed him?"

Ric wrapped his arm around her shoulders and pulled her close. "I'll do what's right, Millie m'love. I'll tell her the truth. She'll either hate me or she'll understand. She's Chanku, sweetheart. She'd learn the truth eventually, just as you did. It's there in my memories, for any one of us who wants to see."

"That was delicious, Millie." Beth leaned back in her chair and patted her tummy. "I've never learned to cook, but I love homemade stuff."

Nick grinned at her. "You don't have to cook. All you need to do is shift, go find a nice rabbit and voilà! Dinner."

Laughing, Beth leaned over and punched his shoulder. "I still want to learn, and I doubt the rabbits will be that easy to find when there's six feet of snow on the ground."

Millie shook her head and sighed. They'd laughed and argued all through dinner, teasing each other like little kids. "Behave, you two. I'll teach Beth to cook any time she wants."

Millie stood up, but Ric put a hand on her wrist and stopped her. "I think Nick and Matt would absolutely love to clear the table and do the dishes tonight, don't you agree, boys?"

"What about Beth? Or you?" Sputtering with fake indignation, Nick stood up and grabbed a couple of plates. Matt did the same.

"I drove, and Beth was the star of the search team." Ric snaked an arm around Millie's waist and she settled on his knee. "Millie cooked. You two haven't done a thing to earn your keep today."

Matt slanted a knowing glance at Millie. She broke into giggles. "I'm not so sure I can say that about Matt."

Ric covered his ears. "I so do not want details. Nada. Nichts. Non . . . how many ways do I need to say it?"

"Well, I do." Beth glanced from Millie to Matt. "Although, to be honest, the real details I want are the ones from Nick, Mik, and AJ. Now that's where I'd like to have been a fly on the wall."

Millie scooted off of Ric's lap and back into her own chair. "You and me both. The idea of three sexy men together . . . just watching them. Not being a part of it so much as sitting back and watching."

Beth sighed. "I agree. I haven't been Chanku all that long . . . I'm still so new to all of this, but it's like my sexual options have opened up and expanded in a lot of directions I never even knew existed. And one thing I've learned is that there's a lot more of the voyeur in me than I realized."

Millie shot a glance at Ric and realized he was staring intently at her. When she tried to see what he was thinking, his mind was blocked. She grinned at him but directed her words to Beth. "Do you think we could talk the guys into it?"

Beth leaned forward, as if whispering a secret. "The three of them, all hot and naked, and the two of us in the bleachers?"

Millie nodded.

Ric turned around and glared at Matt, who was loading the dishwasher while Nick finished clearing the table and scraping the dishes. "Matthew? What have you done with my mate? I already figured out Beth wasn't nearly as shy as I first thought, but this woman isn't the Millie I remember."

Matt sauntered over to the table. "I didn't do anything she didn't suggest first. I am, and always will be, respectful . . . And I always follow orders."

"He did. He was," Millie said, biting back a laugh. "Very respectful. Over and over again."

"And again," Matt said. He snapped the towel at Ric's thigh and jumped out of the way.

Ric leaned over and held his head in his hands, muttering, "I don't get no respect."

Millie leaned close and patted him on top of the head while the kids laughed.

When the young ones all left a short time later to return to their cabin, Millie put the remnants of their dinner in the refrigerator and turned out the light.

"Why do I keep thinking of them as kids, Ric?"

He laughed. "Because they are?"

Millie shook her head. "Not really. Matt's twenty-five, Nick's twenty-four. Beth's the youngest, but I think she said she's twenty-one, or close to it. They've all lived on the streets, been exposed to more life than I'll ever experience. They're not as old as we are, but they're definitely not kids."

"From my perspective, sweetheart, they're still babies." Ric kissed the back of her neck as he walked past her. "Mere babies."

"Well, Matt, for one, does not make love like a mere baby. He's not built like one, either, if you catch my drift."

Ric slipped his arms around Millie's waist from behind and nuzzled her ear. "Oh, I get it well enough. Whatever you did with that boy made a world of difference in his self-confidence."

She leaned back and kissed the line of his jaw. "Mine too, if you want the truth. Growing up with so many rules, so many negatives about sex, I had no idea how inhibited I was. Trying to help Matt lose some of his hang-ups got rid of a lot of mine as well."

She turned in Ric's embrace and looped her arms over

his shoulders. "We had fun, Ric. We laughed and tried stuff I would have been too embarrassed to even suggest to you, and it was all fun."

"Ah, Millie . . . Why would it ever embarrass you to do anything with me?"

"Because you matter so much, you fool! I love you, Ric. More than you can possibly imagine. I don't want you to ever think I'm not worthy of your love, and somehow that all got tangled up in my head with sex and things we do together. I don't really care what Matt thinks of me. Oh, I want him to like me—that's no big deal—but I didn't worry he'd think I was stupid for not knowing things, or that it was weird when I asked him to do things to me."

Ric nuzzled the tender skin between her neck and shoulder. "Hmmmm . . . What kind of things?"

Millie laughed. "I'm not sayin' . . . but if you come with me, I just might show you."

Ric looped an arm around her waist and guided her down the hall to their bedroom. "Good, because I'm so tired I'm ready to drop, and if I do fall over, I want it to be in a bed with you beside me."

"There's no place I'd rather be." She hugged him close.

"Unless it's watching me, Nick, and Matthew getting it on." He stopped in the doorway to their bedroom and looked directly at her.

Millie didn't even blush. She smiled up at him and grinned. "You're right."

"You really are serious, aren't you?"

Ric was smiling that smile of his that meant his mind was spinning circles about something. Millie was certain she knew where those circles were leading.

"When are Daci and Deacon coming?"

"Day after tomorrow," she said. She took his hand and led him toward their big bed. "Which leaves us tomorrow night."

Ric wrapped his arms around her and tumbled her to the mattress. "Tomorrow night it is," he said. "We'll do our best not to disappoint either of you young ladies."

Millie disentangled herself from his grasp and went into the bathroom to get ready for bed. By the time she'd removed her clothes and brushed her teeth, Ric was already asleep. So much for his promises of hot and wild sex. She crawled in beside his big, warm body and leaned over to kiss him good night.

He didn't even stir. She loved him so much it made her ache. Unexpected tears welled up in her eyes. "You've never once disappointed me, my love," she whispered. "I don't expect you ever will."

The caged wolves were settled in their pens for the night. Millie and Ric had run hard and fast with the three young Chanku. They'd cornered an elk, an old bull with one broken antler, that still managed to take a dangerously close swipe at Nick.

He'd rolled out of the way of striking feet and jabbing antlers while Beth and Millie brought the beast down for a clean kill. They'd eaten well and run hard, and had a wonderful time teasing Nick about his near miss. Now, showered and dressed in loose, comfortable clothes, Ric and Millie walked down the path to Lisa Quinn's old cabin where the three youngsters were living.

Millie hadn't felt so mellow in ages. Her thoughts wandered back to those days before she'd known of her Chanku birthright. Before Tinker McClintock had come to the sanctuary and claimed Lisa as his mate.

Lisa had been Millie's link to life as a wolf. She and her sister Tala and brother Baylor were now part of Millie's new extended family, the family of Chanku. Lisa lived in San Francisco with her mate, Tinker. Tala was there as well with both her guys, Mik and AJ, and their brother

Baylor was living in Maine, mated to Millie's daughter Manda.

All of them happy, each with someone they loved. Just as Millie had finally found love. She squeezed Ric's arm. "I hope Nick didn't get upset with the teasing tonight. When he yipped and tumbled head over heels, I thought for sure he'd been gored. It was such a relief to see he was okay, but we were all a little tough on him."

"It's not the teasing that concerns me." Ric paused beneath a large pine. "I don't know if you've noticed, but he's challenged me. He did it during the search and a couple times since we've gotten back. Small things . . . an insult here, a snarl there. A definite lack of respect that's gotten worse since we returned from South Dakota. Matt teases, but Nick challenges. There's a difference to the way the two of them behave. It doesn't fit, as he's not an aggressive man by nature. I don't know if it's his idea, or if maybe Beth's behind it. She's a very assertive young woman."

Millie shrugged. "She's definitely an alpha, but I haven't noticed her acting out of line around me."

"You're not a threat."

"And you are?" Millie laughed. "To whom?"

Ric shook his head. "I'm not sure, but I'm not letting down my guard."

Millie stood on her toes and kissed his cheek. "Don't worry, sweetheart. I'll protect you."

He patted her hand. "I may hold you to that."

Matt opened the door for them when Ulrich knocked. Millie glanced through the open door and burst into laughter. The entire floor of the small front room was one big bed.

They'd moved the furniture aside and placed a king-size mattress from one of the bedrooms right in the middle of the floor. All was in darkness, except for a snake-armed lamp perfectly focused on the middle of the mattress like a spotlight. Extra tables and chairs were stacked against one wall, but the long, low leather couch was now a front-row seat for the impromptu stage.

Celtic music flowed over them, coming from speakers hidden around the room. A chilled bottle of wine sat in an ice bucket on a low table in front of the couch, with five wineglasses already filled from another bottle standing in a line beside it.

"I love it." Millie flopped down next to Beth and took the glass of wine the younger girl handed to her. "When Lisa Quinn lived here, she said she did the same thing one night when Tia, Luc, and Tinker were here. As I recall, it was Luc and Tinker putting on the show."

"Now that's going to be a hard act to follow." Beth sighed dramatically. "Tinker and Luc . . ." She fanned her chest with one hand. "Oh, my. Wouldn't I love those two to myself." Then she took a swallow of wine and sat back to watch.

Ric stood off to one side and studied the women. Millie was such an open, loving spirit. There was no subterfuge in her at all—he honestly didn't think her capable of lying or dissembling. Beth was still an unknown. He didn't have her full measure, yet. He'd thought she was shy at first, but she'd opened up more each day as she got to know them.

What had really surprised him, though, was when she'd wrenched sexual control from him right at the height of her climax two nights before. He thought he'd had her pegged better, and hadn't expected it. In fact, he thought she'd been a little afraid of him at one point, but he wasn't really sure.

He didn't like that . . . not being able to read a person. Usually he was an excellent judge of people, but Beth was one big question mark. Obviously, she liked being in control, but what was her motivation? So much of the time, she seemed tense and on guard, even here in this relaxed setting with her closest friends.

He'd have to watch her, but at least he'd warned Millie.

Nick seemed uneasy, which made Ric even more cautious. The younger man refused to meet Ric's eyes. His focus was definitely on his mate, and he, like Beth, was far from relaxed. Matt wasn't the least bit tense, though he kept glancing from Millie to Ric and back at Millie. Oddly, his thoughts were completely blocked.

The undercurrents in the room, especially between the two younger men, flowed fast and furious. Tensions were always high after a run and successful hunt, but generally it was all due to their highly charged libidos and an overabundance of testosterone. That was part of what made him uneasy. Ric could practically taste the tension in the air, but that wasn't the only reason for his unusual sense of anxiety.

There was something else behind it, something he couldn't identify because of the heavy sexual undertones. Trying to find the source of his foreboding was next to impossible, though, and he couldn't blame all of it on the younger Chanku. He'd been hard since their return—even his shower hadn't helped abate his arousal.

Which made him wonder exactly what he was waiting for. Maybe, once they got things going, everyone would settle down and he could quit worrying. He slowly began to unbutton his shirt. Nick and Matt immediately realized he'd taken the first step, and they undressed as well. When Matt turned, Ric noted the long red gashes on his shoulders and buttocks and had to look away to keep from laughing.

Unfortunately, he looked directly at Millie. He'd recognize Millie's marks anywhere. Of course, he had Beth's and Tala's on his ass, but nothing like the scars of battle Matt was wearing. Grinning, he winked at Millie. She was difficult to see in the shadows, but he knew when she smiled at him and licked her lips. He felt his cock rise, aroused merely by knowing Millie watched him.

Fingers brushed his shoulder. When Ric turned, Matt stood behind him. Nick waited off to one side, watching. The music poured through Ric's senses—piano, the high pitch of flutes and the lower tone of an oboe. Drums in the background kept pace with his pulse.

He signaled to Nick to join them. After a moment's hesitation, Nick stepped into the circle of light. The glow played over his olive skin and accented his high cheekbones, the dark slash of his brows. Ric didn't hesitate—he wrapped his fingers around Nick's erect cock and squeezed. At the same time, he grabbed Matt's shaft in his left hand.

While he stroked both young men with his hands, Ric took a moment to study Nick. He was a mix of races, most predominantly Middle Eastern and Native American. Shorter than Matt with a sinewy build, he possessed a wiry strength about him any man would be a fool to underestimate.

He was larger as a wolf. He'd make a dangerous adversary, in spite of his youth and inexperience.

Ric knew Nick had been on the streets for at least five or six years, long enough to learn survival in a tough environment. He and Beth had bonded from the first, but then Nick had been the first of the youngsters to shift, before any of them even knew what their Chanku birthright was.

He'd shifted and killed a gangbanger who'd assaulted Tala, acting immediately, without any thought toward his own safety, which obviously made points in his favor.

Matt moved closer to Ric and wrapped his arms around him from the back. He leaned close and kissed his neck, and Ric caught the thoughts in the young man's mind—thoughts meant only for him.

I'm not sure what Nick's up to. Watch him carefully.

Beth's on him to do something, but I don't know what it is.

Well, it was nice to know his suspicions weren't totally off the mark. Even nicer to know where Matt's loyalties lay. Silently thanking him, Ric turned Nick loose and slowly went down on his knees in front of Matt. He studied the width and length of his huge erection with undisguised fascination.

Then he opened his thoughts to Matt and Nick, showing both young men what he was thinking. He stroked the silky surface of Matt's shaft, and thought of what it had meant to Millie.

This beautiful cock had pleasured his wife. She'd taken Matt in her mouth, in her warm, wet pussy, even in her ass. For almost a full twenty-four hours, Millie had touched and tasted everything Matt had to share—his genitals, his mouth, his entire body had been her playground. She'd taken pleasure and given pleasure, and she'd learned and changed from the experience.

He sensed Matt's appreciation of his praise, as well as Nick's surprise that he would look so favorably on another male who had given his mate pleasure.

Obviously, there was much Nick needed to learn about the culture of the Chanku. Jealousy was not a part of their society, not among packmates. It appeared Matt had a better understanding of his own sexuality than Nick. Was that the basis of Matt's warning, of Ric's uneasiness?

Jealousy?

Ric cupped Matt's balls in his palm and wrapped his lips around his glans. It had been a long time since he'd taken another man in his mouth, and he'd almost forgotten how much he loved the unique flavor, the texture, the sense of strength.

Even so, while he ran his tongue along the hard length, he couldn't help but think of Nick and Beth, couldn't help but wonder what was going on. The thoughts worked in the back of his mind, all the while he licked and sucked until Matt's hips were dancing in a steady thrust and retreat to the beat of the music and the rhythm of his tongue.

A new cut, with bagpipes this time, came on and the rhythm changed. Ulrich backed away from Matt and turned his attention to Nick. First he looked up and made eye contact. Nick held his gaze for only a moment before looking away.

His behavior was more beta than alpha. Ulrich thought about Matt's quiet confidence and Beth's need for control. Had he totally misinterpreted both young males?

Interesting.

He sat back on his heels and studied Nick, taking stock of his slender build, the lean strength in his long arms and legs. Then he focused on the wiry coarseness of his pubic hair. Nick hadn't been Chanku long enough for his body hair to soften.

Just as his body hadn't had enough time to completely adjust, Nick's mind still didn't accept his changing reality. He didn't fully understand he was as much wolf as human, didn't really appreciate the unique combination of all the things that made him Chanku. Things like the power of the pack, the strength of his newly awakened libido, the respect due the pack's alpha . . . all this would come with time.

And, with lessons.

Nick obviously wasn't immune to Ric's close scrutiny. Even though he kept his eyes averted, his cock had begun to stretch and grow. It filled with blood as his body reacted, whether to Ric's closeness or the personal fantasies filling his mind.

Ric tried to read him, but Nick's mental walls were high and tight. No matter. Ric cupped Nick's sac in his palm and ran one finger behind his balls, tracing the sensitive skin of his perineum.

He totally ignored the erection growing before his eyes. Instead he pressed softly at the puckered ring of muscle between Nick's cheeks, then retreated to once again cup his balls. Nick spread his legs wider. His eyes were closed, his breath coming faster, and Ric felt his mental shields relaxing along with the tightness of his ass.

Ric glanced at Matt. *Lie down on your back with your knees bent.*

Matt complied without question.

Ric cupped Nick's right cheek and turned him, had him kneel over Matt so that his long cock hung directly over Matt's mouth. Beth made a little humming sound deep in her throat. It was ripe with passion, the sound of a woman giving in to lust. The noise startled Ric. He'd been so intent on the two guys he'd totally forgotten their audience.

Carefully he adjusted both Nick and Matt, positioning them in a perfect sixty-nine. There was no hesitation. They had accepted his lead, his role as the pack's alpha. Each of them immediately drew the other's cock between his lips.

At Ric's direction, they kept their hands away, working on one another with nothing more than lips and tongues and teeth. Nick used his hands to hold himself over Matt, but Matt's arms stretched over his head, as if he imagined himself restrained.

Ric sat beside them for a few minutes, stroking and gently squeezing a set of testicles in each hand. He watched Nick and Matt's faces, the way their cheeks sucked in and then expanded. Their eyes were closed, their concentration evident as they used their mouths to pleasure one another.

The Celtic music drifted in and out of Ric's consciousness. The bagpipes were through now and a soft flute played, a sensual counterpoint to the visual of two young men sucking each other's cocks, the physical texture and weight of solid testes in their wrinkled sacs, the way they felt resting in his palms.

Nick's shields had come down almost completely. Ric sensed his elation, that he'd been given the top position as if that somehow meant he dominated Matt. With that came the relief that Beth would approve, confirming for Ric that Nick's position within the pack was much more important to Beth than to him.

No wonder Ric had sensed a challenge from Nick. His mate was the one behind it, and what man among them wouldn't do whatever he could to make his mate happy?

Unfortunately, there was more here at stake than Beth's pleasure. Disturbing an established hierarchy wasn't an act lightly taken, though the youngsters didn't seem to realize the risk of their actions or desires. One more sign of immaturity that he'd need to put a stop to. Ric slowly moved around so that he knelt behind Nick, but he continued to stroke his ball sac and run his fingers along the crease between Nick's cheeks.

Then, moving aside a few inches, out of the spotlight and into the shadows, he grabbed the lube and a condom, sheathed himself as inconspicuously as possible and coated himself with the lube. Then, once again, he took his position behind Nick.

He stroked Nick with both palms, reaching between his legs to cup his sack, trailing one thick finger up the crease between his cheeks, catching the rhythm of the music, the rhythm of Matt's mouth, of Nick's mouth. He opened his mind to the sense of everyone in the room, found the sensual images in Matt's corresponding to the same visuals in Nick's.

He found both women's thoughts—Millie's open and loving, charged with her growing arousal and curiosity—and Beth's. More calculating, more focused on her mate and his actions, on Ric and what his intentions were. She didn't realize he'd sheathed himself, had no idea, at this point, what he planned.

Which meant he needed to act now, before she could

warn her mate. Nick was lost for the moment, entirely trapped in Matt's touch and taste. Ric's arousal grew as he eavesdropped on both men, on the flavors and textures of two young cocks, each massively aroused, on the mental games both Nick and Matt played to keep from coming.

Neither wanted to be the one who shot first, but working to bring off the other was raising the level of excitement for both of them.

A level that wasn't lost on Ric.

His fingers gliding up and down the tight crease between Nick's cheeks wasn't helping, but he knew it felt so good that Nick wasn't going to ask him to stop. He let his fingers pause at the puckered ring of his ass. Pressing gently at first, then with more pressure, he finally breached the tight opening.

Nick grunted, but he pushed back against Ric's fingers. Lost in a haze of arousal, it was obvious he no longer paid attention to his mate. He reached instead for more sensation, more gratification. Beth was beginning to worry about Nick's lost focus, concern leaching from her mind and touching Ric as well as her mate.

Matt seemed oblivious. He worked Nick with his hands and his mouth, as lost in giving pleasure as he was in receiving.

Ric inserted one finger inside Nick and slowly pumped in and out. Nick moved with the gentle intrusion, obviously enjoying the penetration. When Ulrich withdrew his finger, Nick sighed and adjusted his legs, obviously hoping for more. He was still fairly tight, his sphincter not quite relaxed—exactly the way Ric wanted.

This was not so much about pleasure as it was about power.

Aligning the broad head of his sheathed cock against the taut ring of muscle, Ric grasped Nick's hips in both hands and slammed his hips forward, breaching Nick's anus in one powerful, pain-giving thrust. Cursing, Nick jerked his mouth away from Matt's cock and tried to pull away from Ric, but it was too late. Ric held on to his hips and drove into the younger man again, and then again.

"What the fuck are you doing, old man?" Nick whipped his head around and glared at Ric.

"Exactly what you asked for." Staring him down, Ric found a rhythm he knew Nick wouldn't be able to ignore. Matt was still sucking Nick's cock, Ric's thrusts had gentled and finally Nick groaned as sensation and pleasure obviously overwhelmed any sense of outrage.

Slowly, Ric pressed deeper until his balls rested against Nick's. Nick took Matt's erect cock back into his mouth and pressed his buttocks against Ric's groin.

Beth's silent anger exploded as a palpable force in the room. Ric sensed the precise moment when Nick shuttered his thoughts and effectively blocked his mate along with everyone else.

It appeared he'd decided to just go ahead and enjoy the experience, which was exactly what Ric had hoped for.

Matt's fingers wrapped around Ric's sac. Stroking and gently squeezing, his touch immediately dragged Ric's thoughts away from Nick and Beth as Matt raised his level of arousal higher.

Allowing himself the luxury of enjoying the experience, Ric moved now with a sense of purpose, driving deep inside Nick and then sliding slowly out. Aware of hot inner walls and moist, clasping muscles, he was consumed by the intimacy of the act, the sense of communion he felt with both of the men. He cast his thoughts toward Millie and found her aroused but also curious. She didn't truly grasp the undercurrents in the room—the meaning of Beth's anger, Nick's arousal, Ric's sense of purpose.

Or Matt's laughter. He, of all of them, appeared to know exactly what kind of power play was taking place. Totally separate from the game that Ric, Nick, and Beth seemed to find so important, he contented himself with enjoying the sensuality of two other men's bodies completely in sync with his own.

Enjoyed, and shared. Ric suddenly realized he was caught in the current of Matt's desire, caught in the humor of the situation, the failed power play Nick had entertained and Ric's alpha male manner of defusing it. Even Beth's grudging anger faded beneath the powerful tide of Matt's growing arousal and free-spirited joy in the moment.

Shared by all of them, five hearts and souls consumed by the joined sensations of licking and sucking, of penetrating and being filled, of the burn of stretched muscles and the sleek slide of mouths over taut skin, of tastes and textures.

Ric let himself go. Caught in the dark pleasure as he took Nick closer to orgasm, he no longer fought his own. Sharing his own sensations, the clasp of muscles and slick heat around his cock, the power of thrusting hips and bursting lungs. Finally he shared the hot coil of desire pooling in his groin, exploding through his balls to his cock.

Ric groaned and gave up the fight. Thrusting hard and deep, his cock spasmed as he climaxed. He dug his fingers into Nick's sides as his hips and cock jerked with each spurt of his seed. Nick cried out. Matt's fingers tightened around Ric's balls, squeezing him to the point of pain as he swallowed Nick's release while giving up his own.

It seemed to go on forever, yet it lasted only seconds. Without intending to, they'd achieved mutual climax, three disparate minds finding a common thread of desire, shared and multiplied among all of them.

Even the women had joined them. Ric slowly raised his head from Nick's back and looked at Millie and Beth. They lay back on the couch, eyes closed, lips parted as each of them drew air into gasping lungs.

Whatever Beth had wanted from Nick tonight hadn't

occurred. Maybe something even better, had. A new sense of community? A stronger pack? He didn't know. Wouldn't be able to tell for quite some time how things might progress from here on out.

Funny, how Beth was the one who could tell when someone was lying. Did that make her a better liar? Was she better able to dissemble, to evade the truth and hold her own feelings closer than the others?

Something to ponder. Later. When his heart wasn't pounding, his chest wasn't heaving with each breath . . . and the anticipation of taking his mate to bed wasn't the uppermost thought in his mind.

Tomorrow loomed closer with each passing minute. Tomorrow when he would have to look a young woman in the eye and tell her exactly how and why he had killed her father.

It made Beth's plots and plans and power grabs seem petty by comparison.

Chapter 21

Matt wasn't sure what he expected when Daci and Deacon pulled into the parking lot at the wolf sanctuary, but the little Mini Cooper with the sexy brunette at the wheel wasn't even close.

He'd forgotten that Deacon didn't drive. Hell, none of them had driver's licenses except for Logan, mainly because none of them had owned cars, but watching Deacon unfold his lanky body and crawl out of that itty-bitty car had Matt laughing hysterically by the time he shut the office door behind him and walked out to greet the two.

Laughing, but with his heart pounding and a sudden dryness in his mouth that had nothing to do with thirst. Why this sudden reaction, arousal even, to a guy who'd been his best friend from the day they'd first met? Deacon looked great. He'd always looked great, but Matt hadn't realized how much he'd missed him until he got a good look at his buddy.

They greeted each other with open arms and real hugs, not that "slap on the back guy-hug" sort of thing. Matt had to drag himself away, awkward, suddenly, with the desire to do more than just hug. The last thing he wanted to do was embarrass Deacon in front of his mate.

Daci stood off to one side, looking sort of shy and lost

until Deacon wrapped an arm around her shoulders and hugged her close. "This is Daciana Lupei. Daci, this is Matt. Watch out for him. He's sneaky."

"Hey! That's not fair." All that first meeting awkwardness fled as, laughing, Matt took Daci's hand. Then he pulled her close and hugged her tight. "Welcome, Daci. See? I'm not sneaky at all. I merely take what I want. What the hell are you doing with Deacon?"

Obviously flustered, she quickly slipped away from Matt and clung to Deacon. "It's nice to meet you," she said, smiling now that she was back beside the big guy.

Matt's groin tightened as he looked at the two of them. It wasn't jealousy, but he couldn't explain it. This wasn't at all the way he'd thought he might feel. No, it was something else altogether. Something he couldn't quite explain.

Millie stepped out of the office, breaking whatever spell held him in stasis. Matt ran up the steps, grabbed her hand and dragged her down to meet Deacon and Daci. Ulrich showed up a few minutes later, followed by Nick and Beth.

Everyone sort of talked at once, which gave Matt the chance to stand back and watch. Damn but it was good to see Deacon. He'd had a soft spot for the guy from the beginning, long before they knew they were both Chanku. They'd always been able to talk, though they'd never gotten it on. Deacon was as hetero as they came, in spite of the fact he'd worked the streets for dough. Sex with men was, for Deacon, only a job.

Matt wondered with an unfamiliar sense of anticipation, if that might have changed by now. Becoming Chanku seemed to loosen up everyone's sexuality. They'd already begun to pair off in groups while in San Francisco, but it was always Deacon with Logan and Jazzy, and Matt with Beth and Nick. He'd never actually thought of just pairing off with Deacon.

Last night had been spectacular with Nick and Ulrich, in spite of Beth's silly head games.

Which took his thoughts full circle, back to the woman standing beside the man. Daci didn't look like the type to play games. No, she just looked flat-out gorgeous. Damn but Deacon was a lucky bastard to find someone so beautiful for a mate. In fact, both of them were absolutely perfect. He sighed, lost in the futility of his dreams. If miracles happened, if he had a choice between Deacon and Daci, Matt knew he'd take either one of them.

Or both.

Millie led them to a tree-shaded picnic table on the far side of the parking lot. There were a couple of pens nearby with caged wolves, but she'd explained that most of the animals were in larger compounds away from public view. Still, it felt odd to be sitting here with people who could shift into wolves and yet be looking at their wild brethren behind fences.

It was easier to concentrate on the five people Deacon had just introduced her to. Daci surreptitiously glanced from one person to the other, overwhelmed by another group of absolutely beautiful people, all of them Chanku. The most beautiful, by far, though, was Deacon's friend, Matt.

She had to force herself not to spend too much time staring at him. Tall and lean and just plain hot, he was soft-spoken, but funny with a quick sense of humor. It was obvious he and Deacon had a bond. She wondered if they'd ever slept together. So many of these people had screwed each other it was hard to keep track.

She almost giggled and covered it with a cough. Talk about feeling like she'd wandered into the fun house at a macabre carnival . . . less than a week ago, she'd been hunting shapeshifters, trying to prove their existence.

Now, not only had she discovered that the Chanku actually existed, she was one of them, accepting their impossible birthright as her own. Talk about bizarre.

Millie's voice dragged Daci back from her rambling thoughts. "I've cleaned up a small guest cottage near the one where Ric and I live. It's just a studio with a kitchenette, but the bed is comfortable and it's got all the amenities you'll need while you're here. Why don't you bring your car and I'll show you where you're staying."

Deacon stood up. "Thanks, Ms. West."

"Please. Just Millie. We're not very formal here."

Matt turned and grinned at Daci. "It's really hard to be formal with people when you've seen them naked."

"There is that." Daci glanced up at Deacon before she answered Matt. "But then, we haven't seen you naked, yet."

"That can be arranged." The minute the words slipped out, Matt regretted them. Until he caught Deacon's eye. His buddy was grinning as if he didn't mind at all that Matt was flirting with his mate.

"Not yet, children." Laughing, Ulrich Mason tugged on his mate's hand. He paused for a moment and made eye contact with each of them. "Remember, the employees here are not Chanku. They have no idea what we are. Discretion is even more important than it was at Anton's estate." Then he relaxed and tugged Millie after him. "Okay . . . We need to get you two settled. C'mon."

The cabin was perfect, back off the main road and out of sight of traffic, nestled against a stand of cedar and blue spruce. There was a small kitchen with a stocked refrigerator, no table but a nice bar with four stools, a bathroom with a big shower instead of a tub, and an absolutely huge bed right in the main room. There were a couple of comfortable chairs inside, as well as cedar Adirondack chairs on the front deck.

Daci couldn't believe they'd have this perfect spot all to

themselves. It was private, and with the trees right behind them, they could shift whenever they wanted and go right out the back door, directly into a gorgeous forest. She'd thought Anton Cheval's estate was the most beautiful thing she'd ever seen, but this was even nicer.

Smaller. More intimate, and not nearly as intimidating.

Suddenly she realized she'd been staring at the big bed and imagining Deacon and Matt in the middle of it. Someone chuckled and she raised her head. All of them—Nick, Beth, Matt, Millie, and even Ulrich—were staring at her and smiling.

She blushed beet red and hid her face against Deacon's chest. "Oh, Lordy. I was doing it again, wasn't I?"

Laughing softly, Deacon wrapped his arm around her. "Yep, sweetie. Broadcasting."

Matt bumped hips with Deacon. "Personally, I think she's got great ideas."

"You would." Beth sort of sneered at him, though she acted as if she was just teasing. Daci hadn't figured her out yet.

"Actually, I think it's a pretty good idea, too."

Daci raised her head when Deacon spoke, but he was looking directly at Matt, not at her. She was so not ready for this!

Ulrich saved her butt. "C'mon, Matt. We're going to let them get settled in first. You can pounce later."

"Yes, sir. Coming right now, sir." Matt saluted, but he leaned over and kissed Daci's cheek before she knew what he was up to. Then he planted one on Deacon, right on the mouth.

Her biggest surprise came when Deacon kissed him back. It took them almost a minute to break it off, and by then Daci scented arousal from more than one person in the room, including herself.

And here she'd been so worried about talking to Ulrich Mason! These two idiots had managed to take her mind entirely off the reason for the trip, though when Deacon and Matt finally broke apart, it was impossible to tell what they were thinking.

There was no doubt what they both felt. The evidence was right there in front of them, straining at their tight jeans.

Daci was trying to get her thoughts in order and her own arousal under control when Ulrich paused at the open door. He smiled at Daci and lifted her chin in his fingers, almost as if he memorized her face.

"I know you want to talk," he said. "After dinner, why don't you and I go for a run. Is that okay with you?"

"Just you and me?" Daci glanced at Deacon.

"If you like. Or you can bring Deacon along. I thought it might be easier if we got away from everyone. It's entirely up to you, but I've learned that it's sometimes easier to talk about important things from a wolf's point of view."

Daci nodded. Ulrich smiled and closed the door behind him. She stared at the closed door for a moment, turning Ulrich's words over in her mind, even as she sensed Deacon waiting patiently behind her.

"It's so strange, Deac. I just realized it's not that important to me anymore. Everything I've learned about my father makes me ashamed to be his daughter. Why should I care how he died?"

Deacon ran his hand over her hair and swept the tangled mess back over her shoulder. He gently turned her around and wrapped his arms around her waist. "You made a promise to your father that you would find out who killed him, and you're not a woman who breaks a promise. You care because you want closure to that part of your life. You have questions Mason can answer. I think that once you have those answers, no matter what they are, you should be able to put all this to rest. Sweetheart, I'll go with you if you want."

She nodded, thinking of all the things he'd just said. He was right. She did feel a need to keep her promise to her father, no matter what she learned. She looked up into Deac's beautiful face, raised up on her toes and kissed him. "Thank you. I need to think about your offer. I almost feel as if this is something I should do by myself."

"Whatever you like." He kissed her and grinned. "Including inviting Matt to spend the night."

She jerked her head up so quickly, she almost knocked him in the chin. Deacon winked and turned away. "I'll get our suitcases," he said.

He left her standing in the open doorway.

"Daci? You ready to go?"

Ulrich stood by the door, waiting for her. Everyone was either helping Millie clean up the mess from dinner, or they were out on the back porch, talking quietly and sipping wine.

Daci nodded. She'd decided to run alone with Ulrich. She'd started this journey on her own and figured the least she could do was find the strength to see it through on her own two feet . . . or four, as the case might be.

That alone boggled her mind. Would she ever get used to this amazing ability? She could understand her father's fascination with the idea of shapeshifters, but to think he had persecuted them, had tried to imprison so many of the people she'd met and already learned to love and respect . . . that was something she'd never understand.

Ulrich slipped out of his comfortable sweatpants. Daci forced herself not to look at his powerful body when she stripped out of her jeans and sweater and shifted. She still hadn't reached a truly comfortable state with so many gorgeous naked bodies, though Deacon had assured her she'd hardly notice before too long.

She found that hard to believe. Everyone she'd met was physically perfect and she really loved to look, but she put that thought behind her as she waited for Ulrich. He opened the door before he shifted, and then both of them trotted out to the front porch.

Daci turned in time to see Millie close the door behind them. Then she was alone in the darkness with a man she'd only met a couple of hours ago. A man her father had kidnapped. The last person to see her father alive.

Had Ulrich Mason murdered her father?

Did it really matter anymore?

Ulrich leapt off the top step and hit the ground running. Daci caught up to him before he reached the tree line, and the two of them loped at a comfortable pace through the darkness.

The smells here were subtly different than what she'd scented in Montana. The air had a different tang, the ground a different feel. Not better or worse . . . just different.

The wolf running ahead of her didn't smell anything like Deacon, either, though his scent was every bit as attractive to her. That alone was new, the fact she could feel attracted to so many different men, she who had never even had a serious boyfriend.

The air was crisp and cold and she felt the cares of the journey fade away as they raced along well-traveled paths. A wolf howled nearby, and another. Before long, a chorus of wolves were singing in the night. She'd almost forgotten this was a wolf sanctuary.

Millie had pointed out an area where large compounds held small packs of wolves destined to be freed once they were strong and healthy enough. Daci tried not to imagine how those fiercely wild creatures felt, imprisoned behind wire fences.

They made her think of Manda and all the years she'd been held captive. All because Daci's father was curious about her. He'd never done a thing to help her. He'd studied her like a lab rat.

Except rats got better treatment than Manda. Manda had allowed Daci inside her memories before she left. She'd shown her some of the horrible things from all her years of imprisonment, but only after Daci had begged her.

It was like watching her worst nightmares played out in full living, breathing color, with all the physical pain and terrifying fear intensified by the mind of a frightened, confused child who thought she'd been cursed by an angry god.

The only angry god in Manda's life had been a politician named Milton Bosworth. Daci shuddered even now. She'd ended up on the floor in Manda's room, curled into a fetal ball, sobbing as if her heart would break. In some ways, her heart had broken, when she realized what Manda had survived. Daci still couldn't believe Manda actually thought of her as a friend. Not after that. But Manda didn't blame her. Not at all. If anything, she sympathized with Daci's need to find answers.

In fact, she'd done everything in her power to help Daci adjust to this new life. Love like that was totally unfamiliar, almost unbelievable.

Daci wanted so badly to believe.

Ulrich slowed and they trotted side by side along a wide service road. After a while, the road got rougher until it finally disappeared altogether. Ulrich veered off to the right, running through wild forest and thick undergrowth. Daci followed, trusting him implicitly.

The earth was damp here, spongy with humus and the rich aroma of rotting vegetation. Soon, they crossed a small creek. Ulrich followed it until the freshet opened out into a tiny meadow. The grass was beginning to dry and felt crunchy underfoot. Leaves covered the ground, and the shimmer of moonlight gave the meadow an ethereal beauty.

Ulrich dipped his muzzle at the edge of the water and took a drink. Daci stood beside him and lapped up enough to quench her thirst. Then she turned and looked at him, waiting.

Ulrich sat and studied her for a moment. His ears pricked forward, his amber eyes glistened. *Anton doesn't know exactly how your father died*, he said.

His thoughts were crystal clear in her mind.

He told me it was a stroke.

Daci remained standing.

The wolf that was Ulrich Mason nodded. *It was. You've heard that your father had me kidnapped. I was forcibly taken across the country and kept chained in an old barn near where he lived. My daughter and my employees were able to combine their powers with Anton Cheval to rescue me. The men who actually kidnapped me were working on your father's orders. They thought they were carrying out the official wishes of a member of the president's cabinet. They had no knowledge of Milton Bosworth's obsession.*

I understand. I'm learning that my father did so many terrible things. I never knew . . . I'm sorry.

Ulrich touched Daci's shoulder with his paw. *You have no reason to be sorry. I tell you this only so you'll understand that we not only feared your father and the power he wielded through his government position, we hated him, as well.*

Daci had nothing to say. From the things she was learning, she'd begun to hate the man herself. How could she possibly have defended him for so long?

He was a threat to all of us . . . my daughter, my men, Anton's pack. While he lived, none of us were safe. Even now, many of those who pursue us first took up the hunt at your father's bidding. When I was taken, we had no idea he held Manda captive. No idea what atrocities had been committed upon an innocent child in the name of science.

Daci ducked her head, ashamed. *I know. Manda shared*

her memories with me. She tried to keep the revulsion out of her thoughts. Her body trembled with the effort.

Ulrich nodded. *I'm sorry. That must have been very difficult for you.*

Not as difficult as it was for Manda. She's very brave. Daci fought a powerful urge to pace, to just turn and run away before Ulrich said anything else. Wouldn't it be easier not to know? Easier, and definitely more cowardly. *What happened to my father?*

There was something in Ulrich's voice that warned her, some sense that the story the world had been told about her father's death was just that—a story.

Ulrich glanced away, gazing into the dark forest, but he opened his thoughts to Daci, sharing his visual memories along with his words. *I waited on his doorstep early in the morning. I was naked and it was cold out. The sun wasn't up yet. I remember thinking that it was a beautiful morning, much too pretty a morning for a man like Bosworth to die. He didn't deserve a morning this perfect. Not after the things he'd done.*

He stepped out to get his newspaper. I let him see me, recognize me as the man he'd had kidnapped, the man he'd kept chained. Then I shifted and lunged at him, growling. My intent was to rip his throat out, but that leap was all it took. The shock of actually seeing me shift, of having his suspicions confirmed, was too much. He collapsed. I didn't know if it was a heart attack or a stroke at the time. I didn't care. I didn't try to revive him, and I didn't call 911. I left him lying there on his front porch. I put on my clothes—I'd worn athletic shorts and running shoes—and then I jogged away. His wife found his body a couple of hours later. By then it was too late. I must be honest with you. If fear of me hadn't killed him, I was fully prepared to tear out his throat. I didn't have to, but I was willing to. If that makes me guilty of your father's murder, so be it, but you deserve to know the truth.

Daci stared into Ulrich's eyes and knew he would never lie to her. This man had killed her father. She'd seen it in his mind, her father's terrified expression, the knowledge that all he'd believed was true. With that knowledge, she'd seen in his eyes the certainty he was going to die.

A week ago, she would have been running to the police. A lifetime ago she would have blamed Ulrich, called him a murderer.

So much had changed. She had changed, in more ways than her ability to shift from human to wolf. These amazing people—Chanku—her people, had given her a new life. Her own life, not one her father might have directed. She thought of her mother and all the secrets she'd had to hold inside. Had she ever had the ability to shift?

Daci would never know. At least now, though, she knew the truth about her father. She'd fulfilled her promise to him and she could let it go. She'd expected to feel something profound when she finally learned the truth, but all she felt was relief.

Relief that his death had been quick, which was more than he deserved. Relief that this man, Ulrich Mason, one who deserved the respect she could never give her father, had been the instrument of Milton Bosworth's death.

If he'd lived, Manda might still be a captive. Daci might not have discovered her birthright. She might have gone on, trying to please a man who didn't want her, trying to earn some measure of his love. She would never have known what true love really was.

True love was a man like Ulrich Mason, willing to risk everything to help a girl he didn't even know find peace. It was Deacon and Manda, Keisha and all the others, going against their pack leader to do what was right for the one who had come to them meaning only harm. She'd been offered more love in the past few days than anyone had given her since her mother's death so many years ago.

She'd been taken in and treated as if she were family.

And it came to her then, that she was family—they all were. Kinsmen related by blood. The family of Chanku, all parts of a single pack, connected by a shared birthright that would bind them together, forever.

This was the powerful legacy her mother, not her father, had left to her. She, Daciana Lupei, was her mother's daughter.

Daci raised her head and gazed steadily into Ulrich's amber eyes. *Thank you,* she said. *He died a more honorable death than he deserved. Thank you for telling me—for showing me—the truth.*

Then she turned and trotted back along the trail they'd come in on. Ulrich followed her. She was glad he'd told her this as a wolf. The words had never actually been spoken. Their memory would not linger in her ears, merely their whisper in her mind. Milton Bosworth was dead. She'd seen him die. His life, and that part of hers, was over forever.

She would speak no more of her father.

She felt light, at peace. He was finally, truly dead to her. His legacy of hatred and his sick plans could now die with him. She'd been the only one trying to keep his memory alive.

No longer.

She'd gazed beyond Ulrich's words when he told her the story. Not only had she seen his memories, she'd felt the visceral fear he'd had for his daughter, for all the members of his pack.

No more.

Daci carried the legacy of Chanku, a priceless gift from her mother, one given without condition. Her birthright, a legacy she could be proud of.

With Ulrich running close behind, Daci raced through the night, her four feet pounding a perfect tattoo on the trail, following the most direct route back to the one she loved.

Chapter 22

Daci paused just outside the back of the little cabin. It was dark. There was no backdoor light burning, no sign of lights inside. With the shades drawn, it was hard to tell if anyone was home.

Ulrich waited patiently beside her. He'd flanked her all the way back, running just behind her, yet making her feel safe, protected. She'd not felt this sense of security since her mother's death.

Was this what it was like to have family? She decided she really liked the feeling of having people care about her.

Are you okay? He stepped closer. *Will you be all right, Daci?*

She stared into his amber eyes and soaked up the concern he felt for her. *Yes,* she said. *I feel better than I've felt since I was a little girl. Thank you. For your honesty. For caring enough to tell me the truth. For your hospitality.* She glanced toward the small cabin. *It's beautiful here. I'm going to hate to leave.*

You and your mate are welcome to stay for as long as you like.

She shook her head. Not a very wolven gesture, but somehow apropos. *He's not my mate*, she said. *Not yet, but you never know. Thank you, Ulrich. Now go back to your mate and tell her you've done your good deed for the night.*

His laughter filtered through Daci's thoughts. *Oh, no I haven't. Not yet.* Millie's image filled her mind as Ulrich turned and trotted down the trail to his cabin.

She stood and watched him go. Then she climbed up the steps to the back door and shifted. She hoped Deacon was inside. She'd not been gone all that long, but she wondered if he might have decided to go spend time with the others.

She cast her thoughts forward, as she'd been learning. The images that came back sent shivers racing along her spine, building and multiplying until they coalesced deep in her womb.

Deacon was inside. So was Matt. She sensed their arousal and wondered if it was meant purely for one another, or if by chance, she might be included in their fantasies. Her libido responded and her sex grew warm, her body needier than ever.

She'd expected this burning arousal after shifting and the emotional impact of Ulrich's truths. At the same time, a frisson of fear raced along her spine. She knew, deep in her soul, as if the words were burned into her flesh, that if both men wanted her, if she was intimate with both of them, she'd never turn either man free.

She, the one who had been unable to commit to Deacon. Was she ready for an even greater commitment? A lifetime with two men she hardly knew?

Were they?

There was only one way to find out.

Naked and shivering in the cold night air, she opened the door and stepped into the big, open room. Both Matt and Deacon were stretched out on the king-size bed, propped up with pillows while they watched a movie on the small television. They wore jeans but no shirts. Their feet were bare.

They were holding hands, their fingers locked together as if it were the most natural connection in the world.

Maybe, for the two of them, it was.

Did that leave any room for Daci?

Both men were obviously aroused. The moment she stepped inside and closed the door, their heads turned in her direction. She'd surprised them, obviously. Their expressions were filled with guilt.

Her nipples tightened into needy little pebbles, aching, wanting. Daci ignored Matt and Deacon's clasped hands, their guilty faces, the fact they shared the bed meant for Deacon and her. Ignored her own suddenly raging arousal, the clenching in her womb, the slow trickle of fluid on the inside of her left thigh.

Her body practically vibrated with need, the strange lust that arose after a shift. She ignored it as best she could. Put it aside, even though she wanted to throw herself on the bed between both men, wanted to rip their jeans off, taste their bodies, their swollen cocks and flat, male nipples.

No, she had more control. She had to find her center, that part of her that ruled her passion . . . if it even existed anymore. Daci glanced at the TV screen and felt herself beginning to relax. She drew a shuddering breath. "*Star Wars*?" She forced a laugh. "You're watching the first *Star Wars*? I thought from the way you guys looked, you must be watching porn!"

"What do you mean, from the way we looked?" Matt hung on to Deacon's hand like a lifeline, but he grinned and glanced down at his crotch with a look of surprise, as if he'd only just now noticed what shape he was in.

Daci laughed and felt herself relax. Matt's silliness washed the tension out of the room.

Deacon looked down, then back up at Matt. "I think she's referring to our matching boners."

"We were saving them for you, sweetheart." Matt crooked a finger and invited her to join them.

Daci hesitated. She glanced at Deacon. They weren't mated, but she owed him.

"He's harmless, you know." Deacon turned Matt's hand loose and patted the bed between them.

That was all the invitation she needed.

Deacon slipped his left arm around her shoulders. His long fingers brushed her nipple. She felt the shock all the way to her clit.

"First of all, how'd it go with Ulrich?"

Daci leaned against Deacon, almost preternaturally aware of her contact with Matt's jeans-clad leg along her left side. "It went well. Ulrich both showed me and told me how he killed him."

"What? He told you that."

Daci knew Matt glanced over her head at Deacon.

"Yes, Matt. But Bosworth deserved it. He was a monster." She shook her head. "I don't want to talk about him anymore. From now on, I am my mother's daughter, not his. She was Chanku, whether or not she ever shifted, and so am I."

Her body vibrated with need. Her blood raced, her heart pounded and there was nothing else that mattered, nothing she cared about beyond the two men in the room. She glanced at Deacon, and then at Matt and put Bosworth and all he had once meant to her, away, closing those memories up where they belonged, in that part of her mind where they could do no harm.

She smiled at Deacon, and then at Matt. "If you guys are okay with that, what I'd really love to talk about is what the three of us are doing in my bed." This time, she slanted a much more seductive look at each of the men. "And that leads to another important question . . . why are you both still wearing pants?"

Matt tensed beside her. He carefully curled his big body away from the headboard and sat Indian fashion at the foot of the bed where she could look directly into his eyes.

His dark amber eyes, obviously troubled, were exactly the same color as Deacon's. The same color as her own. She fought a powerful impulse to reach out and touch his face, to comfort him. Instead, she clasped her hands against the soft curve of her belly.

"I want to be honest, Daci. I love Deacon. Not just as a friend. I didn't realize how much until I saw you guys tonight, and it just clicked. I know he's your mate, but I can't do anything with either of you without telling you up front how I feel. It wouldn't be right."

Daci frowned and glanced at Deacon. He shrugged. *I never told him that*, he said. She smiled back at Matt.

"Matt, Deacon and I aren't mated. Yes, I love him, but we hardly know each other." At Matt's raised eyebrow, she felt her skin go hot and then cold. "Well, of course we know each other that way, what I meant was . . ."

Matt and Deacon both laughed and her skin got even hotter.

Embarrassed and feeling just a little bit betrayed by the one she loved, Daci scooted away from Deacon and glared at both of them, but her obvious sexual excitement betrayed her even more. It was hard to act all pissed off when her body was humming with desire, when the images in her head were filled with two gorgeous men doing amazing things to each other—and to her.

She straightened her spine and shot mental daggers from one man to the other. They both blinked, almost as if she'd slapped them. She cautiously hid her surprise. There must be a lot more to this *alpha bitch* thing than she'd realized, since the guys seemed to respect her position even more than she did.

One more thing she needed to learn. Smiling now, more confident, she slapped her palms down on her thighs and shifted her glance from one gorgeous guy to the other until her gaze landed on Matt. "My question, Matthew, is whether or not your love for Deacon precludes sex with me, because I will tell you both, right now, that I'm dyin' here and I really, really want to get fucked. Now. Here. By both of you . . . and not necessarily one at a time."

In the silence that followed, a pin dropping would have been excruciatingly loud.

Oh, Lordy, did I really say that? She thought longingly of the deep, dark forest just outside the door, of shifting into her alpha bitch body and running as far and fast as she could . . . except with her luck, she'd probably get lost. Instead, Daci slowly turned to slip off the bed and head for the shower.

Matt caught her arm. "You'd do that? Make love with both of us?"

Deacon touched her shoulder. "Are you sure, sweetheart? I know this is all pretty new to you, but . . ."

She raised her chin and glared at Deacon. "Not all that much newer than it is for you, *sweetheart*. Don't keep trying to protect me, Deac, and don't be condescending. I'm not some helpless sweet young thing. I've had a really wild, very stressful couple of weeks here . . ."

Matt's whispered, "No shit, Sherlock," almost had her laughing, but she managed to keep a straight face.

"And I love you. A lot." She glanced at Matt and huffed out a big breath. "I don't love you. Yet. But I don't know you. Who's to say I won't? Love you, that is. I'm definitely attracted to you. You're obviously attracted to Deacon and he to you. It works for those three in San Francisco, from what Deacon's told me, for Mik, Tala, and AJ, and I'm certainly willing to give it a shot, if it's what you guys want. Tell me this, Deacon. Do you love Matt?"

Deacon nodded and smiled at his buddy.

"Matt, do you truly love Deacon?"

Matt grinned and nodded. "I do," he said. "Very much."

"Goodness. That sounded sort of like wedding vows." Daci grinned and took a deep breath. "The clincher is, Matt, are you at all attracted to me?"

This time Matt laughed out loud and palmed his growing erection, holding his hand over the fly of his jeans. "Oh, yeah. I am definitely attracted."

"Good. We've got that out of the way. So, like I asked before, why in the hell do you still have your pants on?" She tried to hold the stern look. She really did, but it was so hard with both of them suddenly jerking their tight jeans down their long legs, with both men freeing huge erections, cocks that were big enough to scare the hell out of her and make her mouth water and her pussy weep, all at the same time.

It was Matt who moved first. Matt who leaned over and sort of bulldozed her backward onto the bed until he covered her body with his, until she felt the thick press of heat between her legs and knew that, had she been bluffing, this guy had just called it.

But she wasn't bluffing. Not one bit, and the heat of his body, the weight and scent of warm male had her squirming beneath him, searching for the perfect fit. Deacon's package was big, but Matt was even larger. His heavy length pressed between her legs and his lips found hers. Soft and searching at first, then he nibbled at her mouth, sucked gently at her lips and pressed deep with his tongue.

She felt a soft touch against her hair and glanced to her right. Deacon sat beside her, smiling, stroking her hair back from her eyes. Watching.

She felt his intense gaze deep in her core. Felt his love, his need for both her and the man who covered her. Daci's body responded and she arched against Matt's full length, almost lifting him with the power of muscles desperate for more.

"We're not going to rush this." Matt whispered against

her mouth. When she lifted her hips again with the intent of forcing him inside her greedy sheath, he lifted away from her. "Uh-uh . . . not so fast."

Instead he came down in a smooth glide, running his hot length between her sensitive labia, dragging the top of his cock directly over her clit.

Daci moaned and squirmed against him, but he repeated the same, slow move, sliding in her slick fluids, driving her crazy with the subtle pressure that took her close to the edge but not over.

Deacon moved away and she broke apart from Matt's mouth to see where he'd gone. She heard the sound of a drawer beside the bed opening and closing, the sound of tearing foil, and her mind filled with images, Deacon's visuals, of him sheathing his cock, sliding the thin latex over his erection. The vivid images of what he intended next, and Daci's heart thudded heavily in her chest.

He was kneeling now, directly behind Matt with a look of utter concentration on his face. Daci's mind filled once more with Deacon's visuals from his point of view—the sleek stretch of Matt's long back, the taut curve of his buttocks, the sensual rhythm of his body as he moved over Daci.

They'd never done this before, these two friends who had never been lovers. They'd teased one another, made "gay" jokes while they'd wondered, but not once had they acted on needs that had been growing steadily more powerful as their friendship increased.

Daci felt it now, Matt's emotional vulnerability as his friend mounted him, his love for Deacon, his growing desire for the woman beneath him. She experienced Deacon's hesitation, his fear that he might cause Matt pain, that he might not be everything Matt wanted in a lover.

Daci wrapped her arms around Matt and trailed her fingers over his taut buttocks. She felt the bunch and pull of muscles as he slowly slipped back and forth between her legs. She fought the pull of her own climax, determined to help Matt find his.

Trailing her fingers along the sweaty crease between his cheeks, she parted them, holding him open for Deacon. He spread something slick and wet over the tight pucker of Matt's ass.

The touch broke Matt's rhythm and he sighed against Daci's mouth, pulled back just a fraction and slowly slipped his huge cock between her softened labia. She felt his graceful entry, the perfect fit of sword to sheath as he pushed forward, deeper and deeper still, until his sac rested against her buttocks and the broad head of his penis covered the mouth of her womb.

Daci clutched at his buttocks with both hands, holding on and pulling him closer still. Deacon's hands brushed hers and she knew he pressed slowly into Matt, using his fingers to ease the tight muscle, opening him enough to take the broad tip of his cock. He leaned forward and lightly pressed against Matt, opening his thoughts to both Daci and Matt even as he opened his way into Matt's body.

His entry was excruciatingly slow as he savored the reluctant release of muscle, the dark, damp heat of Matt's tight channel. Matt spread his legs a fraction wider, then he held perfectly still as Deacon filled him.

Finally, Deacon's flat belly pressed against Matt, trapping Daci's fingers between the two men. She sensed the moment when Deacon's balls rested against Matt's, knew when he'd filled Matt completely, just as Matt filled her.

The three of them, connected now, their combined lust at a feverish pitch yet still under tight control as each of them experienced the link, the visceral connection of three bodies acting as one, three minds sharing a single thought.

Matt was the first to move, pulling back, slipping his cock almost all the way out of Daci's tight sheath, then plunging forward again. Deacon caught his rhythm and took over the pace so that they moved as one, sighed as one, experienced the sensations of all three as one.

Daci kept her hands in place, sliding her fingers along Deacon's cock with each thrust he made. Matt's erection was impossibly large, so that each thrust he made filled her to the point of pain, stretched her so that the tissues burned, yet still she wanted more. More of him, more of Deacon. She lifted her hips, silently begging for faster, harder . . . and the men complied, until they were pounding, one into the other, their bodies straining, lungs billowing, and the sweat that flowed made their bodies slick and their skin even more sensitive.

It seemed the very room was ablaze with their lust, as if the walls shimmered with their energy, with the strength of emotion, the power of their passion. Daci sensed her climax mere seconds before it hit, a shock of lighting that speared her from spine to womb to clenching sheath. She tightened her fingers around Deacon's cock, arched her back into Matt's powerful thrust and screamed. Shaking, shivering with the strength of her orgasm, she couldn't evade Matt's continued pounding, couldn't avoid the next climax that slammed into her body.

Deacon threw back his head and cried out. The power of his orgasm forced Matt forward, deeper into Daci and she felt it again, the lightning jolt of climax, only this was greater, stronger, because it was Deacon's as well as her own.

Her vaginal muscles clamped down on Matt's cock and he jerked inside her, filling her with spurt after spurt of hot seed and his thoughts spilled over, just as hot, just as powerful as he shared the deepest part of himself, the neediest part that had known rejection and pain for most of his life, the darkest side of the young man who had sold his body on the streets to survive.

This was love. This coming together with Deacon and Daci was the first shot at love he'd ever experienced. Millie had shown him the possibility, but Deacon and Daci had taken him there, shared the reality of what could be his for the asking.

His hips slammed forward as Deacon collapsed across his back. Daci wrapped her arms around Matt and held him close bearing the weight of not one, but both of her men. The hot tears that covered her throat and chest made her own tears fall, a cleansing of mind and spirit she'd not expected.

Deacon rolled to one side and quietly slipped away to the bathroom to dispose of the condom. Matt stayed where he was, his arms around Daci, his face buried in the curve of her neck. She felt the uneven cadence of his chest against hers and knew he wept. Slowly, she brushed his hair back from his face, but she held him close, shared her thoughts of love, of need, of safety, and homecoming.

Deacon returned and lay down beside them. He wrapped his arms around Matt and Daci and held both of them close. "You okay, bro?"

Matt nodded, but he didn't raise his head. Daci felt his embarrassment, that he still couldn't control his weeping. "I think it's going to work just fine, don't you agree, Deac? The three of us." She chuckled. "Instead of a couple, we'll be a triple."

Matt's chest jerked against hers. Daci kissed his forehead and bit back a giggle. If Matt could laugh, he must be okay.

"Or a treble," Deacon added.

"Just not a tribble . . ." Daci said, still running her fingers through Matt's hair. "Remember that old *Star Trek* episode where . . ."

"Enough!" Matt raised his head and leaned across Daci to grab a tissue from the box on the bedside table. He slipped out of Daci and sat back between her legs, wiped his eyes and blew his nose. "I'm having a moment, here, guys. Don't you have any respect?"

Deacon shook his head. "No . . . should I?" He glanced at Daci and grinned.

She shook her head, but when she reached for Matt's hand, she couldn't bring herself to laugh. "More than respect, Matt. I take back what I said. You let me into your thoughts, you shared yourself with me as if we were already a mated pair. I can say with all honesty that I do love you, just as I love Deacon."

She grabbed Deacon's hand, linking the three of them. "It's going to work just fine, guys. The three of us, together. I'm not quite ready for the mating bond thing everyone keeps talking about, but when it's time, I know it will be both of you, if you'll have me."

Deacon leaned close and kissed her. Matt did the same, but he pulled away with a question in his eyes. "I'm curious. Why don't you think it's time?"

Daci scooted back so that she could lean against the headboard. "I guess being around Beth and Nick. You told me they mated really fast, but there's a lot of tension between them. I sensed it as soon as I met them. I don't want that to happen with us. I want to be certain."

Deacon moved over to sit beside her. "Jazzy and Logan were just as quick. They seem really happy."

Daci shrugged. "True, but we're talking lifetime commitment here, boys. I've known I was Chanku for barely a week. I'm coming from a life without any family at all, without ever having a serious boyfriend, and suddenly I'm surrounded by a pack of oversexed shapeshifters and two men who love me. Which reminds me . . . Deacon, what is your real name?"

"Huh?" Deacon turned and stared at her.

"Your name? I can't believe your mother named you Deacon. You have to have a real name."

"She does have a point, bro." Matt grinned at him. "Mine, by the way, is Matthew James Rodgers." He held his hand out.

Daci took it. “Nice to meet you, Matthew. I’m Daciana Rodica Lupei.”

“Rodica?” Deacon grinned at her. “You told me Daciana means wolf, but what’s Rodica mean?”

Daci giggled. “I looked it up. It means fertile.”

It took awhile for Matt and Deacon to quit laughing. Daci glared at Deacon. “And you are?”

He shrugged and held out his hand. “Christopher Andrew March.”

Daci took his hand and shook it. “It’s nice to meet you, Christopher. How’d they get Deacon out of that?”

“Probably his all-American appearance.” Matt chuckled and threw an arm around Deacon’s shoulders.

Deacon glared at him, but it was all in fun. Daci grinned at both her guys. Deac did look like an old-time preacher, and the name fit him a lot better than Christopher.

And both of them fit her. Matt with his innocent beauty and Deacon the ascetic opposite, yet both of them sensual creatures who loved generously.

And both of them hers. Panic slithered along her spine. Could she really handle two men? She, a woman who’d never had a serious relationship with even one?

“Daci? You okay?”

She glanced up at Deacon’s softly spoken question. He looked at her with eyes filled with love. Beautiful amber eyes. “Yeah, I’m okay. Like I said earlier . . . it’s been a really stressful week.”

Matt leaned over and kissed her belly, just below her navel. “I know something really good for stress . . .”

Daci rolled her eyes. “I’ll just bet you do.” But she was more than ready, and so was Deacon. Sighing, she lay back and let both men take her once again over the edge.

Epilogue

Nick trotted along beside Beth, following Daci, Deacon, and Matt down the wide service road near the large compounds. His ass still hurt from Ulrich's screwing the other night, but when he looked back at the way he'd been acting for the past week, he figured he'd deserved what he got and then some.

He wished Beth would lay off. Her anger was so thick he could practically see it vibrating in the air between them. She'd shut him out ever since he'd blocked her constant bitching that night and decided to go with Ulrich's plan, which meant getting his ass reamed out in an obvious display of dominance by the old guy.

Okay. So he got the message, along with some really great sex. Now why couldn't Beth figure it out? There was no point in challenging Ulrich. Nick didn't want to fight him. For one thing, he really liked and admired the guy.

For another, he'd lose.

Ulrich was smart, he was cunning, and he was strong. He had experience on his side and he was a born leader, something Nick knew he'd never be.

Why couldn't Beth accept him for what he was?

He watched Daci, Deacon, and Matt trotting along together up ahead. The three of them had slipped into an amazing union, and they weren't even mated. He and Beth were mates, yet they hardly spoke to one another. He missed Matt and Deacon, missed the fun they'd all had together.

He missed Beth most of all. Missed the girl he'd fallen in love with.

He glanced at Beth and realized she watched him. Was she reading his thoughts? He'd been blocking . . . or at least he thought he'd been.

She veered off the road and followed a narrow trail into the woods. Nick hesitated, then decided to follow her. She stopped after a short distance and turned to face him in the middle of a small meadow.

He halted a few feet away, ears flat, tail down. It was easier this way, acting the submissive role with Beth. It seemed to make her happy. He didn't really care one way or the other.

She shifted. He faced her a moment, still the wolf, then decided to see what the hell she wanted. Nick shifted and stood on two feet, wary and uncertain.

"It's not working." She clasped her hands over her smooth belly. "We never should have bonded. I want out."

Her request came as a relief. At least he wasn't the only one who felt that way. Unfortunately, it wasn't an option.

"Great. So do I, but it's a little late for that, Beth. You heard what Tala said. A pair bond is forever. You wanted me, you've got me."

She jerked back, as if he'd slapped her. "You don't want me?"

Nick shook his head. "Does it matter? You just said you want out. Obviously you don't love me anymore." He realized he was standing up straighter, feeling taller than he had since he'd made his first shift. "So I guess my answer's no, Beth. Not anymore. Not the way you are now. I loved a girl who was sweet and kind, who cared about me. All you care about now is power. You're twenty-one years old, Beth. You have no power. Not over me, not over yourself. Get used to it."

He shifted. *I'm going back to the others. You can come if you want to. Or not.* He glanced over his shoulder and watched her face. She looked like she might cry, but he didn't trust her. Not anymore.

He still loved her, though. Goddess help him, he loved her. With one last look, Nick whirled around and raced back along the trail.

He left her in the meadow, looking lonely and lost. At least she wasn't angry at him anymore, but he didn't feel like he'd won a victory. No, he just felt empty.

Empty and very much alone.

Turn the page for a sneak peek of "His to Reclaim," Shelli Stevens's novella in SEXY BEAST VII, available September 2009!

Chapter 1

"*Gemma!*" The shrill scream pierced through the woods, filtering past the aged walls of the log cabin. "Oh, my God! I can't believe this. *Gemma!*"

The sound of feet pounding down the path mingled with the alarmed whimpers and short breaths of the approaching woman.

Gemma's fingers clenched around the brush in her hand, her pulse quickening as she turned to face the door. *Was it too much to hope that is was nothing more than the caterer having encountered a problem?*

The door flung open, smashing into the wall. Her younger cousin Megan stepped into the room, eyes wild with panic.

"He's really coming."

They were just three words, but they were enough. The brush dropped from Gemma's hand and her body went numb with shock.

This was really happening . . . No! The room spun, and she gripped the vanity table to keep from falling to her knees. *No.* Was he *insane?*

"There's no time." Megan closed the door, hands shaking. "Shift and then run. Run fast. It's the only way you can possibly escape him."

"How far away is he?" Gemma's voice came out remarkably calm as she fumbled to undo the buttons on her wedding dress.

The cold fear began to subside, and a hot burn of rage blazed through her. How dare he? After five years, how *dare* he?

Megan grabbed her arm and tugged her toward the door. "A mile. Maybe. And he's not alone, Gemma. He's brought friends. You must hurry! There's no time to change out of your dress. Run, and I'll find Jeffrey and tell him what's happened."

"My dress will ruin during transition—"

Crash!

The door broke in half and splinters of wood shot into the interior of the cabin like tiny missiles.

Heart in her throat, Gemma retreated, her body trembling as she stared at the man who now filled the doorway. The man who'd just made good on the appallingly dark promise he'd made just days ago in an e-mail. She'd been half convinced it was a joke—someone toying with her heart—and had told Megan as much.

But it wasn't a joke. The proof was standing in front of her eyes. Maybe a couple of years ago she would have wished for this, but not now. Dammit, not now!

Sweat clung to the hard muscles of Hunter's nude body—it was clear he'd just shifted back to human form. A familiar heat crept through her body and she hardened her jaw, refusing to acknowledge it. The same way she'd refused to acknowledge it for the last five years.

It was hard not to, though. With his dark hair and tan body; he was tall and broad, a mass of muscles and ridges. Her gaze dropped and her cheeks burned hot. She swallowed hard, unable to tear her gaze from his hard thighs and the thick cock that rested between them.

The blood raged through her veins, and she closed her

eyes to count to ten. When she opened them again, her gaze was firmly back on his face, unwilling to let her eyes shift any lower than his shoulders this time. That would be a guaranteed diversion from finding a way out of this situation.

Unfortunately, five years had done nothing but enhance Hunter's raw sex appeal.

His eyes, burning like dark blue crystals, met hers. And, like the devil come to collect his due, he advanced into the room, his face a mask of fierce determination.

Oh, God. She needed to act. Now. Swallowing the thickness in her throat, Gemma glanced around the room, looking for anything that might be used as a weapon. She grabbed the chair from her vanity table and lifted it above her head with a grunt.

Hunter lunged forward and knocked it from her grasp, sending it crashing to the ground behind her. Before she could draw in a startled breath, he'd circled her wrists with one of his massive hands and and pulled her body firmly against the rock-hard wall of his chest.

"*No!*" She growled and lifted her knee to tag him in the groin, but he blocked the shot.

Instead he pulled her tighter against him and forced his thigh between hers. His thick cock brushed her hip and she stilled, barely able to breathe as her heart slammed against her rib cage.

His soft laugh feathered warm against her cheek. "You should have listened to your cousin, angel," he leaned forward and said softly against her ear. "You should have run."

The blood drained from Gemma's face and she heard Megan whimper from the corner of the room.

Megan. Hope flared.

"Megan, go find Jeffrey!"

Her cousin lurched away from the wall and toward the doorway, but fell back with a shrill yell.

Two more men—though these ones were clothed—filed through the broken entrance.

"It appears we will have to take the younger one with us as well," Hunter ordered with a sigh.

"Me?" Megan squeaked in alarm. "No! You can't—"

Her words were cut off by the hand that slid over her mouth; then the burly man slid another arm around her waist to lift her off the ground.

Panic resumed in her gut and Gemma tugged at her imprisoned wrists, her mouth in a tight line. "Let her go, Hunter. She has nothing to do with this."

"We will, angel. Tomorrow. We don't want her running off to tell Jeffrey the minute we leave, now do we?"

"*Bastard.*"

His smile came slow. "Now, you know my mother well enough to know that's not true."

Of course he would throw that at her. She bit her lip, trying to hold her temper. It wasn't easy as she watched helplessly as the two men carried her cousin kicking and screaming out the door. Megan's muffled sounds were ineffective at bringing them the help they desperately needed.

Gemma drew in a slow breath. "You know, Hunter, I always suspected you were a bit certifiable. Congratulations, you've just confirmed it."

He caught her chin with rough fingers, lifting her face so she had to look at him. A shiver ran down her spine. Unfortunately, it may not have all been because of fear. His eyes narrowed, until the blue irises were just slits of blue. They burned hot as his gaze scoured her face.

"Am I? You were the one about to marry a human." His gaze darkened. "I gave you fair warning. Call off the wedding or I will do it for you."

"I'll *still* marry him."

"I wouldn't count on it."

"Oh! I'll say it again, Hunter. You're certifiable," she

repeated. As she tried to twist her chin from his grasp, his hold just tightened. "In fact, I'm sure you won't mind if I just call you Certi from now on."

"Angel, I don't care what the hell you call me." His head lowered, until his mouth was just a breath above hers. "I'll just look forward to hearing you call it when I'm riding you in bed."

Shock ripped through her, widening her eyes and snatching her breath away. Heat rushed through her body, curling thick down through her blood before gathering heavy in her pussy.

His nostrils flared, and she knew his were side meant that he could smell the dampness between her legs that his image had created. Heat flooded her cheeks.

"Like hell that will happen, Hunter."

"You want me, angel." It wasn't a question. And there was no asking when his lips crushed down on hers a second later.

Gemma went rigid in his arms, letting out an outraged feline growl that was all jaguar.

He answered with a deeper growl, plunging his tongue past her compressed lips to take control of her mouth.

There was no fighting him. With each bold stroke of his tongue against hers, a little more common sense got swept away. He plundered her mouth, leaving no inch unexplored, controlling her tongue and mind with ease.

The heat built in her body; her breasts swelled, the nipples tightening to scrape against the lace bustier beneath her dress. Five years dropped away and once again it was Hunter holding her, kissing her. Making her forget everything but his touch and the way it made her feel.

His cock pressed hard into her belly, a tangible reminder of his promise to fuck her.

With a groan, he released her chin to plunge his hand into her bodice. He cupped her breast in the palm of his hand, squeezing just enough to send another rush of moisture straight to her panties.

Her head fell back, a gasp ripping from her lips. The calloused pad of his thumb swept across one tight nipple, and her knees wobbled.

His mouth lifted from hers, and he pulled her breast above the bodice. His head swooped down and he wrapped his lips around the hard tip. Hot breath and a moist tongue teased her, before his teeth raked against her flesh.

"Oh God." She trembled, minutes away from hiking up her wedding dress and begging him to fuck her.

Wedding dress? Jeffrey! The name of the man she was supposed to marry in two hours resounded in her head. *Who's certifiable now, Gemma?*

Hunter reached for the hem of her dress, lifting it over her legs to cup her ass.

Now, Gemma. Act now! Knowing she had an advantage—just barely—she grabbed his hair and stepped back enough to slam her knee into his chest.

He stumbled back with a curse, eyes flashing with dismay and rage. It was only a second, but it was the break she needed.

Gemma moved past him and sprinted out the door to the cabin that she'd been using to get ready for her wedding. She leapt off the porch and landed on the dirt path.

Her heart slammed in her chest, her body trembling with adrenaline. Increasing her pace, she growled and willed the change to speed up. It didn't take long. Her twenty-thousand-dollar designer dress exploded into a mass of pearl buttons and lace as her body shifted into its jaguar form.

Seconds later she was on all fours, charging through the resort in a desperate attempt to escape Hunter. The thrashing of branches and trees behind her signaled that is was going to be one hell of a challenge.

* * *

Dammit. How could he have been so stupid to get distracted by Gemma's sweet body?

Hunter snarled and dodged between two trees that appeared on one section of the trail.

He shouldn't have lost focus. As an ESA agent, he was better than that by nature. Their job was to protect and defend all shifter species from threats of corruption, danger, and violence. The Elite Shifter Agency only hired the best of the best. You had to be tough, intelligent, sharp, quick minded . . . *and definitely not lose your focus over a nice set of tits, you idiot.*

His fellow agents would laugh their asses off if they knew he'd gotten completely muddleheaded by a woman.

He hadn't been able to stop himself from touching her. But it had been a costly delay. He should have had her in the vehicle by now and they could've been halfway to White River. As it was, Joaquin and Brad were probably wondering where the hell he was.

Hunter paused and breathed in the air, careful not to lose Gemma's scent.

She wasn't even following the human-made trail anymore. His gaze darted around the lush forest. His ears listening for the sound of her escape. The sudden flash of yellow and brown between the trees was a dead giveaway to her location. Unlike him, Gemma's jaguar form didn't have the luxury of dark brown fur that hid his spots. Though she was desperate in her attempt to escape, she didn't stand a chance.

His resistance softened a bit with pity before he hardened it again. He couldn't afford such a weakness. He gave a low growl and took off after her. Not that he could blame her for running. Not after what he'd done to her so many years ago. But what Gemma didn't seem to quite understand was the cloud of danger lingering over her life right now. And at the center of that vortex was none other than her husband-to-be.

Jealousy, like a hot brand iron, stabbed sudden and deep, twisting inside him. His paws hit the ground hard as he quickened his pace, jumping over bushes as he gained on her.

She shouldn't have been marrying Jeffrey Delmore in the first place. She was his. She'd sworn it. It didn't matter that she'd been barely twenty at the time. It was one promise he intended to see she kept. Gemma belonged to *him*.

Guilt twisted his gut, that he was completely out of line, but he refused to acknowledge it. Not now. Right now his primal side was in dominance and the chase was on to reclaim his woman.

He was only about twenty feet behind her now and she must have realized she couldn't outrun him much longer. He could hear the agitation in the growls she emitted while continuing to dodge through trees and beneath low brushes.

And then she blew it, giving him the final advantage he needed. Her back legs caught on a tree root protruding from the ground and she stumbled, losing her balance before falling onto her side.

She tried to get back up again, but the damage was done. Hunter used her moment of vulnerability and jumped on her. The weight of his body pinned hers to the ground.

Fur flew as she swiped at him with her claws; jaws snapped at his neck but missed. They rolled on the hard earth, fighting for dominance.

He locked gazes with her. "*Stop fighting me*," he said with his mind.

Rage flared in her gaze, and she continued to struggle beneath him.

With a growl of frustration he caught her neck between his teeth, using just enough force to warn her she'd better yield. Relief washed through him when she stilled beneath him.

Shift back, Gemma. Please, I don't want to hurt you.

She tried to swat him again with a claw, but he reared back, missing her attempt.

Realizing fighting was futile, her eyes closed. The fur on her face slowly receded to show smooth ivory skin. She had chosen to obey. Quickly, to avoid crushing her, he rolled off her and shifted back to his human form.

"You have no right," she rasped.

When he turned to look at her, his heart clenched a bit. She sat on the ground, her knees drawn up to her chest as she glared at him.

Her pale skin seemed luminescent against the greens and browns of the forest. The tawny curls of her hair—which had always fascinated him—tumbled over her shoulders, shielding her breasts from him.

His mouth pursed. *Too bad.* He hadn't seen her naked in years, and it was quite obvious her body had changed since then. Her curves were bolder, whereas before they'd been slight.

He lifted his gaze to hers, wincing slightly at how her brown eyes condemned him.

"Let's not make this any more difficult than it needs to be, angel."

"Oh, I think it was too late for that the minute you decided to interrupt my wedding day."

His jaw hardened and he stepped forward. "You will walk with me now to the vehicle."

"What's option B?"

"I'll carry you."

Her nostrils flared and the arms around her knees tightened.

"Let me think," she murmured and then continued to watch him for a moment.

Her lips parted a second later, but words didn't come out. Instead the piercing scream she issued was guaranteed to raise the dead. *Or bring her groom running.*